MYSTERIES AT MATAGAMON LAKE

By

Randall Probert

Sequel of

A FORGOTTEN LEGACY

Published by

Randall Enterprises

P.O. Box 862

Bethel, Maine 04217

Cover photo by Randall Probert

Printed in the U.S
Second Edition

Copyright © 2024 by Randall Probert

All rights reserved. No part of this book may be
reproduced or transmitted electronically in any form
without the written permission from the publisher or
author. For information address Randall Enterprises.

ISBN 979-8884124110

CHAPTER 1

I got up from my desk and walked over to the window. The view from the twelfth floor was extraordinary; the Statue of Liberty and the ocean front. There were many merchant ships in the harbor today, but I was not particularly aware of them. Nor the grand old statue or that the day was extremely beautiful. My thoughts, aspirations and dreams ended this morning when I received an e-mail from my fiancée, Jennifer. I uncrumpled the paper and read it again. "Thomas, I'm going away. Alone. There are things I want to do for me." That's all, no "good-bye, no "I'm sorry," nothing about when or if she'll be back. I crumpled up the slip of paper and this time I threw it in the wastebasket and then deleted it from my computer. I threw her photo in the wastebasket, making sure it was upside down. Then I sat back at my desk and looked at the snowshoes hanging on the wall that Uncle Royal had made for me, the winter I stayed with him at Matagamon. Oh, that had been a grand year. Suddenly all the memories of him and of my stay there, and especially of the canoe trip he had taken me on, through the history of that region came rushing back. Tears welled up in my eyes and made my vision blurry. In my mind I could still see him standing on the river bank where Webster stream and the East Branch of the Penobscot meet, across the river from the Little East campsite. Tears had filled my eyes that morning also.

That had been a long and lonely trip down the lake that morning. I had fallen in love with the region and liked those whom I had met. I really would have liked to have stayed there with Uncle Royal, but I had made a promise that after a year I would go to Oxford University.

I went to Oxford and after the first year I adjusted and rather enjoyed the next three years. That first year was difficult mostly because I refused to change. I arrived still with beard and a checkered green flannel shirt and carrying my snowshoes under my arm. I did have the appropriate attire, but in defiance of the manner in which I was treated I refused to submit to a sports jacket and tie.

I met Jennifer after my bar exams and I had started work at my father's law firm. Outside of the firm Jennifer became my focal point. My world revolved around her. That's why this e-mail message this morning was so profoundly disturbing.

I should be feeling happy and ecstatic today. Yesterday I had won my first big law suit case in superior court. The settlement had netted $1.9 million dollars for Mrs. Helen DuPrey in a wrongful death suit of her husband. The Wellington law firm had received $200,000., and today I'll get a bonus of $10,000. This did little to cheer me. My world had left with Jennifer. Wherever she was going?

I picked up the DuPrey file and stored it in the back room and poured myself a cup of black coffee with a little honey and returned to sit at my desk. My fellow classmates at Oxford never could understand how I could enjoy coffee and black at that. They all sipped tea diluted with milk. This was again beginning to awaken memories of Uncle Royal.

I opened the top desk draw and took out the letter from Don Dudley, telling me of Uncle Royal's death. He had died during my last year at Oxford and I had received Don's letter a month later. I had only written once to Uncle Royal and he had returned with an eloquently written letter. Telling me how much he had enjoyed the canoe trip we had taken. He said that on that trip he had had the opportunity to say some last good-byes to a few old friends and see once again that open wild country that had once been tamed by a few ingenious men.

Don had said in his letter that Uncle Royal had asked him to be his executor of his will when he died and that everything was to be left to me. At this time I still had not contacted Dudley or had any desire to return to the Matagamon region. That is until this very morning after receiving Jennifer's abrupt message.

"Maybe that's just what I need. Some time by myself back there at Uncle Royal's cabin." I chuckled just a bit then. From now on it'll be my cabin. "Perhaps I can get back to enjoying life, once I'm there."

My mother never said anything to me about the death of her remaining brother. And I never said anything about Uncle Royal's fortune or that I was his sole heir. My father did say one day in my office, "Your mother has informed me that your Uncle Royal has died. I'm sorry to hear that." This was two years after his death. He made it sound as if Uncle Royal had just died. Perhaps mother had just informed him. I shrugged my shoulders, "whatever."

I found Uncle Royal's letter in the desk drawer and read it again and reread it. He had beautiful penmanship. It demonstrates his true character.

"Silvia, would you come in here please?" I said into the intercom.

"Yes Mr. Wellington?"

"Silvia, how many times do I have to tell you to just call me Thomas when there are no clients in the office."

"Yes sir."

"Silvia, I'm leaving the firm for awhile."

She looked surprised and asked, "But why sir? You just won your first big lawsuit. When will you return? Where are you going sir?"

Not wanting to explain why I was really running away------I stopped. "Am I running away?" I asked myself.

"Mr. Wellington, are you feeling alright sir?"

"Yes, yes Silvia I'm fine. My uncle passed away some time ago and he had named me as sole beneficiary and it's time I--I took care of things." A lie I realized, but only a small one. Was I really running away?

Silvia was talking again. It seems as though she is always talking. "But Mr. Wellington, you don't have to leave the firm just to administer to your uncle's will, do you?"

"Silvia, I'm leaving. I don't know when I'll return. I have some business up there to attend to." I looked sternly at her without trying to laugh.

"But--what will your father say when he returns next week from London and learns you have left the firm? What should I say to him Mr. Wellington?"

"Silvia, just tell him that I'm taking a leave-of-absence to take care of my Uncle Royal's affairs. He'll understand."

"Okay Mr. Wellington, but I'll surely miss you. What about your cases?"

"I only have two. Give them to George. They both are simple suits and he'll do fine with them." Leaving two cases before either of them were completed might get me disbarred, but at this point I really don't care.

Before I left the office I wrote a short letter to my father explaining why the sudden decision to return to Matagamon. Then I took my snowshoes off the wall and picked up only a few important articles and left. I would cash my bonus check and leave my other accounts as they are. After all Uncle Royal had left me a small fortune.

*   *   *   *

I made arrangements to have my rent payments made automatically through my checking account. I took only what I needed and then before locking the door I went back to the living room and removed Jennifer's picture and threw it in the trash. Now I was all set to leave. The beginning of another new adventure. A complete change over from the life I have maintained for the last five years. I was excited about the possibilities and where my life (destiny) would lead from here. At the same time I was sad and feeling empty to have to leave all memories of Jennifer behind. But that was a choice she had made not me. Perhaps it all had to be this way so I would find my way back to the Matagamon region. Who knows? Perhaps in five years I'll be able to look back and understand these events. I hope so, because now nothing that I am doing seems rational.

My BMW was loaded with what little I had to take. My canoe and paddle, snowshoes, boots and clothes. I figured I'd find whatever would be needed at the cabin. One thing was for certain though, I'll have to go through all of the old food supplies and probably throw most of it out. "I wonder whatever happened to Shep?" Knowing Uncle Royal as I did he would indubitably have known before his death that he was dying and would have turned Shep loose. But Shep was always free to run. The only time Uncle Royal ever hitched him to a rope was when he went hunting. "I wonder if old Shep might still be around. If he is, will he recognize my scent and let me into the cabin or will he protect it." "Keep the ole coyote out Shep!" Uncle Royal would say. I laughed and cried at the same time.

It was a long lonely drive to Maine. As much as I tried to keep Jennifer out of my thoughts, she was always there. Permeating every breath I inhaled. I had been driving in sort of a semi-consciousness. Not really paying too much attention to where I was. I'd only made one stop in Portsmouth for fuel and then back on the road again without eating. Now it was 8:00 p.m. and I was hungry.

A road sign said Howland next exit; 5 miles. I wasn't even aware I had driven through Bangor; that's how out of sorts I was. At the Howland exit I found a small restaurant. The food was good and I filled the fuel tank again and I was on my way. I hadn't driven very far when I noticed the forest had closed in along both lanes of the highway. I remembered five years ago thinking this must be the end of civilization. In a way, I suppose, but more like a change rather than the end. Because Uncle Royal had sure shown me the difference.

Memories of Jennifer were beginning to slide back into the deeper recesses of my mind. I started thinking more about the changes at Matagamon that I would find since I was there five years ago. Would the Dudley's remember me? Tom Chase, Chub and Fran Foster? Was I only fooling myself by coming back? Would I still be thought of as one of the family, or would my absence make me an outsider again?

I was only a short distance north of the Howland exit and darkness had crept in. I found it somewhat disconcerting being alone on the highway. I remembered this long stretch of Maine highway where the forest crowded each lane, but now I was the only vehicle traveling on this road in either direction. I could not see any headlights as far as I could see in either direction. I began to wonder what anyone would do if their vehicle broke down or had an accident out here. I haven't seen a police vehicle since crossing the bridge at Kittery. My question was soon answered, as I crested a knoll. There in the breakdown lane an elderly couple had had a flat tire and someone had stopped to help. Maybe in Maine, but in New York you wouldn't find anyone stopping to assist another motorist on such a deserted stretch of highway.

I was alone once more on the highway. It would appear that in this north woods country at sunset people just don't travel much. Anyhow, to keep my thoughts from slipping back to thinking about Jennifer, I tried to think about what I would do once I was at Uncle Royal's cabin, which would be home until such time as I decided to leave. I knew I wanted to spend another winter there. This time though I'd be by myself and I was finding that just a little intimidating. I have never been completely alone in my life and at the cabin there would be long spells of being locked away without any visitors or means to get out.

Uncle Royal had kept me entertained enough so there was little boredom. Besides, there had been much to see and explore. I suppose it'll take some time to reacquaint myself with the region.

It was 10 p.m. when I drove through Patten. Even at this hour there were people going about their business along the sidewalks. I found a small restaurant still open. The Downtown Deli. It was downtown alright. Only a few people inside but at least it was still open. As I entered the establishment an attractive woman behind the register said, "We're closing soon but the grill is still hot. I can fix something quick for you, but none of the specials are available, " she smiled showing perfectly white teeth.

"All I need Ma'am is a sandwich and a cup of black coffee with honey."

"My name is not Ma'am, it's Sheryl and what kind of a sandwich would you like?"

"A BLT if it's convenient."

"That'll be okay," Sheryl said. "My husband Steve will make it while I cash up."

"Look Ma'am, Sheryl, if you're closing I'll leave."

"No that's okay. It won't be a problem. You're new around here aren't you?"

"Yes, I was here five years ago with my Uncle Royal."

Before I could explain more she interrupted, "You must be young Thomas, Uncle Royal's nephew." "Yes----." "He told my husband and I all about you and your stay with him through the winter." She smiled again at me and said, "That was the best gift you could have given that old man."

What could I say? I sat there in silence, amazed that Uncle Royal would be so personal with anyone outside of the family. While Steve made my sandwich Sheryl brought me a hot cup of black coffee and then she went back to the register. The coffee was strong, but that was okay. I sipped at it gingerly, thinking back to my stay with Uncle Royal.

Steve interrupted my thinking. "Here, I hope you wanted homemade bread. It was the only thing that was still fresh." He sat down across the table from me and Sheryl brought a cup of coffee for him.

"This will be just fine actually." I said and took a bite.

"Do you bear hunt Thom? We got some nice big ones last fall." Before I could answer he continued, "We'll start baiting again in seven weeks. Looks like this'll be a good year for bear too. Everybody is telling about seeing bear while fishing or picking strawberries."

I swallowed what I had in my mouth and said, "No I'm not a bear hunter. Actually the only time I ever hunted was with Uncle Royal."

"You just here for a visit or what? Be around in September?" Steve asked.

I thought he was getting too personal, but I learned five years ago that what I had thought was personal then was people just trying to be friendly. It was their way of saying "Hey are you interested?"

"I came back to take care of Uncle Royal's affairs."

"Yeah, I heard he died some time ago. A year or so, wasn't it?"

"Eighteen months ago."

"How old was he?"

I laughed then, thinking about Uncle Royal's own answer, "He was seventy or so. He never would be exact about that."

"Folks around here thought he was close to eighty."

I ate my sandwich while listening to Steve talk about hunting. He never said anything about any other sport or activity. Only hunting. He had a real passion for the woods and hunting. I'd liked to have known his family's history.

Sheryl finished cashing up and brought another cup of coffee for her husband and one for herself. She slid in next to Steve in my booth. "Why do you come now after five years?" she asked, "He died a year and a half ago. He missed you Thomas."

She wasn't prying into my personal business she just seemed interested and maybe a little concerned about Uncle Royal being alone. "Five years ago I more or less ran away from my responsibilities. My father agreed only if after the year I would promise to go to college at Oxford. I made that promise and when Uncle Royal died I still had a year to finish. When I left Uncle Royal five years ago, he told me to get my education first, then come back if I wanted to. He may not have had a formal education, but he indeed understood the importance of having one today."

We talked for about an hour, sipping coffee too. I paid for my lunch and left a gracious tip and said, "I'll stop again when I'm out this way."

"Good night," they both said.

Once again outside in the cool night air I looked up and down the road. There wasn't anyone around. The shop windows were all darken and there were no vehicles parked along the main street. I looked at my watch; 11 p.m. I was somewhat surprised to find it so late.

As I drove by the Patten museum I thought about Uncle Royal and his brother Rufus, and wondered if Uncle Royal ever came out to visit and have a cup of coffee with his brother. That day five years ago when I had stopped here to say hello to my Uncle Rufus and to tell him that Uncle Royal had said to say he'd be out sometime for coffee. Tears had filled Uncle Rufus's eyes and he was speechless.

There was no traffic and I found Shin Pond village quiet also. As if someone had folded the carpet and taken it inside for the night. There were no more houses, street lights or telephone poles. Only the darkness of night and trees that crowded the very edge of the road. Up ahead I could just see in the headlights, two deer crossing the road. As I thought I was safely by the two, another deer bounded into the road just feet ahead of me and the small deer fell on the road in front of me. I brought my car to a tire screeching halt and the deer then got up and ran off. There were several more deer crossing the road and one huge bull moose. The largest I'd ever seen. Something one might see in an Alaskan magazine. It's antlers in velvet.

Matagamon was close now. I was half way across the long-tangent on the CCC road and I noticed two vehicles pulling onto the road from a small side road, heading west. The same as I was traveling. I caught up to the first vehicle in front of me and I noticed it was an older model Oldsmobile; probably about an '85, dark in color and only one occupant. I followed these two vehicles towards Matagamon. They turned north onto the B.S.A. road that would eventually dead end. Anywhere else this would not have triggered any interest or seem at all out of the ordinary. But here, where everyone retires early for the night, finding these events at this time of night was peculiar. As the Oldsmobile turned onto the Boy Scout road the driver turned his head to look over his shoulder back towards me. I didn't know what this was all about, but I was beginning to feel uncomfortable. He appeared to be somewhat clandestine.

As I drove by the turning Oldsmobile I tried not to show too much interest. But I just couldn't help but look. He was an older man, fifty five to sixty, gray hair and thin build. I accelerated and drove only a short distance and there was the Matagamon store.

Lights were off and the store was closed for the night. Remembering that Mrs. Dudley usually stayed up at the dam house, I decided to drive up to see if any one there might still be up.

The lights were out and everything was quiet, except for the water rushing through the dam gates. I had no choice now but to sleep in my car. Sensing that those two cars that had turned off onto the Boy Scout Road were sinister, I parked in one of Don's empty camp yards, locked my doors and stretched out for the night. Soon my thoughts were centered around Jennifer.

$$* \quad * \quad * \quad *$$

In spite of memories with Jennifer, I slept well in the front seat of my car. I was more tired than I had earlier supposed. I was awakened by someone rapping on my window and hollering for me to wake up. I recognized Mrs. Dudley immediately. As the power window was going down Mrs. Dudley said, "Well! Young Thomas, what are you doing here?"

"I'm sorry Mrs. Dudley about parking in your camp yard, but when I got here last night your lights were off both at the store and house. I didn't want to wake or bother you, so I slept here," I was rubbing the sleep out of my eyes.

"It's Di and not Mrs. Dudley. Come down to the store with me and I'll fix you some breakfast."

"I don't want to be of any trouble."

"You won't. I have to make breakfast for Don. One more mouth won't be of any problem," with that said she left.

I sat at the kitchen table with Don, drinking coffee and talking about the last five years and about Uncle Royal. Mostly about Uncle Royal. Even though it was early, campers and fisherman kept coming into the store for a cup of coffee, a loaf of bread or a six pack of beer. Don and I finally had to go out in the store and talk while he waited on customers.

It wasn't long before Di had breakfast ready and while Don and I ate bacon, eggs and biscuits Di tended the store. Just as we were finishing our breakfast, the morning's busy traffic stopped and Di came back to the kitchen and joined us with her cup of hot coffee.

"After you left five years ago Thomas, Uncle Royal was never the same," Di said.

"What do you mean?" I asked, certainly concerned.

"Oh, nothing serious. It's how he changed. He was always so happy and he was always talking about you. How you were more like a Lysander than your true name
Wellington. He could be a little on the gruff side occasionally, but after you left I never saw that in him again," Di said.

"How long are you here for Thomas?" Don asked.

"I'm not sure. For the summer at least."

Don excused himself and went into another part of the house, while Di and I sat at the kitchen table talking. I asked, "Where's your son and his wife. I can't remember their names."

"Alan and Tabitha, Tabitha is upstairs and Alan is in Warden School. He'll be there for most of the summer."

I was only a little surprised. Remembering how Uncle Royal thought about game wardens. "Ole coyotes;" then he'd laugh. I must have laughed thinking about Uncle
Royal, cause Di asked "What's so funny?"

"Oh I was just thinking about Uncle Royal and how he felt about game wardens. I wonder what he would say about Alan, one of the family becoming a game warden."

Di said, "Actually it was Uncle Royal who got Alan interested in becoming a game warden."

"Boy, that's a switch. I guess Uncle Royal had changed." Di didn't respond.

"Whatever happened to that old warden that was here five years ago? The one that asked me for my fishing license out behind the dam. I can't remember his name."

"Mr. Randall, Jim Randall. He's still here. Getting ready to retire."

"Oh, that'll work out great for Alan I guess. He can stay right here and take over this district."

"They would like him to stay. Dave Sewall the warden sergeant who has this section has talked to Alan about staying, but Alan would like to get out and use what he learned in warden school first before coming back here."

"I guess I don't understand what you mean Di."

"Jim and Dave talked with Alan and told him that here in the woods he'd never (probably) use search warrants, warrants of arrest, assist with drug enforcement much, and I guess this district really isn't a high profile night hunting area. They said this district is probably the best in the state and a good one to have after you get your feet wet first. So Alan decided to go out to the settlement somewhere. Then in a few years if he wants to come back, if the district is open, he can, and he'll already have a place to live. That's something no other warden has ever been able to do; live in this district. There has never been any available housing or land to buy or build on. It all belongs to the paper companies and Baxter Park."

"That shows good thinking on his part," I said. "With Alan's knowledge of the woods he'll make a fine game warden."

Di and I talked some about Alan and where he and Tabitha might go, once he finishes his training. Don came back carrying a box. He set the box on the table and removed a folder of papers. "These are all of Uncle Royal's papers. You'll probably want to go through them. There wasn't anything complicated about his will. He left everything to you. He had a savings account, checking and c.d.'s at the Katahdin Bank in town. He also had stock in the Bangor Hydroelectric Company. Other than that, everything he owned is in this box or at the cabin.

"I went up and stored his canoe and motor and put locks on the garage and cabin doors, here are the keys," as Don gave them to me.

Just then the store door opened and by the sound of the laughter and conversation I'd say they would be friends of Don's and Di's. I noticed that neither Don nor Di got up to go out into the store portion, so I assumed they each were expecting the new visitors to come back into the kitchen.

I didn't have long to wait. I immediately recognized them both. Ted Hanson and Tom Chase. Tom said, "Thomas Wellington isn't it? Come back have you?"

Before I could answer Ted said, poking his friend Tom in the arm, "The Third."

I stood up to shake their hands and said, "Actually it's just Thomas. I dropped the third." I noticed Ted was having a difficult time holding back laughter; chewing tobacco was bulging behind his lower lip. He shook my hand, holding back his laughter, and then he swallowed his chewing tobacco and to my surprise without showing any grimace facial expression. He must have swallowed it before.

Tom shook hands and said, "Are you here for awhile or just to close up Uncle Royals' cabin and take care of his affairs?"

"I'm here for the summer; after that I don't know," I replied.

Everyone sat down at the table and Di poured more coffee for all and then she joined us at the table and conversation. I mostly just listened. Most of the topics were centered around hunting and fishing and the Matagamon area about places that I was not familiar with. Frost Pond; that one had to follow a hidden trail for two miles that was so sparsely identified that unless you knew how to get to Frost Pond, one probably would never find it. There was Lower and Middle Fowler Ponds, that from what Ted was saying was apparently very good fishing this spring. Don and Di talked about how good the fishing had been on the river this spring. Especially during Memorial weekend. Places like Three Mile spring, Stair Falls, Haskell Deadwater, Haskell Rock, Grand Pitch and below the Hulling machine; whatever that was. I wanted to ask about it, but decided to wait for another time, when there wasn't so much conversation. I sat back listening to these people (friends-members of the family) talking about all the places and wondered just how many times through the past that these same four had talked about these same favorite fishing ponds. Probably hundreds, but they were indeed interesting and each of them was apparently just as excited as if the stories had been told for the first time. I sat back in my chair and took a sip of hot coffee and smiled to myself, thinking what a unique friendship these four had.

Di saw me smiling and asked, "Would you care to share with us, whatever it is that's making you smile."

"Oh---nothing in particular. I was only thinking that I am glad to be here instead of back at the law firm." Not quite the truth but sometimes one's thoughts are personal. And this was one of those times.

"Are you going up the lake to Uncle Royal's cabin Thomas?"

"Yes, and I probably should be leaving. As I remember it takes about four hours by canoe from here."

"Well this is your lucky day," Ted said. "Tom and I are motoring up to Second Lake and hiking into Frost, we can tie your canoe to our boat and take you as far as Little East."

"I'd really appreciate it. Thanks."

*   *   *   *

I said good-bye to Di and Don and Di said, "Oh, we'll be seeing you soon enough."

Don again let me park my car behind the Dam House and as he suggested I left my keys in the ignition. Just in case he had to move it. I didn't feel comfortable about leaving a BMW with the keys and unlocked, but Don assured me it would be safe there. While I waited for Ted and Tom to arrive with their boat I loaded all of my gear into my canoe.

As I waited I began to have a peculiar feeling that I was being watched. I looked around behind me and across the channel behind the dam and nothing. But the strange sensation of someone watching was still there. I could hear a motorboat coming and I soon saw Ted and Tom as they motored around an island. I forgot about that peculiar sensation.

Everything was loaded and my canoe tied to the back of Tom's boat, "Here, you'd better have this," and he handed me a life preserver. "If I remember right, last time you were missing one."

It was a slow ride up the lake. We were loaded heavy and the bow was pushing a lot of water. Thankfully the lake was calm. The wind had not started to blow yet. I remember Uncle Royal saying that the lake would generally be calm until about ten in the morning. After that the sun was high enough in the sky to heat the water surface and the wind would start to blow. I never knew if he was correct in his thinking or not, but the lake was still calm and it was 8:35 a.m.

As we headed up across First Lake I looked over towards the distant shore on the right. There was Chub and Fran's house. After I have things settled at the cabin I'll have to come to First Lake and visit the

Fosters. I looked over at the opposite shore line, the bottom of Horse Mountain; to the south of that the Traveler range. It stood majestic against the morning sky. I had forgotten just how beautiful this view was. Then I remembered the view from the Foster's front porch. The view was even more majestic from there.

We motored up through the thoroughfare and over the old bridge that had connected Matagamon village to Troutbrook Farm, and around Togue Ledge. Tom was following the same route through the islands that Uncle Royal had. Then I remembered Uncle Royal saying something about when Don was drawing the lake down that most of the water in the thoroughfare was over a flood plain and too shallow for most motorized boats. "Why are we following the channel now? The water level isn't down," I asked.

"Force of habit. I always try to follow the channel through here, so I don't forget where it is when I need to know," Tom replied.

That seemed reasonable enough. There was a large bull moose swimming across Big Logan Cove. He was not in any particular hurry and Tom steered clear of it and changed course again and we headed westerly, now towards Second Lake. There was a breeze starting to blow, but the water was still calm.

Ted pointed towards the islands up ahead and said, "There's a small fortune in gold coins buried on one of those islands. Last year one of Don's seasonal campers was fishing behind the dam and found an old glass bottle lying up under the bank. There was a note in it and the bottle had been sealed with a cork and wax. This fellow was saying he was sorry for what he had done to his wife and his daughter, Sara, I think was her name, and he drew a map where he had hidden some gold coins he had stolen from The Diamond Match

Company. They had the mill over by that sawdust pile," and he pointed with a swing of his arm. "I saw the paper the note and the map were written on. It looked old to me." Ted said.

"Did anyone ever find the gold coins?" I asked.

"The guy that found the bottle, he and his son came up a few times and then Don came up with him once, but they didn't find anything. I guess one of the landmarks was an old poplar tree--course that would have fallen and rotted away by now. The gold is still here, no one has ever claimed finding it."

"How much gold---coins is there supposed to be?" I asked.

"No one knows. The note only said he had buried some gold coins in a red tin box at the base of a tall poplar tree, next to an oval rock. The note didn't say how big the rock was either. Through the years someone could have moved it, or ice, in the spring as the lake was breaking up.

"Sounds like a hoax to me," I replied.

"Maybe," Ted said, "but back when this mill was operating, times were hard and people were sometimes desperate."

"No one around the lake remembers anything about money being stolen from the mill or a girl named Sara. But that doesn't mean it didn't happen," Tom added. "I talked with the Fosters right after the bottle was found and neither Chub nor Fran could remember anything about it. But Fran said that when the mill was running there were a lot of people around. Some were transients looking for work or a meal and there were a lot of company people."

We motored past the warden's camp. The grass had not been mowed, but everything was quiet around the camp. No smoke in the chimney. There were people camping at Pine Point. There was one bright blue tent and a young man cooking, probably breakfast, and much to my a surprise, there was a young woman swimming and when she heard our motor she nonchalantly got out of the water and walked up to the fire. She didn't have anything on and she wasn't particularly disturbed that three men were motoring close enough to have seen her. She paid us the least amount of attention. You've got to understand, for me coming from New York where you would never see anything like this and the fact that attractive young women are apt to be somewhat stand-offish and prudish, this scene really surprised me.

Tom saw the expression on my face and said, "Happens all the time around the lake. People come up here from outside and they lose all inhibitions. There's something about the Matagamon region that makes people more relaxed, more free. And it also draws some very strange individuals."

"Like what?" I asked.

"If you stay here long enough you'll see. You can't help but run into a few," Tom said as he steered the boat around a piece of floating dri-ki. And then as if an afterthought Tom added, "Yeah, these woods attract some pretty strange people at times." He turned his attention back to guiding the boat through a drifting maze of dri-ki.

"Why is there so much wood floating in the water?" I asked.

Ted spit out some tobacco juice and said, "We had some heavy rain here two days ago. The water was high in Webster and the wood washed downstream in the river to the lake."

That was the end of the conversation until we were around the ledge point in the stream. I didn't know or understand then what Tom had said about theses woods attracting some peculiar people, but in time I would come to understand.

As we rounded the ledge point and headed up the stream there were two blue canoes pulled ashore at the Little East campsite. Smoke from their fire was rising above the spruce and fir trees. As we got closer I could see two small boys playing in the water and around the Little East Point, up Webster Stream were two older men fly fishing. Probably the boy's fathers.

Tom pulled the boat ashore just beyond the old bridge that had at one time crossed the Little East River to the other side. I remembered Uncle Royal telling me how important this Eagle Lake road system was back in the height of the lumbering industry in this country. The flat river bank made an excellent place to unload my canoe and then pull that ashore.

The canoe and gear was all unloaded and Tom and I were talking when Ted interrupted and said, "If we don't get going Tom it'll be dark before we get back from Frost Pond."

"You scared of the dark," Tom said in jest.

"No, but that trail isn't spotted well enough to stay on the trail once the sun is gone."

I held their boat while they got back in, and then I pushed the bow out into the current and the swift moving water swung the boat around; they were soon out of sight. The two fly fisherman and the boys had apparently gone back to their campsite. I was by myself---thinking how many times had Uncle Royal stood here where the Little East and Webster Stream came together. Stood here in peace and tranquility.

How many campers had Uncle Royal terrorized and chased off, saying, "These woods are mine, get!"

I pulled my canoe ashore and shouldered it like Uncle Royal had showed me and took it up the trail where he used to store his, then I brought up all my gear and left most of it with the canoe. Once the cabin was opened I'd come back with the pickup for the rest. I'd drive it backwards for two miles.

I hadn't walked very far when I found my first blow down. There was nothing I could do until I had Uncle Royal's chainsaw. I straddled the tree and continued on my way, only to find that the old road was befallen with trees.

The further I walked along the road the worse the black flies and mosquitoes became. I'm sure that once one of those varmints found me, they went back among the trees and told a whole gang of flies about finding fresh blood. Because they were attacking me now in swarms. In my hair, up my nose and in my eyes and ears and every time I breathed through my mouth I'd inhale bugs. I tried running to get away from them. That worked fine until I came to the next fallen tree.

At last I came to the driveway to the cabin. There were fresh tire tracks here. In and out, and someone had cut up all the blow downs and thrown the wood back. This intrigued me, because the only people who knew I would be here today were Ted, Tom and the Dudley's. And I knew none of them had cleared the road. Had someone found the cabin and knew Uncle Royal had died and had taken occupancy? But to my surprise I found a business card in the door. Don Shorey, Patten, Maine. That was the woods boss Uncle Royal had introduced me to that was hauling that old steam log hauler at the MacDonald camps. The guy with the catcher-mitt size hands. But why would he clear the road of trees? He couldn't have known I was coming. That puzzled me but I'd surely thank him later.

I unlocked the door with the key Don had given me and I was really surprised to find how clean everything was, and there wasn't the musty smell that I would have thought that there might have been, with the cabin being closed up for so long. I opened the windows anyhow. The ones with screens and then I went down to the spring for water. I opened the garage and started the old 59' ford pickup. Still ran like a new one. And only 2019 miles. I thought about that, Uncle Royal had probably spent almost as much time driving it in reverse as he had going forward. I eased the pickup out and then I found his chainsaw, gas and oil. The teeth on the chain were razor sharp---what else? Uncle Royal just wouldn't have a dull saw sitting around. "What if I wanted to use it? Couldn't cut much with a dull saw."

When I came to the first blow-down I shut the truck off and walked ahead clearing the road. When I ran out of gas and oil I'd walk back to the truck and back it down as far as I'd cleared and go again. I worked all day like this not realizing how late it was getting.

By the time the road was cleared and I had all my gear, except for the canoe, loaded onto the back of the pickup, it was six in the evening. I was dirty, tired and hungry. Thank God, Uncle Royal had installed a gas stove. I heated some water and washed up. In all the excitement to get up to the lake to the cabin, I had forgotten to bring any groceries. "I don't suppose there'd be any fresh meat hanging in the root cellar." But it was worth a try. I did expect to find some canned deer meat. When I opened the inner door, I couldn't believe what I saw. There was actually still some ice buried in the sawdust. A small corner of one block was showing above the sawdust. The shelves were filled with can goods, beer and soft drinks and there was twenty jars of deer meat. There were fresh vegetables in one corner of the root cellar, but those had spoiled long ago. I found a can of boiled potatoes, took a can of string beans, and a jar of deer meat and yeah a couple of cans of beer.

While supper was cooking I checked out the one bedroom. It, like the rest of the cabin was neat and orderly. I put my suitcase on a chair and laid down on the bed. Not for too long, because I was afraid of going to sleep too easy, while my supper burned on and ruined. I lay there looking up at the wooden board ceiling, wishing Uncle Royal was here with me. I was having second thoughts (doubts) about living the life of a loner like he had done for so many years. And apparently liking it.

*   *   *   *

After I had finished eating and the kitchen cleaned up, I opened the second can of beer and went to the porch. The chairs and small table were still there. Nobody had disturbed them. Surely one couldn't so freely leave things unlocked or so open as this back in New York. Probably not anywhere else in the world. "I wonder if there are any cigars here. I don't smoke now mind you. It's only to keep the black flies away." I was surely going to miss Uncle Royal. Hell, I was already missing him. The cigars were in the living room right where they had been five years ago.

I sat in the wicker rocker and puffed on my cigar. The aroma was sweet. "Hope it doesn't attract the flies." It was completely dark now. No moon and there was a gentle breeze. An owl screeched from a tree next to the cabin. The sound startled me and again

I realized I was completely alone. Not even a dog to keep me company. A coyote howled, then a loon called from the river behind the cabin.

Thoughts of Jennifer started to creep into my conscious mind. As hard as I tried to think of something else, anything, anything, just so I wouldn't have to feel the hurt of her absence. "Well, she would never have enjoyed being here anyhow." I took another puff on the cigar and blew the smoke above me, "Hell, she probably would never have come up here anyhow, even for a visit!" I took another puff and drank the last of the beer. I was tired and there was nothing to do now but go to bed.

I don't remember falling asleep, but sometime after midnight it started to rain. The sound of the raindrops on the roof was like music. A soft melody. I'd forgotten the sound of rain on a camp roof. At Oxford and then again in New York everyone is always protected from the rain and seldom does anyone get to enjoy its' beautiful sound.

A gentle wind started to blow with the rain. This was too much, this was heavenly music and soon I was back asleep. Coyotes started howling close to the cabin and I awoke enough to roll over and saw that daylight was coming. I closed my eyes, again I was asleep.

It was mid morning before I opened my eyes again. The rain had stopped during the night and the sun was out bright. I got dressed rather hurriedly, cause I had to pee really bad and remembering there wasn't an indoor toilet.

I'd have to go outside to the outhouse. In just my stocking feet I ran out and opened the old door. I was in such a hurry that I didn't see the extremely large and ugly bobcat sitting on the seat until I was inside and the damn cat started to snarl and growl. I just stood there, frozen in place with fear as I pissed myself. I could feel the pee running down both legs and soaking my stocking feet. The cat must have been laughing to himself, he jumped off the seat and brushed my leg as he made his way through the door. After I got my wits back, I started looking to see how the bobcat got in there. The only way was up through the seat, from down under. A porcupine had gnawed a hole through the old boards.

*   *   *   *

There were a hundred things that needed to be done or that I simply wanted to do, but first I had to take inventory of what there was for food and make a list of what I would need. Rather than canoe down the lake to my car at Don's, I decided to take the old ford. It needed to be registered and I didn't feel like making this a two day trip by canoe.

The land company had harvested wood, probably the winter before, right up to where Uncle Royal said the zoned deer yard started. The cut was a good job, with the brush being pulled back with a covering of smaller trees left behind. The road had been widened also and graded. I didn't meet another vehicle until I got to the four corners on the Huber Road. An empty log truck went by; it was traveling so fast and stirring up so much dust I had to wait several minutes while the dust cleared before I could see enough to continue. The main road had been graded recently also. No wonder the big truck was going so fast.

There was no problem getting a new registration for the ford. I had all the necessary papers with me. As

I drove along main street in Patten, everyone stopped whatever they were doing and watched as I drove by. I wasn't sure if it was because the truck was so old or if everyone simply recognized it as Uncle Royal's. Probably the latter.

The people at the Ellis market were friendly and helpful and a young boy helped me carry the bags of groceries out to the truck. "Isn't this Uncle Royal's pickup?" the boy asked.

"Yes, he was my uncle. Did you know him?" I asked.

"Yes, never would forget the only person who always gave me a tip for carrying his groceries out to his pickup."

I reached into my pocket and pulled out all the change I had and gave it to the boy.

"Here, thanks."

As I left town people everywhere were waving. Not at me, but the fact that they recognized Uncle Royal's pickup truck. There were four vehicles parked at the Lumberman's museum. When I had the opportunity I wanted to come back. I realized now that what I saw on that first visit was not just a collection of junky old relics from an era forgotten. The exhibits were very much a part of the history of this area.

As I crossed the Shin Pond Bridge a float plane was taxiing up the cove and a throng of people with camp gear were waiting on the wharf.

It was early evening by the time I drove into the camp yard. Home now. Most of the groceries I stored in the root cellar. Those dry goods that wouldn't spoil I took inside with me. In the morning I'd have to go through all the supplies, in the cabin and what was out in the root cellar and throw out what was no longer any good. I was feeling restless after eating supper so I let the dishes set in the sink and I grabbed a long sleeved shirt and a couple of cigars and went for a walk along the old Eagle Lake Tote road down to the dead water that makes up on the river.

I found a grassy spot and sat down. I lit a cigar to keep the flies away. "I don't smoke now mind you." I laughed out loud. My laughter startled a small coyote pup stumbling up the road. He had no idea I was there until he heard me laughing. The pup didn't have enough energy or strength to get off the road, so he laid down. Probably hoping I wouldn't see him. I sat still where I was for several minutes, not wanting to frighten him and to see if its' mother would come after it.

My cigar was too short to smoke it any longer and I threw it into the water. The pup was still there and no sign of the mother. The pup never made an attempt to run off as I approached. It just laid there with his head laying on the grass between its' outstretched front legs. He was too small to fend for itself and up close I could see dried puss in the corners of both eyes. I picked the pup up and he snuggled into the crevice of my arm.

"Looks like I have a friend," I carried the pup back to the cabin. He didn't move and I wondered if he had died, until I scratched him behind his ears. He liked that and lifted his head. I found an empty cardboard box in the garage and filled it with some dry grass and fir boughs. Maybe these smells would help to make the pup feel more at ease. Then I warmed up some canned milk and put a little butter in it. The pup drank the whole dish without stopping.

As I laid in bed, for the first time I began to wonder if this pup could be an off-spring of Shep. I didn't know what to call the pup. I didn't want just any name. It had to be a name befitting him. And then it came to me as clear as a newly cleaned pane of glass; Royal. What else could it be.

The next day I was up early and checked to see how Royal had spent the night. He was still asleep. I warmed up another dish of milk with a spoonful of butter. I set the dish in the box with him and got myself something to eat. After breakfast I went out to the root cellar and removed all the spoiled vegetables and all the canned foods. Some of the cans were so old the paper wraps were either gone or they crumbled to the touch. When I had finished and the floor was swept clean and more sawdust to cover the ice there was indeed a lot of food. The old food stuffs I took out behind the garage and threw over the bank onto the garbage pile.

With the root cellar cleaned, I decided to go through the cabin and clean that thoroughly. Uncle Royal wasn't in the habit of throwing much of anything away. Particularly if it could be used for something else. As far as dry goods, I threw out anything that had previously been opened. Some of that contained an abundance of mice droppings. Anything that I thought was junk but may perhaps sometime in the future have a purpose I stored in the garage. I tried to separate all the reading material from what looked like important papers. Those I stored on shelves in the bedroom.

I wanted to get as much of the cabin cleaned as I could, so I didn't take the time to look through Uncle Royal's particulars. That is until I discovered a leather bound box in the back of the closet. Engraved in gold letters on the box was U.S. Army. I opened the box and inside were three distinguished medals. There were two bronze stars and one silver star. In the bottom of the box were three official envelopes, in bold lettering U.S. Army. The first one was a letter of congratulations from President Roosevelt. I read through the letter, all the time wondering why Uncle Royal had never said anything about these awards. Instead he kept them in a box tucked away in the back of the closet. Apparently the whole company Uncle Royal was in had advanced to Milan, Italy. They had met heavy resistance there and Uncle Royal's squadron had been pinned down by mortar fire and machine gun nests. Several men had been wounded while crawling on their stomachs, trying to get close enough to throw a hand grenade at the machine gun nest. Some were badly wounded and screaming for help. Uncle Royal had dropped his rifle and removed his backpack and crawled out to the wounded men and brought each one back, one at a time, to the safety of the trenches. All the while being fired upon by the enemy.

The next letter was an award; the bronze star, given to the entire company for the campaign into Milan.

The third letter; again the bronze star, for apparently disobeying orders and taking out a pill box and heavy artillery. There was a new lieutenant who had ordered his men to advance straight into the fire from the pill box. And Uncle Royal being the sort of independent backwoods fellow that he was, had taken it upon himself to break away from the squad and enemy fire and had circled to the right; way to the right and had come in behind the pillbox and heavy artillery and had succeeded in throwing hand grenades inside. All but two of the enemy soldiers inside had been killed and Uncle Royal had heard their screams and had fought his way through the carnage and fire and brought the two out. He probably would have received the congressional medal of honor if he hadn't first disobeyed the Lieutenant's orders.

Probably no one in the family ever knew about his heroism. No, probably not, as I looked back on it. Uncle Royal had come out of the war with a broken heart and there must have been just too much hurt with the memories of Italy and the war. He came here to forget her and the war. That night as I sat in Uncle Royal's rocker on the porch, with the coyote pup asleep in my lap, "And I'm here running away from a broken heart and memories of Jennifer, just like Uncle Royal."

I stayed out on the porch long after the sun had set and it was dark. The only sounds were frogs in the shallow bowgan that makes up on the river. After awhile I got up and put Royal back in his box and continued cleaning out the cabin and picking through all of Uncle Royal's treasures. I don't think he ever threw anything away. Perhaps that came with living a solitary life back here in the woods where you couldn't run to the store to get what was needed. And also during most of his life and I'm sure this is true of all that lived around this region, simply couldn't afford to buy replacement items. If they didn't have a spare something or other in the back closet, one was made. Today a trip out to town and back wouldn't require much at all, but back when life was in full swing around the lake, a trip to town and back would take a whole day, and spare time didn't seem to be a luxury then and probably most people couldn't afford the trip out, let alone the time. Even Uncle Royal, if anything broke and if it could possibly be used for another purpose, it was carefully stored away, and sometimes forgotten.

It was after midnight before I had things sorted out. What to throw away and what to keep. Just in case. The trash I piled next to the kitchen door, there was a lot, and the treasures I carefully arranged back in the closet on shelves where some of the things belonged.

That was enough for tonight. I checked on Royal and he was sleeping soundly. The puss was clearing. I poured a glass of blackberry brandy, a taste I had acquired while in England, and lit a cigar and sat out on the porch. It was a warm dark night. The frogs were still chirping in the bowgan and there were other sounds now too, like the night had finally come alive.

I don't know why but I wasn't tired or sleepy. This seemed somewhat peculiar since I had been busy all day cleaning and sorting out good and bad food. And as I sat here in the rocking chair enjoying the complete quietude, I particularly enjoyed breathing the fresh air accentuated with the smell of the spruce and fir trees and an occasional wisp of pine. I remembered the difference between the various evergreen trees. "Not all green trees are pine," Uncle Royal had said.

After awhile I finally went inside and turned the gas lights off and went to bed. I still couldn't get over the silence. Inside the cabin I couldn't even hear the frogs. There was absolutely no sound at all. If I had not already spent a year here with Uncle Royal, I would have found the complete silence disturbing.

I was up early the next morning; bacon, fried eggs and coffee for breakfast, and of course I attended to Royal. He was well enough to go outside today, but on second thoughts, I decided it would be better to leave him inside and get acclimated just a bit more.

After backing the pickup out of the garage I brought everything out. What was of absolutely no value went into one pile and those objects, some I had no idea what they may be or had been, I piled in a neat stack by the door. Once everything had been removed I gave the dirt floor a thorough cleaning and brushed down all the spiders and cobwebs.

I had almost all of the good stuff back in the garage, put away in nice neat piles, when I bent over to pick up a keg of nails and someone in a green uniform walked around the front of the truck. I recognized him as the same game warden who had asked to see my fishing license five years ago. Jim Randall.

"Hello Mr. Randall," I said. Not knowing what else to say. He had kind'a come upon me by surprise.

"Good morning. Thom isn't it?" He replied. "See you cleaning things out some. You know camp dumps are illegal now. Have been for some years actually. Anything that won't dispose naturally has to be taken out. There's a dumpster at the state sand shed, across the road from the Huber garage."

"Okay, glad you came along. I was going to throw it all over the bank like Uncle Royal had been doing."

Right then and there I decided to drop the Thomas like I had the, third, and just be called Thom. "Yes," as I reached out to shake his hands. "Looks like you're cleaning house. You must be moving in."

Right to the point isn't he. "Yeah, Uncle Royal left me the cabin," and then I added for just the fun of it, "his legacy too."

He looked me over then, from head to foot before replying. "Maybe, but I'm not so sure if you or anyone could live up to his legacy." I wasn't quite sure what he meant. I was sure he wasn't talking just about Uncle Royal's poaching.

All the while he was talking I noticed he was looking things over in the garage like he was taking inventory of the contents. "Would you like a cup of coffee?" I asked him.

"Sure, why not." We went inside the cabin and while the water was heating and I was getting the coffee ready, Randall along with conversing, looked as if he was again taking inventory of the contents. It wouldn't surprise me any, that when he left he would remember everything I had and where it was. I supposed he developed this skill as part of his job.

He surprised me by his next comment, "You know, things just don't seem the same now that your Uncle isn't here. I kind'a miss the old rascal." Perhaps he had a little admiration for Uncle Royal and never wanted to admit to it. Remembering how Uncle Royal used to talk about the wardens and torment them so much; I was beginning to wonder if he had not admired the wardens all this time and had taken a defensive stance behind his cajoling.

"You know, I was just thinking, Uncle Royal would have made a good game warden." Randall started laughing. So hard in fact I thought he might fall out of his chair.

When he finally could compose himself he said, "Yeah, maybe you're right. I'd sure hate to have him on my trail." There was more laughter. "Trouble is, instead of following the trouble, he'd be up front leading the way!" I guess I understood what the warden was saying. Uncle Royal after all did have a notorious reputation for poaching and he liked to make a game out of his escapades by being a prankster. To change the subject I asked, "The other day at the store Di said you were retiring. Is that so?"

"Yeah, but not as soon as I had thought. I was going to retire this fall, but I think I'll stay a couple more years. I wouldn't know what to do with myself if I quit wardening."

While Jim talked I kept trying to guess his age. He didn't look to be old enough for retirement. He had graying hair, but the skin around his neck, face and hands showed no signs of aging (wrinkles). Although he didn't walk with a springy step, he was sure footed and probably could walk the pants off anyone.

"When you left here before," Jim was saying. "You went to college didn't you?"

"Yes, England."

Before I had a chance to finish Jim interrupted and finished for me. "Must have been Oxford. And you probably studied law and you joined some elite firm in New York."

"That's about it." Was he ever astute, I'll bet there aren't many poachers who get away from Jim Randall.

But he started to smile and that turned into a grin. Something was up. "After you left, I'd see Uncle Royal occasionally on the lake or on one of his hunting escapades. We'd talk and after awhile he started inviting me for coffee at his cabin. One day I was out here," he pointed towards the good travelable road, "it was raining and I didn't have anything in particular to do, so I came in and had coffee. I kinda liked his company and I started stopping more often. Sometimes we'd play a couple of hands of cribbage and sometimes we just talked---well he talked a lot about you, stories about the people who use to live and work here and his brother. The one who was a warden, Rufus, and some of his poaching stories. Your Uncle was really unique. He was different than what you would think of a hermit living in the wild. He liked people, although he tried not to let it show too often, and he was an intelligent man for being uneducated. Perhaps a better description would be, he exemplified everyone in the region--even those before his time."

I was seeing a different side of the warden, Jim Randall. This wasn't, at least it didn't seem, to be the same warden I had met five years ago behind the dam. And certainly not the same warden that Uncle Royal talked so much about or tormented and razzed just for the fun of it. But then perhaps Jim the warden, had done his share of razzing and tormenting Uncle Royal also. I could see it in my mind. The two of them going out of their way to play a prank on the other and then sitting back in the bushes watching the whole shenanigan unfold and then later, out of ear-shot, laughing to themselves about getting one over on the other. Yes, I can see now why Jim missed Uncle Royal. He lost his playmate.

We talked and talked and drank two pots of coffee. The longer we talked the more interesting Jim Randall became. He had an encyclopedia of stories stored away in his head and he was having as much fun telling me about them, as I was enjoying listening.

In the middle of one story about finding several women swimming in the nude at the Little East campsite and a troop of boy scouts floated silently around the corner in canoes. He didn't finish the story though, he heard Royal whimpering in the bedroom and that certainly caught his attention and more especially so when he saw the little coyote pup come running out of the room. Royal ran directly to Jim until he heard the familiarity of my voice and then he turned and came over to me.

There was a questioning look on Jim's face, "Where did you get that?"

"A couple of days ago, in the evening I walked down to the dead water and he came out of the tall grass when he heard me coming. He was sick and abandoned, so I brought him back here and fed him. This is the first time he has gotten out of his box. He must be feeling better."

"What do you intend to do with it?" Jim asked. "If you were to keep it locked up in a pen or hooked on a run or leash, you'd have to have a breeders permit from the department to keep a wild animal. But if you were to allow it to roam free like Uncle Royal allowed Shep----well there's nothing saying you couldn't have a wild animal as a friend."

I understood what Jim was saying without him having to come right out and say it. And I must say he surprised me. That's all that was said concerning the legality of keeping a wild animal.

"How long you figuring to stay? Just for the summer or are you going to put in another winter?" Jim asked.

"I'll stay this winter---after that I don't know yet."

The coffee pot was empty and I was hungry. It was past noon and the warden was still here. Apparently this wasn't a busy day, but I wouldn't realize until later that this was the warden's, Jim Randall's way of getting to know if someone new in his district was going to be a problem or not; fish and game wise. I made lunch for us both and another pot of coffee and some canned milk for Royal. Jim sure took a liking to that little coyote Pup; the way he petted it and played with him; letting the pup chew on his fingers.

I'll never understand why I asked the next question. It just rolled out of my mouth kinda natural like. "Do you have any children Jim?"

"None of my own. I've helped to raise a few step kids. What about you?"

"No, I haven't been married yet."

"I'm on my third marriage."

"Must be difficult being married to a warden."

"That's why this is my third. All were good women, no complaints. Just that I found it to be more important to be a good warden than a good mate. Used to be that I was gone from home more than I was home. My second wife complained once that I slept more often on the ground than I did in her bed. Guess maybe she was right too."

It was mid-afternoon before warden Jim Randall left. Two and a half pots of coffee and lunch. I enjoyed his company and talking with him, but at the same time I was feeling a little bit uneasy. There were moments when I thought he might be fishing for something and then he really surprised me with his last statement as he walked towards his truck, "If you're not to busy someday next week perhaps you'd like to go fishing. I've got to hike up to the Fowler Ponds. If you're interested meet me at the store Tuesday morning at 7:00 a.m." He didn't wait for me to reply. He just got into his truck and drove off.

I did some more cleaning, then I decided to go for a walk. I tucked Royal inside my shirt and closed the door and headed out back towards the gravel road. At the end of the camp road where it turns left towards the better graveled road a partridge flushed from under some brushes right beside me. I don't know who jumped more, me or Royal. His toenails were sharp and he scratched my stomach.

Up near the mud hole, the old original Eagle Lake tote road veered off to the left. Moose had used this old road for travel and there was a narrow trail snaking through the alders and raspberry bushes. There were moose tracks and bear tracks; no deer. The only wildlife were rabbits and more partridge.

Remembering how much I liked eating partridge I mentally catalogued this road in my mind for hunting this fall. I wasn't long coming to Turner Brook; water was flowing across the old gravel road, where an old crew camp had once been. I believe this was MacDonald's old crew camp. Upstream was an old sawdust pile and there was rusted tin cans and broken bottles everywhere. Even an old woodstove with fir trees growing up through the lid openings. I tried to imagine how life must have been here back when the mill and woods camp were operating. If this was the same MacDonald woods crew where Uncle Royal had taken me to see the Lombard steam log hauler, then that would put this operation back in the late 20's. Again I tried to imagine how life would be, socked away back here from nowhere and no way to get out to civilization in the winter. Sure couldn't have been much of a life. And what did they get for wages, fifty cents a day. I just shook my head at the idea.

Later that night after supper and Royal was asleep in his box, I lit a cigar and poured me a glass of whiskey and water and sat in Uncle Royal's rocking chair. I puffed on the cigar until a pillow of smoke filled the screened-in porch, forcing the night bugs to retreat, and I took a sip of my drink, silently wishing Uncle Royal was still here.

As I sat there rocking, puffing on the cigar and blowing smoke, listening to the loons; what a beautiful sound,---then suddenly for no apparent reason that I could explain something triggered a memory cell in my brain, and for just a moment I could see a glimpse of a dream I had had the night before of Jennifer and I together. I sat out there on the porch long into the darken hours of the night.

The next morning I was up early; not early like Uncle Royal would have been, not daylight, but 7 a.m. is early. Today I would take Uncle Royal's canoe and motor and go down the lake. Visit the Fosters and then have coffee with Don and Di. I put Royal in the garage with food and water and I could hear him whining as I walked towards the pickup.

About half way down the Eagle Lake tote road I decided there had to be a better way than this. Driving the pickup truck backwards for two miles was no easy task. Tomorrow I'd go to Houlton and buy me an ATV. That would certainly be easier than all this driving in reverse. Besides, the bushes and trees needed to be trimmed back if I was going to continue to use the truck.

At the junction of Little East and Webster Stream I pushed the canoe out into the current and brought the bow around with the paddle so I was going with the current before starting the motor. To my surprise the motor started with the first pull on the starter cord. I set the throttle just fast enough so I'd have steering control in the current.

No one was up yet at the Little East campsite; there were three blue canoes pulled up on the shore but not turned over; they would fill up with rainwater. "Neophytes, they'll never learn." I was remembering my experience when I had not turned my canoe over. "Hell, I didn't even pull it ashore. That was the morning when I had first met my Uncle Royal.

The lake was still calm, like a mirror almost. I cracked the throttle some more and I was surprised how fast this three horse motor could push this canoe when there was but one person and no camping gear. I motored down the center of the upper part of Second Lake. I was surprised to see the point of pines campsite empty. It looked like a beautiful place to camp. The ole coyote den, the warden camp, was there and no one there. The grass hadn't even been mowed. That was strange, the warden always kept the grass trimmed neat.

When I came to the islands on the lower end of Second Lake I remembered what Ted had said about some gold coins supposedly had been buried on one of the islands, and I decided what the heck, I might as well stop and see for myself; the small islands I just motored around. The only trees were jack-pine and Ted had said the note had said at the base of a tall popple tree next to an oval rock. So I avoided the islands, for now, that had only jack-pine on them and concentrated only on those with popple trees. But those islands were so big it would take me a long time to investigate each one thoroughly. I chose one and pulled my canoe up on some grass turf and tied it off. I walked the length of the island, back and forth spacing only about ten feet each time until I had walked over the entire island. I didn't see anything that resembled an oval shaped rock.

I'd spent enough time looking already and decided to leave the treasure hunting for another day. I had things I wanted to do today. I remembered what Tom had said about following the channel through the narrows; even in high water. "It makes for good practice," he had said.

As I motored around the point at Togue Ledge I noticed a green canoe had been pulled way up on shore and as I rounded the point I saw for the first time a girl about my age standing on the other side of the ledge. She had just taken off her bikini. She heard my motor and she stood up and turned towards me. About this time I was only twenty feet or so away. At first she seemed surprised. Who wouldn't? Then she regained her composure and said, "Good morning, it's a beautiful day isn't it?"

"Yes," I replied. "It certainly is at that." She smiled back and dove off the rock into the water. I kept motoring, trying to stay in the channel. As I motored around the next island I saw a young man, maybe a little older walking down where the girl was swimming.

I scratched my head in bewilderment. I couldn't imagine seeing a sight like that back home. She wasn't embarrassed at all with me motoring by so close. "There's something strange about this area." That's what Ted and Tom had said too.

At Louse Island I turned east towards Deep Cove and Chub and Fran's. Down here on the bigger lake there was a gentle breeze and a small chop on the water. I motored by the Jake Day camp, or Edmund Ware Smith's camp. All was quiet; no one there. It was quiet at Chub and Fran's also. The grass needed mowing and fallen tree branches littered the lawn and door yard. There was no smoke in the chimney. There were no fresh tire tracks in the gravel driveway. The sheds were locked as well as the boat shed. "That's strange."

I sat on the front porch steps drinking in the beautiful panoramic view of Horse Mountain and the Traveler Mountain Range. I had forgotten just how beautiful the view was from here. If only my friends at Oxford could experience just a moment of this. For some reason I was really beginning to feel lonely. Now I discover that Chub and Fran are not here either. Uncle Royal is gone and now the Fosters. But before I could finish being lonely I noticed movement out of the corner of my eye. A tall dark complexioned man in a rather striking blue uniform came around the corner of the house. I wasn't familiar with the uniform, but I did notice that he was carrying a handgun. That meant he was some kind of law enforcement.

"You looking for the Fosters?" The tall man asked.

"Yeah, but I guess they aren't around. My name is Thom Wellington," I walked over to him and extended my hand. I noticed then his insignias. His shoulder patch identified him as a Penobscot Indian Warden.

He shook my hand and said "My name is Kirk Loring. I heard your motor when you came ashore and I came over to make sure no one was trying to break in. I have a camp through the woods, there," and he pointed.

"Beautiful view isn't it." Kirk said.

"This has got to be the prettiest spot in the world."

"Just about. Not surprising Chub wanted to die here, instead of going into a nursing home," Kirk said.

I looked at him and from my expression he said, "You didn't know did you?"

"I'm assuming your saying Chub has died."

"Fran too, she didn't last long after Chub went." Then as if Kirk could read my thoughts he added, "Their son Kerry owns this now. He lives in New Hampshire.

"How did you know the Fosters?" Kirk asked.

"My Uncle Royal introduced me to them five years ago."

"Your Uncle Royal's nephew? Now there's a hard ticket. He was quite an enigma. A juxtaposition. He had been a loner all his life; preferring to be left alone, but then he truly enjoyed the company of his friends."

"He once told me that loneliness was a welcomed companion. Yeah, he was an enigma certainly." I was a little curious about Kirk's usage of the word juxtaposition. I wonder now where he had gotten it. Uncle Royal; perhaps.

We went over to Kirk's camp. He said he had coffee brewing. "How do you take your coffee?"

"Black, thanks." I was looking at the moose antler carved into an eagle's head. "This is great. Did you carve it?"

"No, my father carved it for me. The eagle represents a special deity in our culture." There was a pause while we both sipped our coffee and I was surprised with his next statement. "All this used to belong to us once."

Not sure what he meant I asked, "All of what?"

"This land, those mountains, the lake. A hundred and fifty years ago my people would make this their summer camp. They would hunt caribou when they migrated, fished for salmon and trout. This was their winter food."

I interrupted then. "And they made their camp at the beach on Second Lake. Uncle Royal told me about finding arrowheads and spearheads there."

"Now we own half the township. It's tribal land. After the 1980 Indian Lands Claim Act the tribe bought this and other territories in the state."

"Where do you live Kirk?" I asked the obvious question.

"Indian Island, Old Town. I'd like to live here but my wife won't have it."

Not to change the subject, but I asked, "How old was Chub when he died?"

"Ninety seven."

"Were they alone? I mean Chub and Fran. It would be an awful burden for her if they were, seems to me."

"Kerry's wife was here with Fran. At least I think she was his wife. I only met her once. The warden was here too, Jim. At least the afternoon before he died. He spent the whole afternoon with Chub and Fran."

This certainly wasn't the picture in my mind I had conjured up of Jim Randall. After my initial encounter with him five years ago and the stories Uncle Royal told of him, I pictured a hot nose arrogant man. A grizzly bear of a personality. But after talking with Jim back at the cabin and now what Kirk had said about him spending the afternoon here with Fran, I guess I have to change my opinion of him.

Kirk started laughing then and I waited for him to compose himself. I was sure another story was in the offering. And I was correct.

"Jim and I went to warden school together and we became good friends. After he transferred to this district we worked together some each fall. Sometimes he'd help me on tribal land and I'd help him working night hunters. That's where this story is going. We caught quite a few night hunters, but last year was the most extraordinaire. I mean, it was like a voice coming right out from heaven saying, "Look at my watch!" Kirk started laughing again.

"That night we had arranged to use my decoy deer, Jim and his assistant Alan Dudley, he's a game warden, in training. Well we set the decoy up at the murder field. That's what we called it. It was a small clearing on the Huber Road just above the garage. Jim had a nice hiddie-hole where he could get his pickup out of sight. Alan and I were on foot next to the road so we could see everything as the scene unfolded. The decoy wasn't up long before the hunters started coming out. The first vehicle, a pickup, stopped and started to turn to put the headlights on it. But there were three other vehicles coming up behind that one. They took off and stopped down at the garage. I could see the truck but not what they were doing. I thought maybe they were just waiting for the other vehicles to come out. Alan and I both were getting excited. I just had a feeling that as soon as traffic was clear that this first pickup would be back. Now Jim is sitting in his pickup, for a chase vehicle, and he can't see any of this unfolding.

"Then headlights come on at the garage and the same pickup starts back. Just before the pickup got to Alan and I, it turned in the road, jigging, and illuminated the decoy with the headlights. I hadn't positioned the decoy for traffic from this direction. The head wouldn't pivot fully around so the eyes were illuminated. But I had rigged one front leg to pick up with an electronic servo and the limit switch would kick off and the leg was spring loaded to snap back, as if the decoy was stomping the ground. Like they'll do just before running off.

"The head didn't pivot right and that dam leg stayed up. The limit switch wouldn't disconnect." Kirk started laughing then. Finally he composed himself enough to continue. "There stood this deer on three legs and the head not turning enough for the eyes to illuminate---well, I guess it didn't matter that much if the deer was standing on three legs or not. The pickup, before it had come to a full stop, a shot was fired from the truck." Kirk started laughing again.

"This was Jim's signal to come out. He pulled out and directly behind the pickup and he turned his blue light and head lights on. Alan went to the passenger window and I went to the driver's side," here Kirk started laughing again. This time it was quite awhile before he could continue. "Then---there from above me, out of heaven I first thought; came this voice that said 'Look at my watch;' then the voice said again, 'What time is it?' I made sure the driver wasn't going to try anything stupid and then I just had to look up to see where this voice was coming from. I shined my flashlight up, there was a body cab on the pickup and Jim was standing on top holding his light and a rifle and a second subject that, Jim was telling to look at his watch and tell him what time it was.

"I heard the guy say 'It's ten minutes to six.' then Jim said, 'It's an hour and a half after sunset, so there shouldn't be any question about time in court, should there?'

"Why did he do that for?" I asked.

"Well he had just lost a good case in court because the defense attorney confused the judge about the time. Lawyers are the scourge of this country," Kirk added. I didn't tell him I was one of those scourges.

"Jim passed the rifle down to me and I unloaded it and secured it in Jim's pickup and left Alan to secure the other three guys in the front of the pickup.

"To this day I don't know how Jim got up on top of that pickup so fast. I mean, he had to have turned his lights on,---then there came this voice saying 'Look at my watch.'"

"That seems like an awful dirty trick, putting out a decoy deer for some poor unfortunate hunter to be tricked into shooting," I said.

"There have been a lot of fellows who have said the same thing. But you know, I've only heard that from those who have been caught.

"Alan frisked the occupants inside the pickup and by now Jim and the shooter were back on the ground. But things weren't over yet. Jim has an inner instinct or something like that. He had a gut feeling there was more to this. I took charge of the shooter and Jim opened the back of the body cab and started looking through their dunnage. And you know what he found! I'll tell ya. There buried amongst all their gear was another deer. No transportation tag attached to it and it was hot too. We did a postmortem on the deer right there to determine the time of the death."

"I didn't know or never realized you wardens were so scientifically advanced with your investigations," I interrupted.

"It's a proven science that has been recognized by the courts. The time of death of this particular deer was too close to call. So the shooter and driver were both charged with night hunting, illegal transportation of a deer and oh yeah, it was a doe and none of the four had a doe permit."

"Jim said he was taking the driver and shooter with him and asked one of the others to follow him in their pickup. The two said they didn't have driver licenses. So Jim asked their age and they said nineteen and twenty. 'I don't understand why you two don't have licenses if you're nineteen and twenty,' Jim said. They all were smoking cigars and drinking beer. Then the oldest one spoke and said, 'We're Mennonites and we don't drive.'"

"Then Jim said, 'Well, you're drinking beer and smoking cigars, I thought Mennonites were suppose to be religious?'"

"The driver answered then and said, 'Some are and some aren't.'"

"This really blew Jim's mind and he started laughing so hard I thought he was going to pass out. 'Some are and some aren't,'" and Kirk started laughing and he spilled his coffee.

"So what did you do with them?" I asked.

"They didn't have any money at all and the bail amount was $1,125 each. So we had no choice but to take them to the nearest county jail in Bangor, 120 miles. That was the longest ride those two ever made."

"That seems like an awful long distance to the nearest jail."

"This is awful big country." Kirk started laughing again; remembering the scene and the voice from heaven saying, 'Look at my watch.'

We drank more coffee and Kirk told me stories of catching fish hogs over in western Maine and on other tribal land; Alder Stream Township, stories of chasing people around the islands in the Penobscot River near Milford and Indian Island. Of using a decoy moose for early moose hunting before their sustenance hunt began in September. But the one I liked the most was of Jim Randall on top of the pickup telling the shooter to look at his watch. As I think on it now it would appear to be comical, especially in the dark when you couldn't see where he was.

I told Kirk that he was welcomed anytime and if he was working in the area to stop by for a hot meal. "I'm on my way to see the Dudley's." He held the canoe while I got in and then he pushed me off the rocky shore. I said good-bye and, "I'll stop in again."

There was more wind but the water hadn't gotten rough yet. As I neared the boat landing behind the dam I throttled the motor back. There were people fishing offshore and I didn't want to make a big wake for them. I pulled my canoe ashore and checked my car. It was okay and instead of driving down to the store I felt like a walk. Everybody I met on the gravel road or at a campsite, said good morning and asked about the fishing. People from back home wouldn't say good morning to you. But then I thought, some of the vehicles had New York plates on them. What is it about these woods that changes peoples personalities so much? The same people who happily greet me here wouldn't give me the time of day, if I asked, back in New York.

There were several vehicles parked at the store and most of them were from out of state. The store was crowded with vacationers buying fishing licenses, canned goods or having a late breakfast. Di saw me as I came in and motioned for me to come out into the kitchen. "Whenever we're busy Thom just come around through the other door."

She poured me a cup of coffee; I was about coffeed out but I didn't want to hurt her feelings, "Would you like some home fires and eggs?"

"Yes, that would be good." I replied. I wondered if they ever ate anything for breakfast besides eggs.

"What are you doing today Thom?" Di asked.

"Well I had planned to visit Chub and Fran.. I met Kirk Loring there and he told me that they had both passed away. We talked for awhile and drank a pot of coffee and then I decided to stop by here before going back up to the lake."

I had lunch with them; we shared a pizza. Di makes the best pizza I have ever eaten. I wonder if she's Italian. All the while I was visiting, customers came and went and neither Don nor Di seemed to behave as if I were imposing.

"The game warden Jim Randall stopped by the cabin for a visit the other day. He was there several hours. You know, I've formed a different opinion of him now, than I had five years ago. He even asked me to go along with him next week to the Fowler Ponds.-- said the fishing was good. By the way, I'll need to buy a license. I guess I might as well buy a combination, I'll be here hunting in the fall also."

"You'll enjoy that trip," Don said, "He'll probably take you up the back trail. The park really doesn't like people using it, but there's very little they can do about it. People were using the trail long before there was a park, even ole Baxter himself used it a time or two with Chub Foster. At one time everyone drove into the Mitchell Camp and parked beyond the camp out of the way, but the Mitchell's put up a cable to keep people out. So Jim found a way around the Mitchell's and spotted the trail with blue paint. He didn't want to be called out at night to look for someone who had wandered off the trail and had gotten lost. When the lumber company cut wood there they pretty much obliterated the old trail. Jim cut out trees laying across the trail and cut back the bushes. There's still a lot of people who use the trail and it's a lot shorter hike to the good fishing. You'll see for yourself." More people came into the store then and this time Don got up to wait on them.

By the sounds, it would seem that they were looking for information concerning the park. "Jim was at Middle Fowler Pond right after ice-out." Di said. "He caught three fish hogs. He went for an early swim too."

When I looked somewhat confused about the early swim she continued. "It was the eleventh of May and the ice had only been out for two days. It was cold and windy, only about fifty degrees. He watched from the opposite shore as these three guys cleaned, cooked and ate fish. They had used the back trail and Jim knew they had to come out on his side of the pond. So he waited. They each were carrying just their legal bag limit and when Jim said he had been watching them, they said they had eaten hot dogs. Jim knew better than that and asked about the fish tails in the fry pan. I guess there wasn't much said after that. Jim apparently knew where they were camping. They left and Jim crossed to the other shore and he could see fish heads in the water. He took all of his clothes off and went in after the fish heads."

"I don't know if I would have been that dedicated." I said.

"Well, there's probably a lot of wardens who wouldn't be. They lied to him and I guess that made him angry enough to go in. He caught up with them at the Sebosis campground at the river. "Yeah I know where it is." He charged all three for the fifteen trout over the limit. Oh Yeah! He found a paper plate one of them had thrown away and he charged each of them with littering also. And if all of that wasn't bad enough, he wrote a letter, he's famous for that, to the park authority and had the three banned from ever using the park again. They learned an expensive lesson."

"Yeah," I said, "don't cross the warden!"

"They haven't been back since. They used to come up here every spring, from mid-Maine somewhere, to pick fiddleheads for commercial retail."

Now this is the kind of warden Uncle Royal had told me about; not the one I had had coffee with at my cabin. I had then seen another side of the man.

*   *   *   *

The boat ride back up the lake was extraordinary. The wind blew almost as strong as it had when I was with Uncle Royal. We had just left the Fosters and had to spend the night on Louse Island. I motored along the westerly shore and the wind and waves were not that heavy until I rounded Martin Point and started through the devils' throat.

Something didn't look right, or the same on Martin's Point. Then it occurred to me. The big log cabin was no longer there. I know Tom wouldn't have had anything to do with the removal, but I couldn't imagine who would be fool enough to demolish a nice cabin like that. Then I remembered what Uncle Royal had said about the park authority and how the authority had burned all of the old timers homes around the lake when this region became part of the park. I shook my head in disbelief. "The fools."

The Martin Camp and those responsible for its destruction were soon forgotten. The wind whistled threw the devils' throat and me and my canoe were being precariously thrown about. The lake was calm in the shelter of Louse Island. So once again I headed for its rocky shore, prepared to spend another night there waiting for the wind to ease off.

Once I was directly behind the island the lake surface was once again flat and calm. I found the same shoal that Uncle Royal and I had used before and I pulled the canoe up and tied if off to a tree. Rather than just sitting there waiting for the wind to drop off, I went exploring about the island. I found some early blueberries and ate until I had filled my stomach. I found the remains of an old building. Probably this is where the men were de-loused in the spring when they came back from their winter camps. The thought of lice made my skin crawl and naturally I began to itch.

From the high point of the island I looked up the lake towards the thoroughfare and Togue Ledge where I had seen the girl earlier this morning. I shook my head in disbelief and rubbed my eyes. But they were still there. There was a small group of canoes. "What in hell are they doing in water as rough as this?" There were two canoes lashed together. Not a bad idea, but they were also bracing a small sail which in this wind was carrying them quite well. There were two boys and two girls in those two tied together. Not adults yet, upper teens. The boys in the other four canoes were considerably younger; maybe twelve to fourteen. Probably boy scouts from the base. But what of the girls? Don't say boy scouts now have girl counselors? I thought about that. Younger boys just entering puberty and girl counselors old enough but still---? Boy, not when I was a boy scout. How things do change.

I was glad they couldn't see me ensconced here on Louse Island. Did I dare chance it? Then I thought that as skilled as Uncle Royal was with the canoe, he didn't take any unnecessary chances. No, I'd wait until the wind subsided.

I walked around the island again, paying close attention to the ledgey shoreline. Behind one ledge rock and almost covered over with tree roots I found several old boom chains. Then I found where these chains were probably secured to the ledges, because I found four old iron bolts embedded in the rock. Not knowing anything about booming wood down the lake I couldn't begin to fathom how the booms would be stretched out across islands or an inlet cove. Let alone understanding the mechanics of getting the wood from one end of the lake to the other. I know what Uncle Royal had told me about towing huge booms full of wood; sometimes using capstans and winches. But never having seen a boom of logs before, it was difficult for me to understand just how it was accomplished. Yes these early woodsmen were indeed ingenious.

The wind finally subsided at 6 p.m. I started off up the lake again. It would have been easier and a shorter distance to go straight across the flats instead of following the channel through the thoroughfare; remembering what Uncle Royal had said about that section of lake that looked so inviting. That just beneath the surface lay a hundred acres of stumps. The remains of trees that had to be cleared when the dam was built. I had paddled my canoe up through the stumps five years ago, but with a motor hanging over the side would only be tempting good fortune.

At Togue Ledge the young couple were sitting on grass on top of the ledge. They both waved and I waved back.

The sun was setting by the time I had pulled the canoe ashore and turned it over. And by the time I was back at the cabin it was dark. Clouds had settled in and there was a fine mist in the air. "Glad I didn't have to spend the night on Louse Island." After that whenever I ventured anywhere in the canoe, I also took, a survival pack; dry clothes and some food, compass and a lighter.

Royal was glad to see me. He was hungry. I took him off milk and started feeding him solid food from my plate. I left the dishes for morning and Royal

and I went out on the porch. It was a dark quiet night.
Except for the frogs. They were singing quite a chorus
tonight. The mist had changed to a steady rain and
before long I could see lightening flashing off in the
distance, so far away I couldn't hear the thunder. I
remember one particular lightening storm five years
ago. The flashes and the thunder claps were
instantaneous; the strikes were that close. The sharp
splitting noise bothered me, but Uncle Royal sat in his
rocking chair and carried on a conversation like there
was nothing to the noise. "You get used to it boy.
These hills are so full of iron ore that it draws that
damned lightening to it. Be a wonder if we don't have
some fires come morning," he had said.

The rain was coming down real hard now, and I
was enjoying the sound on the porch roof. Royal was
subdued by the sound too, as he lay curled up in my lap.
The lightening had stopped; I thought. I hadn't seen
any more flashes for some time. But just as I was
thinking this, a bright bolt of lightning struck across the
river from the cabin and the ear splitting crack deafened
me. I was sure I could feel the concussion of air against
my chest. Royal felt it too, he jumped off my lap in
surprise and started whimpering. I laughed, only a little
and said out loud, "What would you ever do if you were
on your own out in the woods?"

The thunder and lightning kept up its barrage
even after I went to bed. The rain came down so heavy
I thought maybe the log cabin might wash down into
the river. The next morning I checked around the
cabin, garage and root cellar for water damage. There
didn't appear to be any. I guess Uncle Royal had long
ago made sure everything was proofed from the
weather. I don't know how much rain had fallen but

there were puddles everywhere; even behind the cabin in the moss.

After breakfast I decided to go to Houlton and buy an ATV 4 x 4. There was a lot of this country I wanted to explore and an ATV will only make the exploring easier and fun. Besides, that's just what I need to haul my gear down to the canoe at Little East and back again. Not the pickup.

I found a Polaris Four Trac at Tidd's Sportshop. It wasn't new but it was clean, good tires and it had been well maintained. "What about a utility trailer, do you have any?"

"The best place to get what you need is in Patten, Kathadin Welding. Steve Crouse. If he hasn't got what you want, he'll make it."

Two days later I picked up my utility trailer built to my specifications. Nice job too. The ATV and the trailer were just what I needed to get back and forth from camp to Webster Stream.

Tuesday morning finally arrived and instead of taking the canoe down the lake, I decided to drive around in the pickup. It was just 7 a.m. when I pulled into the driveway at the Dudley's store and Jim was already there. I was surprised when I saw his pickup. Without thinking too much about it, I just simply assumed it would be clean and polished like I've seen the state police vehicles. But Jim's pickup was covered with mud from the front bumper to the rear. And the rear bumper had old blood caked to it and then I saw a puddle of fresh blood on the ground. As I walked by his pickup I saw a dead deer laying in the back.

Don was waiting on some customers and Di said from the kitchen. "Come right out here Thom. You're just in time for breakfast." Tom and Ted were there at the kitchen table with Jim, drinking coffee and chewing tobacco. I watched Ted and he never spit the juice out.

"Heard you were going up to Middle Fowler with Jim. Better have your hiking boots on," Ted said.

"The fishing has actually been better at Long Lake and Billfish. Before the day is out you'll see for yourself," Tom said. Only later would I come to understand what he was implying.

When Di set breakfast on the table I was surprised to see oatmeal and not eggs. Maybe she had overheard my thoughts last time. I shrugged it away and ate breakfast and two more cups of coffee. Jim, Ted and Tom kept up a continuous conversation from fishing, to coyotes, to what the Red Sox were doing and back to fishing.

I noticed Jim kept a vigilant eye on all traffic going in towards the park. I suspected then that there probably was some particular individual that he was watching for. He never said, even after Ted and Tom left. Di went out into the store and Don came back and had a cup of coffee with us. Still I thought Jim was waiting for something in particular. He kept looking at his watch.

I was beginning to wonder if we'd ever get to Middle Fowler. It was 8:45 a.m., "Be at the store by 7:00 a.m. Tuesday," he had said. That was almost two hours ago.

"Well it's time we were on our way. Fish must be biting by now," he stood up, "Thank you for breakfast Di," we left.

The inside of his pickup wasn't as cluttered with necessities of the job as I would have thought, except for the radio, there was nothing. Jim must have wondered at my surprise because he said, "I travel light."

We crossed the bridge over the Penobscot. There was a father and two children fishing over the side. We turned left off the paved road and headed south along a wide gravel road that had recently been graded. Jim pointed to a smaller road on the right and said, "That's how people used to get to the back trail until the gate was put in." We drove for another half mile and Jim stopped the pickup in a gravel pit. "We'll walk from here."

Across the road was a narrow footpath blazed with blue paint. After about five minutes the trail turned sharply through some bushes and we came out to an old log landing and about 150 yards away was the Mitchell camp. The blazed trail followed an old skidder road up over the height of the land. The terrain was steep and I was sweating profusely; so too was Jim. We came to the end of the skidder trail and from here the footpath wound its way through tall old growth trees. The terrain was too rough for tree harvesting equipment.

Before we got to the top, the trail broke out into a huge beaver pond, ringed with tall swale grass. We had to cross over on the dam; I got my feet wet. Rugged rocky cliffs ringed the beaver pond. What a beautiful spot. But Jim wasn't wasting anytime looking at the scenery. He kept the pace, once we had crossed the dam.

Jim pointed off to the left. There was a pond there. "That's Little Fowler. It empties into Middle Fowler. The fishing isn't as fast here, but the trout usually run bigger. Not many people bother with it. It's best early in the spring."

Jim slowed the pace, trying to be quiet. I knew we must be getting close when we veered off the trail to the right and came up behind an out cropping of ledge on top of a rocky knoll. I still couldn't see the water. Jim took his pack off and pulled out a camouflaged shirt and binoculars. He inched around the rocky ledge and kept a small spruce tree between him and the pond. He scanned the shoreline looking for fishermen. He was soon satisfied and stepped back behind the ledge. "There's four fellows across the pond. They are the ones I want. There are more people at the lower end. But we won't worry about those until we've finished with these four."

"You knew these guys would be here didn't you?" There, I wanted to ask that ever since leaving the store. I felt as if he was waiting there at the store for a reason.

"Yeah, I got a tip from the warden in Houlton. They drove by the store right after you got there. I wanted to give them enough time to get here and do some fishing before we got here. We won't have to sit on'em as long that way. That is unless the fishing is really slow.

"You might as well fish yourself. Go over on that shore," he pointed, "and drop below them some and fish down towards the other end. I'll catch up with you when I'm finished with these guys. Right off that point there," he pointed again, "is an underground spring brook that puts into the pond. The water runs off the mountain and the ground is so porous the brook actually flows underground for about the last one hundred yards.

"Oh, and don't get your feet wet. It's no fun hiking with wet boots."

From that last statement I guessed we had a long trail ahead of us. I crossed to the other shore and when I walked by the four fellows Jim was watching, they sneered at me, so I went to the point Jim had described.

I made several casts before I hooked my first trout. It was only eight inches or so, so I threw it back. As I fished, I kept an eye on the other four. They were keeping every fish they caught. I looked across to the other shore and the rocky ledge and hoped Jim was seeing the same as I. Then I thought, of course he is, that's why he's here.

Right then as my thoughts were across the pond, I got a heavy strike on the line. I set the hook and started reeling in. It fought hard and jumped clear of the water once. This would be a keeper. I didn't have a net and I certainly didn't want to lose it, so I backed up into the alders and pulled the trout onto the rocky shore. I noticed the other four were watching.

The trout was thirteen inches. I broke its' neck and cleaned it. "Trout ain't no good if you leave the guts in it," Uncle Royal had said. "Soft trout aren't any good to eat."

The trout stopped biting after that. Cast after cast and nothing. I didn't really want to leave,--cause I wanted to see Jim over haul these fish hogs.

The sun was hot and the sky was really blue. The bluest that I can ever remember. And the mosquitoes were as bad as I had ever seen. I threw the baited hook out and let it settle to the bottom and I set the pack down so I could light up a cigar, hoping the smoke would drive some of these flies away. I hadn't noticed it yet, cause I was too busy swatting mosquitoes, but the four had pulled up and were coming towards me. Was Jim close by and would he over haul them now?

"How's your luck?" one of them asked. "All we could catch were too small and we had to throw most of them back."

"I kept that one," and I pointed to the crotch alder branch I had strung it on, "and I threw one back."

"Well you've done better than us. We're going to try it from that large rock, across that cove. Sometimes it's pretty good there. You're in a good spot here too." The same fellow said.

They left and I watched as they made their way to the rock. They set their spinning rods down and just sat there on the rock smoking. Almost as if they were waiting for something. Had they seen Jim? I doubted that. Were they waiting to see if there was a game warden there at the pond? They were being cautious that was obvious. I'd still like to know where Jim was. With binoculars he'd have a good view from the rock ledge, but could he get here fast enough if they were really going to pack up and leave?

Twenty minutes or so went by and I caught one more trout about ten inches. I kept it and cleaned it. It looked like the four were packing it up to leave. They each shouldered a pack and broke down their rods. I wanted to see this, so I put my two trout in my creel and put that in my pack and left. Walking nonchalantly in their direction. I stepped in behind them and followed along the trail to the lower end of the pond.

There were two couples fishing from the ledges at the lower end. By the looks they were doing more playing than fishing. Still no Jim. Where in hell is he?

"Hey, you going out? The one named Bruce asked.

"Yeah, I was going to fish Lower Fowler before going out." I really wanted to see them over hauled.

"Might as well walk along with us. Maybe we'll stop at the lower pond too. I'd like to have something to take out. You know that's fly fishing only. Hope you're no damned warden," Bruce said.

Right now I was wishing I was. What kind of trouble am I getting myself into? All I could say was, "Okay."

I had no way of knowing where the trail went that we were following; only it was suppose to take us to the lower pond. Where was Jim? Had he gotten delayed at Middle Fowler? After about ten minutes we left the trail and headed downhill through the trees. As I was sliding through some fir trees the fish hook on my line snagged and the line broke inside the reel.

Once at the lower pond the other four started gearing up and baiting their hooks. Nailed to a tree just fifty feet away was a poster, covered with wire screening. It said very clear, "Fly Fishing Only." It was ignored. I was still trying to fish my line out of the spinning reel.

I heard twigs breaking behind me and before I could turn and look. "Hello boys. How's the fishing?" Bruce turned around and answered, "Don't know for sure we just got here.--hiked up from Fowler Green."

"You fellows know this is fly fishing water only."

"Yeah, figured you'd catch on. Glad we didn't catch any."

"Yeah, that would cost you more; for each fish." Jim said.

He asked for their licenses and while they were finding them he said to me, "It's a good thing your line was caught up inside your reel or perhaps you'd be getting a summons also for illegal fishing. But I will have to see your license also."

I think he was telling me to play along. So I produced my license and he said, "Thank you."

As he wrote the summons he had a good time joking with the four. As he was writing the last summons he asked, "Did you get any fish?"

"No, like I said we just got here. We haven't had enough time to catch any." Bruce said.

Jim handed Eric the last summons and said, "This has been an expensive experience." And I thought he was about to let them go, they were all shouldering their packs, without finding what they had for trout. "Boys, I'll have to see what you each have in your packs."

Eric said, definitely, "You got a search warrant?"

"Nope, I don't need one. You see I've been watching you most of the morning and I followed you down along the pond. You went by Dudley's store at ten minutes before seven. That's all of a search warrant I need."

Jim found nineteen trout total in Bruce's pack; making him fourteen over the limit. Eric had fifteen total, David had seventeen total and Charlie, the quietest of the group, had twenty one total. Jim wrote each of them another summons and gave each five trout and he took the rest. "Now boys, have a good day and I wouldn't do any more fishing on the way out if I were you." They just grumbled and left.

After they were out of ear-shot I burst out laughing. "I thought sure that you were going to let them go without finding their cache of trout. Where were you? I never saw you following."

"They had to come back this way, so I observed them from the other shore across the pond. There's another campsite on that side and from the knoll I could see a tent there, so I checked them over before I caught up with you. How was your fishing?"

"I kept two pretty nice ones. Where do we go from here Jim?"

"Long Pond, and we'd better be on our way."

"Down this trail?" I asked

"Nope, through the woods," and he turned uphill off the trail and strode out across country. No maps, no compass; he just knew where he was going. He had me totally confused. We never walked in a straight line for more than a couple of minutes. We went around a knoll, uphill, downhill through a wetland and thirty minutes later we were at Long Pond.

We stayed back from the water and any openings! We stayed behind bushes while Jim scanned the pond with his binoculars. "There's two parties camped and one lone fisherman.

"If you want some good fishing, stay along this shore and I'll meet you at the other end in the pines by the campsite. I'm going to work these parties and then meet you later. If you find the fishing good, remember to save one for another pond on the way back." He disappeared into the bushes and I wasn't to see him again until late afternoon.

The fishing wasn't that great. At least I didn't think so. I caught one about fifteen inches. A nice trout by any means. I wondered how Jim was doing. Later in the afternoon I was tired of fishing and was just moseying along looking at the view and watching two rabbits in the pines.

"Hello there," a young woman spoke from behind me.

I turned around to see who was speaking. "Hi," I replied.

"Are you camping here also?" the girl asked.

"No, I'm just resting for the hike back. I'm Thom. I live up the lake along the Eagle Lake tote road," I knew that would confuse them.

I told them about the cabin and where I was really from and not mentioning anything about the game warden being around.

"We're on our honeymoon," the young woman added.

I was silently hoping that Jim wouldn't have to issue these two a summons. Just then I saw Jim step out from a bush. The young couple hadn't seen him yet. Not until he spoke.

"Hello, wow you sure have nice weather for camping. Where are you folks from?" he asked. Again I was seeing a different personality in Jim.

"We're from Woodstock, New Brunswick. We came here for our honeymoon," Jeb said. "Susie and I were here last year and we wanted to come back."

By now we had walked over to their campsite. I knew there was a reason why Jim continued the conversation; he knew something.

"Some of the best eating trout I've had have come from this pond," Jim said.

"I know what you mean, I caught one late yesterday and we ate it for supper."

"How long will you folks be here?"

"We have to leave in two days," Susie replied. "I have to go back to work."

"I'd like to check your licenses please." Here it comes. Good guy turns grizzly bear.

"Ah, --we don't have any. We had intended to stop at the store, but we were running late. I'm sorry."

Jim asked for Jeb's drivers' license and wrote a summons for no license and Jeb even signed it. Then Jim put his summons book back in his pack and said,

"On your way out stop at the store and buy a three day license. Just one. I'll check to see if you do. If you don't I'll mail you a copy of the summons. Wedding Gift."

From there we went to High Pond. The only thing there to see was a flock of ducks and an otter. From High Pond we cut through the woods to Round Pond. No fishermen there only a young couple sunbathing in the late afternoon sun. We didn't interrupt their privacy, instead we continued on through the woods to Billfish Pond.

There at Billfish the water was the bluest that I'd ever seen in my life. We had come out to a peninsular. "There's a campsite over there," and Jim pointed, "We'll have to be quiet. We'll walk out here on the peninsula, from the point we can pretty much see the whole pond."

I followed Jim out onto the peninsula trying to stay low, down behind the bushes. Part way out Jim stopped and pointed to old rusted pieces of iron. "See those iron wheels? These rail wheels were used back in the 20's when there was a tramway here to get the pine and spruce logs off the mountain down to the river. Once the logs were at the river they were piled up until the river drives in the spring. It was expensive building this tramway but it was the easiest way to get the logs down. It was a lot of hard work building it and a lot of ingenuity to come up with the idea. The crew camps were over there behind that thicket of trees. These old trolley wheels are the only remnants of that era.

"Do you know what a tramway system is?" Jim asked.

"Yes, Uncle Royal had described for me the one that had been used between Eagle Lake and

Chamberlain. He had some old photographs of that tramway."

"Well," as he scanned the pond with his binoculars, "I don't see anyone out fishing. They're probably back at the campsite."

"Anybody you know?" I asked.

"Not really. I checked at the gate house yesterday afternoon and their records show that three guys from the Portland area are supposed to be here for three days. It's a long hike to bring three day's provisions with you; four miles."

We didn't go straight to the campsite. Instead we circled around to the west and came back onto the foot trail that goes to the sight. "This way they'll think we just stumbled onto them." No more explanation than that.

We walked right into their sight and two bearded fellows were frying trout in an aluminum fry pan and not having much success. "It would be easier to wrap your trout in aluminum foil and put it in the coals. It'll taste a lot better too."

"Thanks, we'll try that next time," the shorter of the two said, "My name is Jake---Jake Pirinnian."

I didn't like the look in his eyes. His dark hair was unkempt and scraggly and down on his shoulders. His eyes were as dark and menacing looking as his hair. The taller one just sat there and never did say anything.

"How's the fishing?" Jim asked.

"Slow, but when you get one, it usually is a good one."

"I'd like to see your licenses please." Jim said.

"Yeah, no problem," and Jake had his in his shirt pocket. The other guy, Bill, had to look for his in his dunnage.

"How long you staying?" Jim asked.

"We're going out tomorrow about noon."

"That's good. It's supposed to thunder shower tomorrow night."

"Well Thom, we'd better get going if we intend to be back to the truck before dark." We left and headed back out along the foot trail that goes back to the perimeter road. We walked along the tops of two knolls, not very far at all, then we stopped.

"I thought you said there was suppose to have been three guys there?" I said.

"There is. The third guy is out hunting." When I looked surprised Jim continued. "Did you see all those .22 shells on the ground behind the fireplace."

"Yeah."

"Well, this is a wildlife sanctuary. No firearms allowed."

"What makes you believe the third guy is hunting?" I asked.

"First of all; a gut feeling. Second; neither of those two mentioned a third person in their party. And third; those two are nothing more than thugs. Capable of anything."

"So what do we do now?"

"We wait, and listen. If I'm not mistaken we'll hear gun shots before dark." We moved off the trail, on top of a knoll and hunkered down behind some small fir and spruce trees. I was hungry, but the excitement of the chase made me forget just how hungry; and how tired I was.

"What do you think the third guy is hunting for?" I asked.

"My guess would be partridges. There's quite a bunch in through these mountains where they're protected from hunting. The birds will be roosting soon, before it gets dark."

And the shots came and just like Jim had said, only minutes before dark. You know in all the excitement I never gave it a thought about how we were going to get out of here in the dark.

"We'll follow the trail back to the campsite and wait for that fellow to come back."

We didn't have long to wait. A shadowy figure walked into the site from the direction of Round Pond and he was carrying something in each hand. Jim took his pack off and suggested I do the same. He removed a long handled flashlight and said, "Follow me and be quiet."

The three never knew we were there. They were engaged in oohing and aahing over the partridges and how good they would taste for breakfast.

Jim snapped his light on and said, and this I still can't believe he said it, "Wow? Those are nice birds. Plump and both are cocks. But---I'll have to take them you know." His demeanor was anything but antagonistic, almost friendly. "What if I say you're not," the guy holding the birds said.

Then very firmly and direct, Jim replied, "Then I will arrest you and walk you out of here tonight. No matter how long it takes. It's your choice."

The guy held out the birds at arm's length and Jim took them and said, "The .22 handgun also," and he put the two birds in one hand and held out the other for the gun. I must admit, he has nerves of steel. Jim handed the two birds over to me and he unloaded the .22 handgun. Then he handed that to me also.

Jim walked over to the picnic table and pulled out his summons book from his back pocket and sat down. By now the atmosphere had subsided some and the earlier hostility was gone. Bill even offered Jim a cup of coffee, "Thanks." He took a sip and set the cup down, then he began to write out the summons by the only light he had; his flashlight.

When he had finished writing he said, "I've issued you summons for; one, a closed season violation; two, hunting in a wildlife sanctuary and three, possession of a spruce partridge. I could also give you one for possession of a firearm in a wildlife sanctuary but I think the courts would consider that too much. But I am taking your handgun and if you want it back, show up at court.

Fred took the summons; he wasn't smiling. "How much is this going to cost me?"

"Oh, probably about four hundred dollars plus cost of court and the victim's fund."

"For two stinking birds!" Fred said.

"It was your choice Mr. Tucker. Now gentlemen have a good night." Without saying anything more Jim got up and started back out the trail. And me not far behind him. He left his flashlight off; why? I'm not sure. But he was able to navigate the trail flawlessly. Neither of us spoke until we were back where we had left our packs.

"That could have been close," I said. "Did you see the look on that guy's face when you said you were going to take his handgun plus summons him? He was angry."

Jim still hadn't said anything and we were shouldering our packs and I asked, "What do we do now Jim?"

"There's a beaver dam across the cove down here a ways. We can cross over on that to the other side." The walking was easier on the other side in spite of the steep shale bank. Instead of thick underbrush, like there was on the campsite side, this was open hardwood and easily navigable. We followed the ridge, always climbing to the top, towards the lower outlet end. When we finally stopped I looked back towards the other shore and we could see their campfire.

Jim built a fire in front of a large rock and in the firelight I could see a stack of wood already there and an abundance of dry kindling.

"You've done this before I take it?"

"Sometimes when I make this trip there isn't enough daylight to get out, so I camp here and walk out in the morning."

"We can see their fire from here. Certainly they can see ours. Won't they think you're watching them?"

"Perhaps. It might do some good if they think they're being watched," Jim replied not seeming to be too concerned.

"Give me your biggest trout and put the rest and these confiscated trout in the spring. It's about fifty yards behind this rock."

When I got back Jim had the trout and the partridge breast on a stick roasting over the fire. "Why didn't you cook both partridges?" I asked.

"You ever tried to eat a spruce bird?" "No." "They taste awful."

"Won't your wife be worried when you don't come home tonight?"

"She's away visiting her sister." Then he took out his portable radio and called the police barracks in Houlton and notified them that he would be out of service all night. I wondered how many times he had stayed out all night when his wife wasn't away visiting her sister. Had he always been able to have the barracks call her and let her know, her husband wouldn't be home that night? I wasn't sure if Jim would ask the barracks to call his wife or not. I keep seeing a different side of his character. It kept changing with every event.

"You surprised me back there."

"How's that?"

"You said after talking with the first two that they were thugs. You knew the third had a handgun and was illegally hunting and we're what four-five miles from nowhere and oh yeah, it's dark and you go walking in with your hands in your pocket acting like you're a friend, instead of the law. Then just as cool and calm as you can be, you tell that thug that you're going to take his birds and his gun and if he didn't like it, you would arrest him and walk him out of here! You could have at least had your gun out."

"That would have only antagonized him and made them mad as ole hell. It wasn't necessary."

"What if they had been doing drugs?"

"Still wouldn't have been necessary. The only time you, or any officer, pulls his gun out of the holster is to shoot someone. Not to scare or intimidate some thug into submission. You pull your gun, you want to damn well be ready to shoot someone."

"Police officers pull their guns all the time. Even to make a simple arrest on the street and oh yeah in daylight."

Jim was quiet, I knew he'd have a good answer to that. I waited. He turned the trout and breast over, then he answered. "I had asked an old time warden a similar question, Warden Sergeant Duane Lewis; he said 'That if you couldn't get yourself out of a mess with your mouth then you don't deserve to wear the uniform.' You won't find any police office going more than fifty yards off the hot top without calling for a game warden to do the chasing. They don't like to get their uniforms dirty and they certainly don't feel comfortable in the woods. Those guys back there, they expected me to come barging in with a drawn gun acting like a cop and when I didn't and I came in calm and friendly they didn't know how to react. They were confused and they had, and will always have from now on, a lot of respect for me, for the manner in which I handled the situation. They may never like me, but they'll certainly have respect and they won't forget.

"I'll tell you a story. This actually happened. I wouldn't lie. Some years ago I received a call from a woman that her daughter and boyfriend had taken the daughter's eight year old boy fishing on the Mattawamkeag River and hadn't returned yet. It was 10:30 p.m. The night was warm and clear and I assured her that they probably just had gotten caught in the dark and had holed up for the night, and that I would head right out. She had said they hadn't taken a compass, so I knew they'd probably stay on the river instead of striking out through the woods. I knew the river and knew that the only place where there would be enough water to fish, for that late in the summer, would be at Four Foot Pitch, about two miles below the bridge on Route 11. Walking along the river would have taken all night. I knew of a gravel road that would get me close, at least I thought. I ended up hiking two miles through a cut over area and then through a swamp. I came out on the river right at Four Foot Pitch and they were on the other side with a fire going.

"I had no choice but to wade the river. They were all okay. They had just stayed too late and didn't have a flashlight. I really didn't want to go back the way I had come. I wasn't sure if I could get back to the end of the road where I had left the truck. I knew of a closer road. So we crossed the river and another large brook and then uphill through raspberry bushes that were taller than the young boy. But he never complained. We came out to the road; about two miles off another paved road, so I radioed the state police and they sent out a trooper. After awhile he called back and said he'd have to wait for us at the mouth of the road. He said there were too many bushes closing off the road. I walked that eight year old out another two miles. And all because that trooper didn't want to get his clean cruiser muddy or scratched. By the way the road had recently been graded. True he would have had a few scratches from bushes, but---."

He didn't finish, but I understood what he was saying. "What about when you catch a night hunter? Do you use your handgun then? I mean you're facing someone who has a loaded rifle or shotgun."

"Still never felt like I had to. Sometimes you become a friend, like we did this evening and sometimes you scare the living hell out of them. That usually takes the fight out of 'em."

We sat there in silence. Jim was turning the trout and partridge breast and I was deep within myself. Thinking about what Jim had said about using his gun.

Suddenly not more than fifty feet behind us a lone coyote howled. I jumped and exclaimed rather vehemently, "Jesus Christ! Is he close! He scared the crap out of me!"

Jim just sat tending to his cooking, "He must have smelled the meat cooking. He won't be back and he's just a lone coyote. After we leave tomorrow he'll be back looking for scraps."

"What happened to the Martin Camp?" I asked.

"Park tore it down, hauled it off and burnt it." I noted a bit of bitterness in his tone. "Tom retired and the authority took it down.

"Same thing is going to happen to our camp also, the Davignon camp. I think at first snow the director will send the rangers up and burn it."

"Everything?" I asked.

"Yeah, probably the tall spruce trees will be burned too. A lot any of them care."

"What about the asphalt shingles?" I asked.

"I don't understand. They'll probably burn everything."

"Well if they do, that'll be an environmental violation. It's against the law to burn any asphalt shingle in an open fire. Asphalt is considered a hazardous material and must be disposed of properly; either burying in the ground or burned in an appropriate incinerator."

"How do you know all this?" Jim asked.

"Remember, I'm an attorney at law. An officer of the court," we both laughed.

"If it hadn't been for that camp, there is a reasonable chance that I wouldn't be here tonight cooking your supper," he turned the partridge breast and trout over.

"Well are you going to tell me the rest?"

"It was a few years ago, middle of January, -20°F that morning. Don was snaring coyotes for me on the river just above your camp. Dri-ki dam; you know where it is?"

"Sure, I've been there."

"Don had to go to Augusta that day for some meeting or other and he asked me to check his snares for him. I've been out in colder weather than that, but still it was dam cold, especially going up the lake on the snowmobile. I had an arctic cat - super jag then. Nice sled, I simply wore it out. It was cold, so I put my olive green refrigerator suit on over insulated pants and sweatshirt. It was bulky but warm.

"The snares were beyond the park line. Hell it's legal to trap in the northern townships of the park anyhow. Except that is when biologist are doing a pine martin study in the northwest portion of the park. I dropped off two beaver carcasses for bait. Coyotes had knocked several snares down and I reset those.

"Through the years between Don and Ted they have removed near a hundred coyotes from the river there at Dri-ki dam. That has saved a lot of deer from the coyotes.

"On this day in January I didn't have any coyotes, but they had been there and the beaver carcasses that Don had frozen into the ice were almost gone. From there I rode upstream just to see what the coyote activity was like. There had been four run right up the center of the dead water and over Dri-ki dam. I drove my sled right up close to the dam so I could look at the tracks closer and the engine shut down on its' own. That wasn't a good sign. The state couldn't afford an electric start, so I pulled---pulled and pulled, until I couldn't pull the starter cord anymore.

"I have to be real careful in cold weather. I sweat profusely with the slightest exertion. Then I freeze because I'm soaking wet. Well, I pulled that cord until I was wet. I lifted the cowling and the plug wasn't firing. It was getting gas but no fire. I figured the coil had shot the bed. I closed the cowling and pulled the started cord one more time. Nothing.

"I dug out my portable radio from my pack. I was so far back from nowhere that I didn't think I had a prayer of ever reaching anyone. I turned it on and switched it to the State Police channel and screamed into the radio, if there was anyone out there that could hear me. The state police dispatcher came back and asked what the problem was. I advised him that my snow sled had quit running and I was twelve miles from my pickup at Dri-ki dam. I asked him to call the park and to have Charlie, Barry or Tom come to Dri-ki dam because I was broke down. Charlie, Barry and Tom were the only ones who knew where Dri-ki dam was. In a few minutes the dispatcher called back and said that the Director was not going to send anyone out. I tried to call back to the dispatcher but I was unable to get through. The battery had discharged enough in the cold, so the radio was now useless.

"It was twelve miles back to my pickup. But---I had no choice. I put my snowshoes on and started back. Remember now, how I was dressed. Insulated pants, sweatshirt and that refrigerator snowsuit; no hat only a helmet. I hadn't snowshoed a hundred yards and I was wringing wet. And to make things worse, the trees and branches were all covered with new snow. But honestly I wouldn't have been any wetter if I had fallen through the ice. It was -20°F."

I interrupted then and asked, "Why didn't you go to Uncle Royal's cabin. Sure he wouldn't have turned you away."

"No probably not. But back then I didn't know Uncle Royal real good. There was another reason though and I guess that one kept me going," he turned the breast and trout over again.

"What would that be?" I asked.

"My wife. She doesn't get home from work until about nine forty at night. I didn't want her to come home to a cold house and worry about where I was."

"Did you really think you could snowshoe twelve miles dressed as you were?"

"I didn't see how I had any choice."

"I don't understand you Jim. You could have stayed with Uncle Royal; warm and food to eat, but you risked your life so your wife wouldn't worry?! I don't know if I could have done the same; knowing what I was faced with. I mean twelve miles in a refrigerator suit," I shook my head.

"By the time I got to the lake I was soaking wet and tired. But I didn't dare rest, because of the cold. By now the wind was blowing a gale and had erased my snow sled tracks across the lake. At times the wind blew so hard there was a complete whiteout there out on the lake. But I had only another eight miles to go to my truck.

"It was two miles to the camp. At Pine Point I knew I'd never make it back to my pickup. So I swung left for the camp. The cold had frozen the outer layer of my clothes, I was cold and getting more tired. I had a real difficult time snowshoeing up the hill to the camp from the lake. I fell once and decided it would be easier to crawl the rest of the way.

"The camp was cold but I managed to get a fire going. That's an awful good woodstove. At least it used to be. I took my clothes off and hung them up on the clothesline I had put up by the stove. I figured that as soon as my clothes were dry, I'd strike out again. I ate a can of cold beans and pulled a chair up beside the stove and wrapped some old towels around my legs.

"As soon as my clothes were dry I got dressed and was getting ready to leave when I heard snowmobiles running. It was Don and Alvin Theriault, another game warden. Alvin had heard the radio traffic and knew that if I was calling for help, that I must be in a real fix. Alvin had never been up the lake nor did he know where Dri-ki dam was, so he stopped at Dudley's store. Don's meeting had been cancelled so he was there. The thoroughfare can be real dangerous in the winter. One day it might freeze over and the next it could be wide open. Don didn't want Alvin going up the lake alone so he got dressed and went with him. Don knew that I would sometimes start a fire in the stove, so I could stop and warm up on my way back from Millinockett and Millimagassett lakes.

"Don said that he had seen smoke coming out of the chimney, but he knew I'd sometimes start a fire and then come back; he and Alvin decided to check the camp regardless, even though they couldn't see a snow sled there or any activity. I was sure glad they showed up. It would have been a long and cold snowshoe hike down the lake. The wind was still blowing and the chill factor was probably about -30°F or colder.

"The Davignon camp saved my life because I was left in the cold, and the idea that the commissioner of Inland Fish and Wildlife is just going to stand by and watch it go up in flames is reprehensible. I'd like to see that man left in -20°F weather with twelve miles to snowshoe."

"And---you never told your wife what you went through out there, did you."

"I told her I'd been left out in the cold after my snow sled broke down and that I'd hiked back to camp and Alvin and Don came up after me. There wasn't any need to go into details. No sense worrying her for no reason.

"Here I think these are done enough now."

"They sure smell good. No wonder that coyote came around."

When we had finished eating there wasn't much left except for a few bones. Jim put some more wood on the fire and I laid back on the ground. The night air was cooling but I was still warm. The stars seemed to be exceptionally bright tonight. Loons were calling and I found myself suddenly sleepy. I pulled out a heavy weight shirt from my pack and put it on. I noticed Jim was doing the same.

*   *   *   *

We were both up early the next morning. The sun wasn't yet above the ridges at the lower end of Billfish Pond. "Come on, you going to fish or sit here?" Jim asked. "This is the best time to fish this pond. I use worms myself. I see no sport when trying to get something to eat.

"That spring out back goes underground to the pond. That's the best fishing in the pond. I think the biggest trout in the state are right here. At least the largest one ever caught that I know of came out of here. Eight pounds two ounces; Alan Dudley caught it. He made a wood carving of it later."

"Why do the trout grow so heavy here? No fishing pressure?"

"Shrimp. This pond is full of fresh water shrimp. About the size of a quarter."

The water was already greenish blue and the sun wasn't even up yet. "What makes this water so blue?" I asked.

"I'm not sure; just the mineral concentration in the ground, I guess."

We made several casts and nothing. I decided to let my line sink to the bottom and then bring it back slowly, dragging along the bottom. When my hook was about twenty feet out and Jim was reeling his in almost beside my line, he got a hit and I watched as he let the fish run with the line before setting the hook. He didn't waste any time playing with it, he brought it right onto shore. It was a beauty. "Twenty inches I'd say, maybe about five pounds," Jim said.

That whetted my appetite. On my fourth cast I hooked into one and I set the hook like I had seen Jim do. Mine was about an inch shorter and almost as heavy.

After that we packed up our gear and headed down along the shoreline to the outlet and then down the rugged and steep side of the front slope. Jim pointed to two old rusted bolts embedded in the ledge and said, "This is where the tramway was anchored to support its weight down the mountain.

It was downhill all the way and we came to the park entrance road just beyond the end of the paved road. We had made a complete circle, now only we had two miles still to walk back where his pickup was parked. "How often do you make this trip?" I asked.

"Once in the spring and then whenever I hear there's a party that needs watching. Sometimes only once a year, sometimes three or four. I hike into Middle Fowler and then back quite often."

By the time we got to his pickup my legs were tired   and it felt good to sit on a soft seat. When we were back on the paved road, just before crossing the bridge back to the store, we met a lone man walking and carrying a backpack who seemed somewhat confused. We stopped and Jim got out and asked, "Can I help you?"

The man turned his head away from Jim before answering. "No---I'm okay."

"Which way are you going?"

He pointed towards the park and said, "Ellsworth. I have a job there." Again he turned his head away from Jim before answering.

"Well Ellsworth isn't anywhere around here. It's below Bangor on the way to Bar Harbor." He was obviously confused. Lost?

"I tell you what, why don't you come down to the store with us and I'll buy you breakfast. When was the last time you had anything to eat?"

The guy pulled two hotdogs out of his pants pocket and said, "I've been eating these, I'm okay." It was clear he had some problems.

"Where are you from?" Jim asked.

"Four days ago I was released from AMHI."

"Do you have any identification? Anything that would tell me who you are?"

He pulled out a slip of paper from the same pocket as the hot dogs and handed it to Jim. Written in pencil was, "My name is Sam Broder and I am sane."

"Thom, I think I'd better take him with me and get him some help. Perhaps it would be best if you get out here. I think he'll get in if it's just he and I."

"No problem," I replied.

"Look Sam, why don't you get in with me and I'll give you a ride out and get you pointed in the right direction."

"Okay." No fight at all. But he turned his head before answering.

As Jim drove out of sight across the bridge I shook my head. He never knows what he'll run into out here. Thugs, poachers, mentally impaired, what next? And he carries a gun that he feels he'll never have to use.

I had breakfast with Don and Di and told them about our hike in the mountains and showed them the big trout I caught at Billfish. Don weighed and measured it. Nineteen and a half inches and almost five pounds. Before leaving, I tried to pay Di for the breakfast, but she only waved her hand and said "your family."

CHAPTER 2

I had really enjoyed the trip with Jim, but now I was glad to be home. Royal was glad to see me too. Later, I had taken care of my fish, cleaned up, opened a can of beer and lit a cigar; only to keep the black flies and mosquitoes away you understand. I don't smoke. Then I sat on the porch in my rocking chair, simply enjoying being here, being alive.

I started comparing my life to Jim Randall's. I came from an influential family. I had the privilege of studying overseas in probably the most astute college in the world. I didn't know anything about Jim's background; but the main difference being he had chosen a profession that he had dedicated his whole life to, something that he obviously enjoyed and he was also very good at it.

*   *   *   *

For the next few days while the weather was reasonably cool, I worked on firewood for the winter. I had the local heating oil dealer in Patten install an oil fired heater and two fuel tanks. I bought a small propane generator and a television set. I was looking forward to spending the winter alone here, but I was not going to become a recluse. I put in extra propane tanks and finished with putting up enough firewood. All except for some dry cedar for kindling.

Royal went with me every day. He wasn't afraid of the noise from the chainsaw and he rode behind me on the ATV. I didn't take him with me when I went to town or down to the lake to visit the Dudley's. He was growing fast and his fur was different than Shep's had been. Where Shep had had coarse wooly fur, Royal's was finer and the guard hairs longer. He was mostly gray and brown, whereas Shep had been white and gray.

I took him with me scouting the hunting trail across the river. There were a lot of blow downs in the trail and I was two days clearing the trail. We saw deer and Royal never paid the least bit of attention to them.

When the winter's firewood was finished and I had plenty of oil and propane I decided to explore some of the country. Places I haven't yet seen. Jim had said the river road would be a good place to ride the ATV and explore. So the next day I was up early and loaded the ATV onto the trailer and drove around to the lower end of the lake.

I stopped at the Matagamon store first to buy a lunch to take with me and to say hello. "You can unload and leave your pickup at the turn around, by the park garage at the end of the paved road. That belongs to us." Don said. "Your pickup and trailer will be okay there."

I started down the new road where Jim and I had parked at the beginning of the back Fowler trail, and turned off onto the old road that followed along the river. It was a nice ride. The river was calm and wide and the best thing was the absence of people. I had it all to myself.

At two and a half miles I did meet another ATV rider; an older gentleman. He stopped and I stopped beside him, "Good morning," he said. "Going far?"

"Don't know really, I'm just out exploring." I extended my hand to shake his and introduced myself, "I'm Thom Wellington."

He shook my hand eagerly and said, "I'm Al Ellis, my wife and I have that camp back this way," he pointed behind him, "on the sharp curve. My two sons own the grocery store in town."

"You'll have to stop by the camp sometime for a cup of coffee. I'm on my way to Matagamon now to do some fishing on the lake."

At six miles I came across a dead water that makes up on the river and at the lower end of that Haskell Falls. There was a huge rock in the middle of the falls. This was really a beautiful sight when the river was high. I continued on and the road divided. I stayed to the left, following the river. The road forked again after a mile. The left was now only a footpath. Well used at that. I parked the ATV and took the key out and decided to follow the trail to see what was the popular attraction. It became very clear in a short distance. I could hear the roar of falling water. The more I walked the louder the roar. I wasn't long coming to a section in the river where the bowels of the earth had split open and separated eons ago. It was a jagged narrow cut and at the lower end of the cut was a twenty foot deep pool. Tall pine and spruce trees lined both sides of the river. A magnificent setting. Only later would I discover that this is Grand Pitch. It was still morning, but I ran back to my ATV and got my pack and ate an early lunch on top of the ledges at Grand Pitch.

This was a very beautiful and tranquil place and I could have stayed all day, only I had more exploring to do. On the way back along the foot trail I met a group of boy scouts portaging around the gorge. The same young girl councilor I had seen on the lake was among them. As I was walking by her she turned and said, "Didn't I see you a while back on the lake? Hi I'm Ronie," she extended her hand and I shook hands with her. I was surprised how delicate her hand felt.

"Yes, you have an exceptional memory. My name is Thom, I live north of Webster stream and the Little East campsite, along the Eagle Lake Tote road."

"You must mean Uncle Royal's cabin?"

"Yes he was my uncle. The cabin belongs to me now."

"I only met him once. My family was camping at Little East and we went for a walk on the other side of the river. We had an unforgettable encounter with your uncle. What an old grouch!"

I laughed and said, "You're correct about first impressions, but as I learned, he was a very caring person. He was a true juxtaposition."

"Hey, I can't talk with you now. We've got to portage all this gear below the gorge. Maybe I could come by sometime," she said.

"That would be fine. Come anytime; you can usually find me home."

"I'll do that. See ya," and she smiled. Ronie had sparked some kind of a happiness inside of me, and it confused me because I couldn't identify with it.

Back at my ATV I noticed the road narrowed, only passable with an ATV. Not knowing where it would lead me, I decided to follow. The trail followed what appeared to have been an old, old woods road at some time. Little did I know then that this old road I was following was indeed the same Eagle Lake Tote road system that ran by my cabin. In time I'd learn that on the other side of the river was another road system that was nearly as diverse as the Eagle Lake Tote road; the American Thread Company road.

The ATV trail was still following the river, through mud holes and raspberry bushes. Finally I peeked out on a knoll and saw a set of buildings on the further side. Beside the driveway, on the upper side was a small pond and a woman was standing there throwing something into the water. I continued following the trail, now it was resembling a gravel road only one seldom used by four wheel vehicle traffic. It was somewhat confusing and I went around in a loop twice before I found an exit off the circuit. And that exit led me to a narrow iron suspension bridge that crossed the river. It was just wide enough for my ATV and a snowmobile. The road went through the middle of, what looked like a set of wilderness camps.

There was a big red log truck unloading, I suppose, firewood. The operator waved. I waved back, not knowing who it was, other than the name on the truck door Probert Trucking. There was someone working in the garage, in the center of the yard.

He saw me, as I stopped and he walked over, "Hello," I said and I shook his hand. Everybody around here is always shaking hands.

"I'm Jon Smallwood."

"I'm Thom Wellington," I replied.

"Yes, we met several years ago. You and your uncle were at Dudley's store."

"You have an excellent memory."

"It helps, running a business like this."

"What exactly is it?" I asked.

"Year round sporting camps. Hunters to snowmobiles and ATV riders to horseback riders.

"Come on in and meet my wife Betty. She was down feeding the trout. She should have a fresh pot of coffee on." He led the way to the main camp that overlooked the river. We sat down at the kitchen table. There's something about this region; guests are always being entertained in the kitchen, over a pot of coffee. Everywhere I go, people are always pouring coffee into me.

A woman came in from outside through another door, "Betty, this is Thom, Uncle Royal's nephew. Thom this is my wife Betty."

"Hi Thom. Coffee is fresh and I've got hot cookies in the oven."

Jon and I sat at the table while Betty got us coffee and then she pulled a sheet from the oven with peanut butter cookies. She put a plate full of cookies on the table and said, "Here, they taste better when hot."

"Thank you," I said.

They both told me about raising their family eight miles from the CCC, or Matagamon Road. The hardships of winter travel out of here and the expense of transporting their children to school activities. The lean years after they bought the camps from Wayne Chapman in 1967. How Jon had to work in the woods during the cold months of winter, in deep snow. As the reputation of the camps spread to new sportsman and widen out across the northeast and even Europe, the business increased sufficiently so Jon only worked in the woods because he wanted to do so.

"Charles McDonald built the original camps here in 1896. He was a woods contractor for Great Northern and the Eastern Corporation. About 1919 he built an out camp on Traveler Mountain, near the pond. But when Baxter bought the land, the authority made Chapman move it. So he numbered each log, disassembled the entire cabin and hauled the logs by horse teams down just below the town line and set it up again about fifty yards below the park line. This didn't bother old Baxter none, but it sure did irritate the authority. And it's presence today still irritates some.

"The fishing at one time was grand in Traveler Pond, but through the years the water got so contaminated by acid rain that the water went sterile. Like the lakes died off in upstate New York. There the conservationists neutralized the acid with lime. This gave me an idea. I hauled bags of lime up and put it in the inlet to the pond and around the pond. Today you go up there and you can catch a nice mess of trout."

"How do you get out of here in the winter?" I asked.

"When the crews are working in here in the winter cutting wood, they'll keep the roads open. What they don't plow, I plow with my pickup. When the crews aren't working then I have to plow all the way to the CCC road. I have an old grader to push the snow banks back with. But when we first bought the camps, we had to leave the vehicles out at the end of the road and go back and forth with snow sleds."

"You certainly do have a nice place here and what a unique lifestyle. These cookies are delicious Mrs. Smallwood."

"Thank you and it's Betty. Jon, before Thom leaves---take him down to the pond and show him the trout."

I walked with Jon down to the small pond he had dug. The water was cold from a natural spring.

"These fish double in size every winter. Of course we feed them pretty good too, even in the winter."

"Do you ever catch any?" Or allow your guest to fish?"

"Sometimes the larger trout have to be taken out. They get too aggressive at times."

As we were walking back up the driveway I noticed a sign that said Bowlin Pond camps. So I asked the obvious question. "Where is Bowlin Pond?"

"It's two miles out, or six miles in from the CCC road. It's right beside the gravel road. The original camps were about half way out. They were crew camps during the winter. Then as the crews cut further south the camps were moved here."

We walked back to my ATV and I noticed for the first time that the big truck had left. It's odd I never heard it. I would have thought that a truck that size would have made enough noise to be heard even inside the building.

I said, "Thank you for the coffee and thank your wife for the cookies."

As I crossed the suspension bridge I noticed some kids swimming in a deep hole in the river on the lower side of the bridge. I followed the snowmobile trail signs, as Jon had said to do, to a good gravel road and then I turned left at the T, and soon I came to another better gravel road and took that south until I came to a right in about a mile. Then Jon had said to follow this road up the mountain and stay left at the junction of the only other road. At the very end I would find an ATV trail on the left that would take me to his camp on Traveler Mountain and a foot trail from the camp to the pond.

I must say he gave easy directions to follow. Perhaps that comes with running a set of sporting camps in the middle of nowhere.

The trail to the camp was getting rough so I parked the ATV and hiked the rest of the way. The log cabin was like you'd see in some old wilderness movie or photograph. And as Betty had said each log had been numbered when Wayne had to move it from the pond. I walked around the cabin and used the outhouse. Apparently a family of mice had taken up residence in one corner; it was full of dry grass and white birch bark.

As Jon had said I could almost spit and hit the park line. I located the trail and started the trek to the pond. The climb was steep, but I wasn't long before I was on top.
Jon had said to look for an area where dwarf beech trees grew. "This is where the camp was originally."

The foot trail took me up a slight knoll where low lying bushes and dwarf pine and spruce trees grew. When I reached the top, "What a beautiful view." The pond was below me and from here I could see the bottom very clearly. "What pristine water." No wonder Chapman hated to move the cabin.

I had forgotten about how late in the afternoon it was getting. I was so enjoying myself. As the sun dipped behind the mountain I decided it was time to leave and start for home.

*   *   *   *

Later that night as I was sitting on the porch with Royal, reminiscing of the day's events and the people I had met. What an exciting life Betty and Jon must have at the Bowling camps and what a beautiful setting there beside the Penobscot River. I was still filled with the tranquility that I found on top of the mountain, looking down into the pristine water of Traveler Pond. I would return there someday, but before then there was a whole lot more to see in this absolutely fabulous, mysterious country.

Remembering what Uncle Royal had told me of the early history of the Matagamon region, I now agree with him that it was a crying shame that the authority had so blatantly burned the hotel building at Trout Brook Farm instead of turning the building into a museum and preserving the history of this region. There was an abundance of history here.

After breakfast the next morning I put up a lunch and loaded my gear on the ATV and drove down to my canoe at Webster Stream. I had decided to spend the day exploring around the lake. The first place I wanted to see was Norway Dam. I motored passed the warden camp that would be burned come first snow, and I felt a real sadness that the authority was so blatantly going to remove another piece of history. A piece of history that if it had not been for the fact that the camp was there, and Jim had been able to start a fire and wait for help after the park director had left him stranded in -20F weather at Dri-ki dam, he probably would not be here today.

I motored passed the island in the thoroughfare, staying to the north shore. If there was time on my return, I'd look for the gold coins on as many islands as I had time. As I turned the point and headed up the cove towards Norway Dam a pair of golden eagles landed in a tall dead tree not more than fifty yards away. These were magnificent birds.

A little further into the cove and I saw two deer feeding at the shore line. At the head-end of the cove I had to make another turn into the mouth of yet another long narrow cove. Both shores were ringed with high ridges. The north shore grew red pine and the south shore supported tall spruce trees.

I came to a narrow gorge on the right, I could see where a cabin had once stood. This had to be the infamous Amos Steen's camp. One of the older game wardens that had chased Uncle Royal on occasion. It was easy to understand why he had been so bitter about being told he would have to vacate and the authority burning it to the ground.

I motored through the gorge to a pond like area and then at the head of this was sort of a natural dam made up of ledges. This had to be the Norway dam. I had to lift the motor and pole my way through the rocks to a huge deadwater upstream. The water was shallow but plenty deep enough for my motor. There were flocks of Canadian geese and ducks. There were deer, moose and a beaver that startled me when it slapped the water with its tail beside the canoe.

The deadwater twisted and wound its way through a huge meadow that was probably two or three miles long. Almost at the head end of the deadwater I noticed an opening on the right and what looked like a well used trail. I was exploring, so I beached my canoe and followed the trail just a short distance to a picturesque old log cabin. The logs were standing upright and not laying horizontal like most cabins. I started laughing out loud when I noticed the park line, again with this cabin, within spitting distance. Tall spruce and red pine grew around it, with shorter fir and cedar in amongst the taller trees, shielding it from the deadwater.

I tried the side door and to my surprise it was not locked. As I thought about it later, this unlocked door was not that surprising once you consider where it is and the character of this land. I felt obligated to go inside. There was a note on the table. A business card from Jim Randall. He said he wanted to talk with whomever owned the cabin about purchasing it. There were some old magazines in a cupboard and I checked for an address label. Robert Steen. "Well I'll be damned!. This must be where Amos had rebuilt his cabin after the park took possession of his. Fifty feet behind the line!" I laughed again, enjoying the irony of it.

There was another trail that led off to the east for a quarter of a mile before turning north up a steep ridge. The footpath broke out to an old road that still had wooden corduroy in the wet places. This corduroy road soon turned into a skidder road and the woods on both sides had been harvested a few years earlier. I followed the skidder road out to the log landing and a wide gravel road.

I took my time walking back to the cabin. From the harvest area to the park line, the land dropped off sharply, with jagged ledge and gorges; covered with a layer of moss and huge spruce and pine trees grew out of the crevices and gorges. Instead of motoring back down the deadwater I decided to lift the motor and paddle. I took my leisurely time enjoying the serenity. I ate my lunch at Norway dam. The sky was blue and the sun was hot. I wished I had remembered to bring my fishing rod. The dark deep water in the gorge looked like a likely spot for big trout.

I motored back out the cove to the thoroughfare and turned into Big Logan. It was a long cove, about a mile. I motored along the shoreline and soon came to the park line and a sign indicating that I was now on the Penobscot Indian Nation Reservation land.

The water suddenly turned shallow and littered with old stumps. I turned up the other shore and found an old camp hidden out of sight on an island. I motored by it and back to the thoroughfare, where I had a strange encounter with a lone canoeist. On both sides of his canoe was painted in white paint "My Lord."

I pulled up alongside him. He appeared as if he wanted to talk. He was in the center of his canoe on his knees. No life preserver, no lunch, no fishing equipment, clothes or anything, except for his paddle. "It's a beautiful day to be out here," I said. "Are you camped at one of the sights?"

He sat there grinning at me. At first I wondered if he had heard me. Then he said, "No,"--a long pause, then, "here to find and experience peace, tranquility and the wonderment of God. Have you seen it?" he asked.

"Hi there, my name is Thom," I tried to start over.

"Hellooo---. My name is," and he pointed to the side of his canoe, "My Lord."

I decided right there I'd better let this one alone. "Have a nice day," and I started my motor.

"Peace brother." I looked back occasionally until he was out of sight. He just sat there in his canoe. I don't know if he was high on drugs or just burned out from too many drugs. Or, then I suppose maybe he had found his wonderment. Who's to say?

There were many islands in the thoroughfare between First and Second Lakes. It would take all afternoon to check each one of them, looking for the buried gold coins. I started with the first one I came to. Searching up and down the island looking for an oval rock. Then the last island before approaching the apple orchard, where David Hannah's farm once stood, I did find a long cylindrical rock. More like a rock fish than oval, but it was the closest to an oval that I found all afternoon.

There was no poplar tree however. But that in time could have blown over and washed away in the spring ice out. I found a piece of solid dri-ki and dug in the dirt around the base of the rock and again I didn't find anything. Had someone been here before? Was this the oval rock described in the map? Or was this even the correct island?

That's a mystery of Matagamon that will probably always remain one of its mysteries. Then as I thought about it; why not? This is a mysterious and enchanting region.

From the island near the Hannah Farm I crossed to the west shore and motored along a long and high ledge peninsular with short red pine trees growing on top. There was a sign that said, "Boody Brook Campsite."

I pulled my canoe ashore. This is the best campsite I had seen on the lake. The grounds were clean, a credit to the park.

My next stop was at the sawdust pile where the Diamond Match Company mill had operated during the fifties. I walked around the pile of sawdust and wondered how many spruce and pine trees all this sawdust accounted for. I found metal pieces of the old mill half buried in the sawdust and mud. There were rivulets of water that ran off the pile to the lake. Of course there was no water running in the rivulets now. They were dry. But each time it rained, water flowed off the sawdust pile like a spring gusher; and taking sawdust with it into the water. All of this sawdust piled so close to the lake; right on the shoreline; tannic acid had to leach into the water. That would account why the water was so dark. Did tannic acid have any effect on the fish? I didn't know.

I stood on the sawdust pile and looked across the lake at the warden's camp, thinking how much of a shame it'll be when the park burns it. How many jokes had Uncle Royal played on the wardens at that camp? I thought about Jim Randall and how the park director had left him in the cold and if it had not been for that camp being where it was, Jim might not have survived that day.

How many memories would go up with the smoke?

Now that I was thoroughly depressed, it was time to be heading for home. As I turned the corner in Webster stream by the ledges I could see several canoes at the Little East campsite.

*   *   *   *

I stayed up late that night. Another thunder shower blew in and I was enjoying the sound of the rain on the roof and watching the spectacular displays of chain lightning. The whole sky would stay alight for seconds with each bolt. So the next morning I slept in. It rained heavy until it stopped around mid-night. So everything would be wet this morning. In the afternoon it would be dry, so I'd feel more like doing something.

It was ten o'clock and I was still lying in bed playing tug of war with Royal. There was a loud knock on the kitchen door and a girl's voice, "Hey! Thom, you home! This is Ronie."

I don't know now if I was more surprised that someone was knocking on the door or that Ronie was here. I pulled on a pair of jeans and an opened shirt, barefoot and opened the door. I saw she was wet, but I just couldn't say anything. I just stood there and probably looking stupid. She started giggling and said, "I'm wet! Can I come in?"

I stepped aside and held the door open; still unable to talk. "No fire? Don't tell me you were in bed."

I was finally able to talk, "Yeah, I was up late last night and just felt like laying in this morning." I went to work kindling a fire in the stove. "Do you drink coffee?"

"I'd love a cup," she replied.

There was a pool of water where she was standing. "Hey look your soaking wet. I'll give you some dry clothes and you can get out of those."

She went into my bedroom and closed the door. I finished dressing and combed my hair and put more wood in the stove. "Ronie, do you want breakfast?"

"Yes, I haven't eaten yet. Hey! There's something growling under your bed!" She was only a little bit alarmed.

"Oh that's only Royal. A coyote pup. He's friendly."

I put on some bacon, scrambled eggs and the coffee was done. "Hey, breakfast is ready. Is everything okay." she had been in the bedroom for--- well longer than I thought it would have taken to change into dry clothes.

"I'm coming. I was playing with Royal. He's cute. Where did you find him?"

"Where the Tote road meets the river. He was sick and abandoned." As Ronie walked out of the bedroom Royal was nipping at her heels playfully.

"Are you cold?"

"I was, but these dry clothes feel good." The clothes were big on her and she had taken the time to dry her hair somewhat and combed it out. She was really quite attractive.

"You must have left early this morning."

"Before breakfast. Is it alright if I hang up my wet clothes over the stove?"

"Sure, while you're doing that I'll set the table and serve the bacon and eggs."

"These eggs are delicious," she said.

"Where are you from Ronie?"

"Berlin, New Hampshire. This is my second year at the scout base. Last week was the last group of boys. I'm one of the councilors, and we're finished for the summer and I'll be returning home in a couple of days. I left the base early this morning because I wanted to see you before I left."

"That's a long ways to paddle," I said.

"I used one of the base motors. I wasn't long at all motoring to Webster Stream. Once I started up the old road--well I was wet pretty soon and I wasn't exactly sure how far up you'd be."

"I'm glad you came by," she smiled.

We ate breakfast and had more coffee, all the time carrying on a constant conversation. It was so easy talking to Ronie. Royal had curled up in her lap and was sleeping. I was a bit jealous.

"This is a nice setting for a cabin. It's far enough from the lake so most people wouldn't be venturing this far. Your Uncle saw to that," we both laughed and I told her about my first encounter with Uncle Royal.

"Where does the road go out this way?"

"This land all around here belongs to the Huber Corporation and this road joins the main woods road that goes back out to the CCC road or to Beatle Mountain." I explained to her how the original road, the old Eagle Lake Tote road had gone all the way to Chamberlain and Eagle Lake further to the north, and that this stretch through here was the only passable portion of the original road now.

As I began clearing the table and putting the breakfast makings away, Ronie took her clothes off the clothes line, "They're dry," and went back into the bedroom to change back into her own clothes.

I took this opportunity to finish dressing and cleaned up somewhat. "Are you in any particular hurry to get back to the scout base?" I asked hopefully.

"No. I don't actually have to go back at all except to return the canoe and motor and pick up my few belongings."

It was said so subtly; was it a pass, an invitation? I'm afraid she'd have to be a bit more obvious. "I was wondering if you'd like to go for an ATV ride to,"---she interrupted before I could finish.

"I'd love to go. I've never driven one myself so I'd prefer to ride with you." There it was again. Or was I simply imaging that she was making a pass. However.

"You'll have to ride with me, I only have the one machine. Have you ever seen the giant king's pine tree up near Beatle Mountain?"

"No. I have never even heard about it," she replied full of excitement.

"Well, have I got a treat for you." While we packed a lunch I told her about the history of the king pine tree and how a hand full of determined lumbermen had declared war on the entire British Kingdom. "To settle the timber trespass laws established by Canada to prevent Maine loggers from cutting the giant pine which were geographically within the Maine boundaries settled by the 1783 Versailles Treaty.

President Andrew Jackson had privately offered Maine an unusually large cash bounty, plus one million acres in Michigan Territory, if the Aroostook lumberman would back down and concede the county to Great Britain. Finally in 1838-39 after threats of declaring war against Britain, Daniel Webster was sent to the county to negotiate a settlement."

"You sound like a historian. Where did you learn that?"

"Some from Uncle Royal, but when I was at Oxford I did some research about the dispute. It was all about who owned the giant pine trees. Something the politicians, of that time, could not see the value of the pine or the huge expanse of forest. And the only way the lumberman had to get Washington's attention was to declare war against Great Britain. It worked."

Ronie was silent for a moment before saying. "That's a very important event in history. Not just for the state of Maine, but for the unification of this country in its' formable years."

"Yeah, I agree the history books document the Treaty of Versailles and Ghent, but the Aroostook War, or the Bloodless War as it was sometimes called, only received a brief mention and not what brought it to the surface.

"You know Ronie, some of these people up here even today that I have met, still have that same stalwart determination, as those early lumbermen."

"Hey enough about war, let's ride." When we were outside Ronie linked her arm in mine and walked so close I could feel her leg brush mine.

I put a boat cushion on the luggage rack on back for Ronie and she climbed on and wrapped her arms around me so tight, I could feel her exquisite breast pressing against my back.

I found the Beatle Mountain road and the raspberry bushes had almost completely inundated the road. There was two miles of these to endure. I thought about stopping and walking the rest of the way, but that would have been more difficult than trying to ride through them. We endured and when the noble giant came into view as we rode up a slight incline I heard Ronie gasp, over the engine noise and exclaim "Holy Christ! Look at that sucker!"

We had to walk off the road a short distance through a thick tangle of second growth hardwood. I pointed to a scar on the southern exposure side of the tree and said, "Uncle Royal said that the Crown's land cruiser mark the giant pine on the south side of the trees by burning a broad head arrow design into the bark. The woods boss for the land company Don Shorey believes that this scar, since it is on the south side and no possible explanation for a scar to be here, that this is one of the King's Pines."

"What did the King of England want with them?" Ronie asked.

"For the Royal Navy, for building ships and tall sturdy masts."

"You could build a whole house with boards cut from this one tree," she said.

"And there'd be some left over, would be my guess."

Ronie crawled under the root that jutted out from the trunk. It was a tight squeeze but she said, "I just wanted to be able to say I did it."

She kept walking around and around the giant, looking up she said, "How high up do you suppose the first branch is?"

I stood back and looked. "I'd say about one hundred and twenty feet." There wasn't a dead limb on the entire tree.

"This tree should be a national monument." Ronie said.

"Yeah, I kind of agree with you. This tree with its healed over brand represents the tough individuals who secured this portion of the state."

We left the big tree and fought our way back through the raspberry bushes. I didn't want to return home just yet. I was really enjoying Ronie's cheerful company and the feel of her arms wrapped around me holding on. So after we came to the end of the raspberries, we started exploring every side road we came to. Every road ended at an old log landing. It was always one way in and out. We didn't care though. By now I knew Ronie was enjoying this as much as I was. We explored all afternoon. Finally I said, "We had better start back."

"What time is it?" she asked.

"It's about six. By the time we get home, there won't be much daylight left for you to motor back in."

"Who said I have to leave tonight? That is unless you don't want some company for the night," she hugged me even harder.

I had no idea at all where we were. But I knew it would take us a least an hour to get back. I hadn't planned it this way. It just sort of happened. We were having so much fun exploring and enjoying each other's company.

The return trip actually took us longer than I had supposed. By the time I put the ATV away and started preparing something to eat the sun had already disappeared.

While I prepared supper, Ronie took Royal outside and played with him.

When we had finished eating, we sat on the porch and listened to sounds of the night. The one thing that impressed me most of all about Ronie was that we never stopped talking. She always found something of interest to talk about. We played cribbage until I was getting tired of counting cards and moving match sticks for pegs.

I think Ronie had had enough also, we sat there and looked at each other and soon we were both laughing. I took her in my arms and kissed her gently at first and then when she responded, I kissed her with passion and picked her up in my arms and carried her into the bedroom. Royal was put out and the door closed.

She was already removing her clothes. I was ecstatic but I tried not to let it show. All day I had fantasized about sliding her blouse over her shoulders. I watched as she unfastened her pants and let them drop to the floor. I took a step closer and cupped her face in my hands and she looked up at me and smiled. Her skin was brown from the summer sun and she was firm and sensual.

She pulled the bedding back and slipped between the sheets with the grace of a queen. I blew the kerosene lantern out. The full moon was shining through the windows and the room was still brightly illuminated; also with her womanly essence. She smiled again and I was so engulfed with her beauty and her charisma that I forgot about what was illuminated, the bedroom or that the moon was even shining.

We made love over and over; each new climax took me to a new height and each time I found my awareness expanding to the point where I was becoming completely cognizant with, not of, Ronie. We finally collapsed from total exhaustion. Ronie laid her head on my chest and I put my arm around her.

We were still sleeping in this position when the first morning rays began to filter through the windows. I feigned sleep; if I moved I was afraid of waking her and I didn't want to spoil or lose what I was experiencing. I had never experienced anything close to this with Jennifer.

Daylight waned to early morning and Ronie was beginning to stir. She moved her head off my chest and looked at me and smiled. "Hi."

*　　*　　*　　*

All good things eventually come to an end. We got up and had breakfast. "I've got to go you know," Ronie said as we looked at each other over our coffee cups.

"Yeah, I know. I'll get the ATV out and give you a ride back to your canoe."

She held onto me so tight it was difficult to breath; but I wasn't going to complain. I pushed the canoe back into the calm eddy and straightened up and said, "There's no wind so you'll have a good trip down the lake."

She kissed me full on my lips and I held her, not wanting to let her go, but I knew I must.

"See ya." and she climbed into her canoe and I pushed her out into the swift current from Webster Stream and she back paddled once and brought the bow around and she rode the current downstream to the lake before starting the motor. I stood there and watched as she disappeared around the ledge point. I was sad to see her leave. I suddenly realized she never told me what her last name was; nor her address or how I could get in touch with her. I ran along the Tote road towards the lake trying to catch up with her. By the time I got to the point, she was well out into the lake. I hollered and whistled, but she couldn't hear me over the noise of the motor. I raced down the road again to the old boy scout campsite. I stood in the clearing hollering and waving my arms, trying to get her attention. But she was so positioned in the canoe that she was looking towards the other shore. She motored out of sight, never knowing I was there. "How dumb can you be?"

I walked back along the old Tote road towards Webster Stream. I sat down on the riverbank where the old bridge had once crossed the stream at Little East. I sat there in silence feeling sorry for myself.

"How could I have been so stupid?" I was so taken with Ronie and she suddenly arriving at the cabin, I had never thought about asking for her last name and address. I laughed then, at myself, when I thought of Tom Hanks in the movie "Forest Gump" when he says "stupid is as stupid does." I guess I certainly qualify there.

*   *   *   *

There was only two weeks left before the partridge season opened and I spent that time exploring. I walked up and down both sides of Webster Stream and up along Little East as far as I could go. Always, Ronie was at the forefront of all my thoughts. Jennifer! I never thought of her again. She was gone and so too was the hurt and loneliness. I saw birds; partridge, those you eat, everywhere I traveled.

I used a tank of gasoline in my ATV every day. Sometimes the sun had already set by the time I got back to the cabin. I was immensely enjoying myself. My new life. Yes, I now understood why Uncle Royal had stayed in the woods; loneliness being his only companion.

I hadn't yet formed a companionship with loneliness. In fact there were days when I needed the company of someone to talk and converse with. Three weeks after Ronie's departure I boarded my canoe and decided to take, probably the last trip of the year, a trip down the lake and visit Don and Di. The river was low and I had to keep the motor up.

When I got to ledge turn I understood why the river was so low. The water was gone from the lake. All I could see were brown mud flats and a channel snaking through them. The water in the channel was deeper than the river and I put the motor back in the water and started it. For the life of me I couldn't imagine what had happened to all the water. After several minutes I motored around a sharp bend and now I could see the lake, or what was left of it.

There were piles of rock; square cribbing at the mouth of the channel and another far along the now present shoreline. I remembered then, Uncle Royal telling me that when the Matagamon Dam had been built in 1942, the dam had flooded more of the low lying areas than the original wooden dam that had been built in 1876. I looked back at the channel and understood that back before the dam the channel had actually been part of the river. And these rock piles had been boom anchors for the huge log booms. Boy! What an experience this day was being.

I also remembered Uncle Royal saying that when the water is down, is a good time to look for Indian artifacts at the beach. Before I got to Pine Point I found another rock boom anchor, out in the middle of the lake. There were sandbars protruding out of the shallow water everywhere. This was an eerie trip. The grass on the lawn at the warden's camp was knee high. "What a shame to lose another historic land mark." I'd always remember the story Jim had told me, about being left in -20F weather, whenever I thought about the Davignon camp. And so too would Jim Randall.

The water was so shallow at the beach I had to lift my motor and step out of the canoe and pull it ashore. The sand was dotted with pieces of white flint. I walked back and forth along the beach and was just about ready to quit when I noticed a complete flint arrowhead lying in the sand at my feet. I picked it up and washed the dirt off it. It was perfect and in one piece. I looked around me and made two more trips up the beach. I put the arrowhead in my pocket and pushed the canoe back out into the water and continued on my way down the lake.

The water was so low I had a real difficult time trying to find the channel to the thoroughfare. Which was the outlet to Second Lake before the dam was built. In desperation I finally lifted the motor, got out and dragged the canoe through the shallow water until I found what looked like the beginning of the thoroughfare channel.

The thoroughfare now was only a narrow brook connecting the two lakes. There was too much shoreline now at Togue Ledge for campers to pull a canoe ashore. But then who would be using the lake this late in the season? I motored on and underneath the old bridge, or let's say between the abutments where the old bridge once stood, I felt like I was sitting in a land mark, fixed in another time. What daring tenacity those early lumbermen must have had.

The channel from the bridge snaked by Trout Book to Louse Island, it wound back and forth like a side-winder snake. Near Louse Island I found another boom anchor of rock and cribbing. As long as I stayed out away from shore I really couldn't see that the lake had dropped. But I was surprised to see how many large rocks were now out of the water along the shoreline and the ledgey rock shoals that I had misunderstood as deep water.

Nearing the dam I found another rock cribbing, boom anchor. The water was so shallow right behind the dam, where I usually pulled my canoe ashore, that there wasn't any way I was going to get it up the bank. So I tied it off as best I could.

From the noise I surmised Don was dropping a lot of water through the dam. I walked out onto the dam to see. I was right. There were three gates fully opened. The water below the dam was churning into a white foam. Probably the pool below the floodgates were crammed full of togue and trout. Being the pool was the only calm water there was.

The warden's truck was parked at the store when I got there. He and Don were having a cup of coffee. "Good morning Thom," Di said. "The boys are having coffee in the kitchen; go right through."

The first question I asked; the obvious one, "Why are you lowering the lake so much Don?"

"The hydro wants to do away with this dam and the Telos Dam. No one wants the dams and the state won't even take them as a gift. They have threatened to pull the gates and let the lake drop back to its original level, before the dam. They want to show folks what the shoreline will look like with the gates pulled. They're hoping this will get someone's attention. I still have to draw the lake down another eighteen inches, by October 15th, then close the gates."

"Why doesn't anyone want the dams?" I asked.

"Everyone is afraid of the liability and in a few years they both will have to be re-licensed. And especially with this one, if it shouldn't happen to pass inspection it would cost a fortune to repair it. That's what everyone is afraid of. Actually both dams are in good condition."

"I noticed coming down the lake how much shoreline there was everywhere. Campers wanting to use the Togue Ledge site wouldn't be able to get close in a canoe or a boat."

Jim Randall cut in there, "If the water level was left where it is now in two years alder bushes would fill in the shoreline and campers wouldn't be able to see the water from the sites. I doubt if people would use the sites much then."

"What about the camp owners. They wouldn't be able to launch a boat. Then in time they wouldn't be able to see the lake either, once the undergrowth and bushes started growing taller."

"Exactly," Don said, "but no one wants to take over the dams."

"What will happen if no one does?" I asked.

"Like I said, the Hydro will pull the gates and the water level will be eighteen inches lower than it is right now."

"Why does the Hydro want to do away with the dams?" I asked.

"The insurance cost and property taxes amount to several thousands of dollars annually. The Hydro has a generating dam at Mattaseunk; the Weldon Dam. Even without the Telos Dam and this one, the Hydro will get the water, no matter who owns it or if the dam is removed. It's attrition; cutting operating costs.

"These dams were originally built for the early log drives, but when the environmentalists got the river drives stopped, these dams became a big expense." Customers came in and Don went out to the store to wait on them.

"I haven't seen you around much for a few weeks. What have you been doing Thom?"

"Oh making sure I have everything ready for winter and I've been doing a lot of exploring with my ATV. I've done a lot of hiking too. Just looking."

"Have you been out to Hay Lake?"

"Probably not, I'm not sure where you're talking about," I said.

"It's back this way," and Jim pointed up the hill towards Patten, "about three and a half miles. It's a pretty lake to canoe around. Fishing is no good but the view from the upper end is great."

"When the CCC built this road during the Great Depression there was a base camp there where the forestry camp is now."

"I'll have to make a point to go out there. Not to change the subject, but last week I was out back here on my ATV; I think it is the road behind the red gate." Jim nodded his head. "I found an old burned car at the end of the road. What happened? It looks like it was a hot fire?

"It was. They used an accelerant," Jim said.

"What was it a stolen car?"

"I'm not sure really. I found it in July and reported it to the State Police barracks in Houlton. I don't think they ever looked into it. The license plate was gone and so too was the vehicle identification tag. From the looks of the car and the burned gravel I'd say it was torched in June. The landowner wants it removed. I talked with the woods boss yesterday."

"There had to have been two vehicles and two people. That's too far to walk out and not be seen." I said.

"So much time has gone by now, I doubt the investigators could come up with any information." Then as a second thought, Jim added, "If the State Police were interested."

Don came back out to the kitchen then and the conversation switched back to the dams. "The camp owners around the lake are trying to form a cooperative to manage the dam and the water level in the lake and the flow in the river. If we can form a co-op the Hydro will give us the dam." Another customer came in and Don had to leave.

"You know if the lake is kept this low, canoes and boats won't be able to get to Second Lake. Coming down the lake I couldn't find the outlet channel from Second Lake. I had to drag my canoe through the shallows and mud to the thoroughfare. The water was so muddy I couldn't tell where the channel was."

"There isn't a channel there anymore. Through the years silt has filled the old brook bed in. You're correct though, boats and canoes couldn't get through in low water. But I doubt very much if you'll ever see the lake this low again. I think the Hydro did it just to get the state authority's attention.

"If you've got the time would you like to ride out to Hay Lake? I'll show you where the old CCC camps were. It won't take long."

"Sure."

There were two pickups parked off the road at Hurricane Deck and five middle age men leaning against the blue pickup; talking and drinking beer. The five looked up to see who was approaching and then; I still have a difficult time understanding why he did it at all, but one of them in defiance tossed an empty beer can over the bank. I knew Jim saw the act too and I also knew he couldn't just drive by.

Jim got out and nonchalantly walked over to the five fellows; with his hands in his pockets.

"Hello boys," he said. "There's no problem with you drinking a beer, but you'd be better off if you didn't do it right here by the highway. There's a deputy sheriff on his way in to one of the camps and he probably wouldn't just talk to you."

Much to my surprise they all dumped what was left in their cans and threw the empties in the back of the pickup. Jim looked squarely at the tall fellow who had thrown his over the bank and said, "Probably I wouldn't have to give you a summons for littering, if you were to go get that empty Budweiser can." The guy just stood there glaring at Jim. Then without a word he went over the bank after his empty beer can.

While the guy was over the bank Jim casually talked with the other four. "Are you going to do some late season fishing?"

"No, we forgot our fishing gear. We've got a camper to bring up for the first week of bird season and we're looking for a place to set it and do a little early scouting."

"Where you boys from?" Jim asked.

"Winterport area." The Budweiser guy came crawling back up the bank and threw the empty can into the back of one of the pickups.

"Have a good day boys. Let's go Thom."

Once we were on our way again I asked, "You didn't summons anyone, how come? I thought sure you'd summons the guy who threw the empty. And how did you know he'd go after his empty can? He could have as easily told you to screw off."

"If I had summoned him for littering then I'd have to go after that can and crawl back up through that garbage. This way I stayed clean and he's the one that is foul smelling. As far as expecting or knowing that he would do it---Well did you notice him considering the alternatives at first. He wanted to tell me to screw off or worse. But I'd just given his four friends a break. He didn't want to take the chance that I'd summons his buddies if he didn't"

"What about the sheriff?" I asked.

"They'll be gone already, but there ain't no sheriff." He couldn't hold it back any longer. He started laughing and I joined in, but I think he understood more about what had just happened than I did.

"What was over the bank that was so foul smelling?" I asked.

"Someone had dumped several barrels of rotten bear bait there and some rotten bear guts. I'm surprised you couldn't smell the mess." We both laughed some more.

"Those boys aren't all from Winterport either. I'll have to watch'em this weekend."

"How'd you know that? I never heard any of them mention anyplace except Winterport."

"There were empty beer cans and soda cans in the back of the first pickup that you can only get in New Hampshire. I didn't see any shotguns, but they were there somewhere. Trust me."

We stopped at the ranger camp at Hay Lake. There was no one there. We walked up to the huge stone fireplace and chimney. Driving by I thought this was just an outdoor fireplace. "There was a building here once fifty feet by thirty feet and another down below amongst those trees," Jim pointed with a wave of his arm. "These two buildings housed the CCC crews when this road and the Sebosis river bridge were built in 1933. James Sewall of the Maine Forest Service directed all the CCC programs."

We walked in silence down to the next huge stone fireplace. This one was even larger. "What happened to the buildings?" I asked.

"When forestry and the CCC were finished with the road and there was no more need for the buildings they were burned."

"Most of the work done on this road back then was done by hand. That's why the road today is so crooked. They didn't have the equipment back then to straighten the road, so the road was built around the wet holes, gullies and ledge precipice."

We walked down to the shore of Hay Lake. It was a beautiful view looking up the lake, and then as if Jim could read my thoughts he said, "The view from the other end is even grander. Especially in the winter."

On the way back to Matagamon I asked, "What about those five fellows we saw at Hurricane Deck, what will you do there?"

"Well, this evening after it's dark I'll look around and find where they're camped and sit and watch'em until they go to bed. Then I'll be in here early tomorrow morning and watch them again. If they are the kind of fellows that I think they are, I won't have to wait for long."

*   *   *   *

Motoring back up through the thoroughfare I noticed something, a lot of some things swimming just under the surface of the water. The water was so muddy that I couldn't see what it was. I cut the motor and made a dip with my net and pulled out a hundred or so red fin shiners. They were all swimming in the same direction, as if they were being chased by something. I waited quietly in my canoe.

It wasn't long before I noticed the black backs of large fish, probably trout and togue, arching their backs above the water in pursuit of the shiners. I couldn't let that pass me by. I made another scoop with my net and brought up a huge trout. I made two more dips with my net and brought up two more large trout. I had enough. I'd eat one for supper and the other two I'd smoke and can for winter.

By the time I had finished eating supper that night, it was late and I left the kitchen until morning to clean. I poured a drink and grabbed a cigar for the porch. "Come on Royal, you coming outside?" I sat there and rocked back and forth listening to the night sounds. A coyote howled, a loon called and something broke a dead stick. There was a sharp snap and then everything went quiet. All the creatures were listening too. Deer, moose, bear? It didn't pose any threat and in a few minutes the night sounds returned.

As I sat there listening to the quiet, I couldn't help but think of Jim Randall today and how he had handled the situation with the litterer. How he had toyed with them without any of them understanding what he had done. And where was Jim now? Had he found where they were camped and was he now sitting quietly behind a bush watching? Probably.

I picked Royal up and set him in my lap, "You know fella, Jim has the cunning and tenacity of a wolverine. Hope we never have to cross his trail."

CHAPTER 3

There were two days left before the opening day of bird season. Royal was big enough now to go with me on the ATV and on long walks. So, during those two days we spent roaming the woods, looking for deer signs. Everywhere we went we flushed flocks of partridge. They were everywhere in large numbers. One day we hiked down the Tote road all the way to the lake. The water level had dropped even since I made my last trip down the lake. The mud flats were beginning to turn green, as new grass started to grow in the fertile mud.

But what was even more unbelievable were the deer tracks in the mud going out to the new grass. There were literally hundreds of tracks in the narrow crossings. There were beaten trails in the mud three to five feet wide. There were large buck tracks, pointed perfectly designed doe tracks and little lamb tracks. I also found moose and bear tracks. All coming from the north side of the lake.

I thought this would be the place to be on opening morning. That is, until I remembered what Uncle Royal had taught me about deer hunting.

Because the meat could spoil in warm weather, I would patiently wait until the end of November and cold weather. It would however be an awful temptation to take a small deer opening day, for camp meat. Besides, who would be around here then. Then the image of Jim Randall flashed in my inner mind and I saw him following my tracks back to my cabin. Sweat beaded on my forehead as I thought of him on my trail. No, I would not have early camp meat. I'd wait for cold weather.

On the way back home I decided to hitch the trailer to the ATV and haul my canoe and motor up and store it for the winter. There were seven partridges under the first apple tree at the orchard, and at the upper end of the orchard eight more flushed from under another apple tree and five of those landed in a nearby tree. Tomorrow was October first, but Sunday. I'd be here Monday morning that's for sure.

Rain started beating against the roof, softly at first, the next morning before daylight. I rolled over on my back listening to the soft melody. The rain began to come harder and harder and the noise was almost deafening. But for me it was still a welcomed melody. Thoughts of Ronie flooded my conscious mind then, and I forgot about the rain. At least for a brief interlude.

I didn't know if she would be at the scout base next summer or not. I didn't know where she lived. Hell, I didn't even know her last name. But still I was warmed and comforted with thoughts and desires of Ronie. With these strong feelings coming through my protective aura, I began to wonder if the warm feelings were because at that exact same moment she was lying in bed thinking of me, and our two psyches meeting on the invisible plain, creating so much joy that my conscious mind was overwhelmed with her; her touch, her kiss, her warmth and essence.

And then without warning her psychic presence was gone and I found myself listening again to the melody of the rain on the roof. I laid there in bed for a long time listening to the rain, before I fell asleep. When I awoke in the morning I remembered only fragments of a dream I had had sometime during the night. I could only remember a lovely woman and a white cloud. Before breakfast was over those too, were erased from my memory.

The rain had stopped sometime during the night, but the forest was too wet to go exploring today. I sat at the table and made a list of the supplies I had and another list of supplies I would have to get before there was too much snow to drive the old ford out through.

With nothing more urgent to do, I decided to drive to town and pick up what I could now, so that I wouldn't be backed up against the wall when and if the weather suddenly changed and we were dumped on with snow.

Living alone, one day ran into another and I really didn't pay too much attention to the day unless I was supposed to do something, or if I had to be somewhere. So it never occurred to me that today was Sunday until I got to town. Main Street was relatively quiet compared to a normal weekday. For a small town, downtown Patten I found was usually busy. Richardson Hardware store was beginning to close as I walked through the door, but the owner Steve said "Take your time, I'll close when you leave."

"Thanks. I need some gas light mantles; probably a box of them and a half dozen kerosene lantern wicks." While Steve was after the mantles and wicks I roamed through the store picking up some oddities.

"Something to read."

"What was that?" Steve asked.

"Oh, I was just talking to myself. I just remembered I should get plenty of reading material before winter."

"Sorry I can't help you there."

I picked up a few groceries and found several good books there. Before leaving town I stopped at the Deli. I figured to have a cup of coffee and a piece of their homemade apple pie with a scoop of ice cream on it. Steve was just going out the door with an order to go. "If you're going to have lunch I'll be back in ten minutes."

"Okay," not really knowing what he meant. There were two cooks and two waitresses inside.

I ordered my coffee and pie. It was delicious. Just as I was finishing the pie Steve returned and sat down and across the table where I was sitting. "Hi Thom," Steve said, and then before I could answer, "any bear up there where you are?"

"I haven't seen any recently, although I saw tracks on the mudflats where Webster Stream puts into Second Lake," I replied.

"All the bear camps around here had a good year. A lot of big bear were taken. Between me and my brothers we killed nine; one three hundred and fifty and the biggest went four and a quarter. The others were pretty small."

"How many brothers do you have?" I asked.

"Oh we didn't kill the bear ourselves. We outfit hunters with bait and stands. We used to run dogs, but that's a lot more work, and you stand the chance of losing a good dog. Do you hunt bear?" All in one breath.

"Well I did when I was here before with Uncle Royal. I may later if it gets cold early. That's the only way I have to store fresh meat. I like cooking with bear fat though. Did you ever fry up a mess of potatoes in bear fat?" I asked.

"No, can't say that I have. We used to eat a lot of bear meat. We had a large family and sometimes that was the only meat my father could get. The wardens used to watch our place a lot."

Someone else came in that took Steve's attention. He came over and sat down beside me at the same table. "Brian---did you find your dogs?" Steve asked.

"Yeah, he was at Glen Kennedy's this morning. I figured he'd go there when he crossed Route 11 by the high school and Buck's road. The guy I was guiding had had enough for one day and there wasn't any sense chasing Ole Dude anymore, he has been in the woods behind Glen's enough so he'd know how to find his way to Glen's barn."

"Bri, this is Thom, Uncle Royal's nephew. Thom--Brian Glidden."

Someone named Val was hollering for Steve. It was one of the cook's apparently. Steve got up to go back to work. "Thom if you like bear stories Bri has one." Oh boy, another bear story. Frankly I'd rather be talking about some pretty girl. But before Bri would finish with his story I'd find myself captivated.

"I knew your Uncle Royal. He was quite a woodsman and hunter. Like to test the temper of game wardens. I had an uncle just like that, Uncle Jack Craig. Uncle Jack and Uncle Royal never met, but they knew each other through the stories told of each."

"What about this bear story you were going to tell me." I figured it would be some tall tale. That is until Brian pulled up his pant leg exposing his wounded lower leg.

"He started chewing here and then he let go and bit on my upper leg. If there was only the girls here I'd lower my pants so you could see those bites. Just so you'd know this actually happened."

"Guess you wouldn't lie with wounds like that."

"I was guiding a bear hunter from Virginia; Teddy Rackcliff. Just a young fella, small, maybe a hundred and fifteen pounds soaking wet. I was using another bear hunters dogs from Tennessee; they hunt mostly swamps and when the bear trees his dogs back-off, they weren't accustomed to fighting with bear.

"I had a bait behind Glen Kennedy's farm on the Happy Corner Road just south of town. It's a good bait, my dogs strike easy off that bait. The Tennessee dogs struck a scent and took off. There's no sense trying to keep up with the dogs, cause sometimes they'll chase a bear for miles before the bear trees and sometimes the bear gets away.

"Most bear dogs have radio collars to make tracking them easier. When the bear trees we can coordinate the location on the radar screen and find a closer road to the bear, so we don't have as many miles to chase through the woods.

"The Tennessee dogs struck good and took off. From the sounds of the dogs barking that bear took a zigzag course through the woods, behind the Sherman Lumber Company mill and crossed the lumber company road and it treed near Look-Out Mountain in T3-R7.

"I drove around to Buck's Road and got a new fix on the radar screen. Once we were close I took a compass course on the dogs barking and we were there in no time. Once we got to the tree the dogs backed off and laid down. I stayed near the tree to keep the bear up it and told Rackcliff to get back where he could get a good head shot. I think he was nervous; hell scared. He didn't take his time and he hit that bear in the ass and he fell out of the tree. When the bear fell, I knew it wasn't a very good shot. That bear got to his feet as soon as he hit ground and with head down he started running. It didn't matter where, he ran straight at me. Right between my legs! I did a complete somersault over his back. As soon as I hit ground I tried to scramble out of there. But that bear was on me before I could get up. Did you know bear really stink up close. Real bad breath.

"He jumped on me and bit into my left leg. He had his jaw around my whole lower leg. It hurt. I hollered back for Rackcliff to shoot him. All this time I was trying to get a clear shot off myself at the bear's head. I had a new thirty caliber Irving automatic handgun. But that frigging gun jammed. I had to do something. I didn't know where that kid was. If I had had my own dogs they would have been right in there and on his back chewing at him. The Tennessee dogs for all I knew had probably run off. As I said, I had to do something, so I started beating that ole bear across the head with my gun. Stop at my house sometime and I'll show you the gun. I hit him so hard I bent the barrel. I was still hollering for Rackcliff to shoot him. Well, I guess I kinda pissed that bear off, hitting him across the head, he stopped chewing on my lower leg and bit right here," and Bri touched the inside of his upper left leg. "Now that really pissed me off. It hurt like hell too. I hit him across the head again and stuck my thumb in his eye. I had that sucker almost out of the socket when he let go. But he bit into my lower leg again. Rackcliff came up then and I hollered to him again to shoot that gawd dam bear. This time he did right between the eyes with a 30-.06. When he shot, the bear had my leg in his mouth."

"How big was the bear?" I asked.

"He was an old bear, four hundred and twenty two pounds. When we got the bear back to my house I skun it out for Teddy and told him I was going to keep the skull. You can see the bullet hole. I kept that worthless gun too. I'll have something to show my grandkids someday and quite a story to tell'em too."

"How did you get out of the woods? I mean you must have lost a lot of blood."

"It was surprising, but I wasn't in much pain. And he never severed an artery. Although I did lose quite a bit of blood, I tied a bandana around my thigh and one around my lower leg. Then we walked out to my truck. It wasn't that far. We left the bear and dragged it out the next day."

"And you still bear hunt?" I asked.

"Sure do. Except I now carry a .44 magnum revolver and I always take at least one of my own bear dogs."

He got up and poured himself another cup of coffee, "Do you want more?" as he offered the pot.

He changed the conversation then. "Yeah, I knew your Uncle Royal real well. As I said before, he was a good woodsman. I got acquainted with him at the Clarky Camp on Second Lake. Some of us from town used to go up there and spend the weekend. Fishing, hunting and partying. Some of us were young then, but that didn't bother Uncle Royal none. Anytime he knew we were there he'd come down. Yes sir, those were some good times."

"Where is the Clarky Camp? I only know of one on Second Lake; the warden's camp." I said.

"It isn't there now, park burned it like they did every other camp. It was at Pine Point. All you can see of it now is where the thick cluster of jack firs are growing."

A big red log truck with a loader turned down the road and Bri got up and said, "There's my driver, I've got to go."

*   *   *   *

On my way home I kept thinking about Brian's ordeal with the bear. He was lucky he wasn't killed or maimed for life. He and Steve both seemed very passionate about their bear hunting.

Everywhere I went and everybody I talked with had a story of uniqueness to tell. Something they had experienced. And another thing I had discovered; the people who live here were actually part of this region; the uniqueness that separates this extremely interesting country from that where people simply exist. These people were as uniquely interesting as were their stories. I'm not part of this land; I'm just here.

Back home that night, after all the supplies were put away and I cleaned up after supper, I got Uncle Royal's old shotgun out of the gun cabinet. I pulled an oil rag through the barrel and polished the wooden stock and barrel. I laid that and a box of shells on the table. "After breakfast Royal, I'll get us some fresh meat."

I fell asleep with excited anticipation in my veins and that same anticipation was still there when I awoke. The excitement was because today would be the first day that I would be all alone on a hunt. Sure I had hunted with Uncle Royal, and we had been apart for most of the day. But today, there would be no one else to help me, to guide me or to keep me company. This activity today of going alone on a hunt would be the true epitome of a loner. So far, I had not until this very moment considered the fact whether I was ready or even wanted to be a true loner like my Uncle Royal. I had been having so much fun and there was so much to do to prepare for winter that I had never felt alone.

I wrangled with this over a cup of hot black coffee. Was I prepared to cache myself here for the rest of my life? With no one to share my life with? Wow! That idea was beginning to eat away at my insides. Did I really want to become an old reprobate, grouch, like Uncle Royal had become, where his greatest enjoyment in his life was pulling tricks on the local game warden? I wasn't sure, but I'd have the winter to think about it.

My coffee was gone and now it was time to go shoot a few birds. "No Royal you'll have to stay here." I put him in the garage and closed the door. It was a cool morning in spite of the bright sun. I had my sights set on the orchard down by no-name brook, where I had seen the flock on Saturday.

I walked along thinking about the orchard and a partridge flew up not six feet in front of me. The bird surprised me so, that I never even brought my shotgun up. Disgusted I moved on, but walking slower and paying more attention to the road. When I got to the river I noticed movement up ahead to the left, under a spruce tree. I brought my shotgun part way up to my shoulder; placing one foot ahead of the other.

Everything was still, no movement, but I was sure the partridge must still be there. But as I got closer, I could see there was nothing under the spruce tree. I just stood there dumbfounded. I knew I had seen a partridge move, but how could it just disappear without me seeing it. Then there was a flutter of wings up ahead and behind some bushes and the partridge was gone. "Damn! This isn't going to be as easy as I thought."

I didn't see anything else until I got to the orchard. Then at the top of the apple tree furthest off the trail sat a lone partridge. It was facing away from me towards the sun. I slowly walked around the alders and the gravel berm. I didn't dare chance getting any closer. I took a fine bead on the head and squeezed the trigger. The partridge tumbled to the ground, but before it hit the ground five or six more partridges took to flight in a flutter of wings from beneath the same tree. I started laughing. I had been so intent on the one bird I failed to see those on the ground not fifteen feet away.

I put the partridge in my jacket pocket and continued on down the Tote road to the lake. I wanted to see the mud flats again before Don closed the gates. Just before I got to the shore below the ledge point, I could hear a bunch of coyotes yipping out on the flats. I eased my way through the dry leaves and fallen branches, trying to be quiet.

About a hundred and fifty yards out there were five coyotes trying to bring a small doe down. They kept running around it, preventing the doe from escape while the others kept biting the doe in the flanks and tearing out chunks of raw flesh. I wanted to shoot them but I knew my shotgun could not reach out that far. All I could do was stand there and watch as the coyotes ate that deer alive. Finally the doe could no longer stand and it fell. All five coyotes now biting and tearing into its flesh. Not bothering to kill it first. Some chewed away at the tender under belly while some continued chewing on the flanks. The doe laid there helplessly bleating. Then the doe was quiet and the coyotes ate their fill.

I waited there at the shore hoping to get a shot at the coyotes, once they were finished eating, if they should come towards me. But when they were finished they crossed the flats, swam the shallow channel to the opposite shore of the lake. Even though the biologists say that's only part of nature, I still hate to see it happen. Seeing a deer eaten alive is something all the anti-hunters and do gooders should see.

The coyotes were gone and there was nothing more I could do here. Ravens had gathered at the carcass and were beginning to feed. After watching that deer die I was not as excited about hunting as I had been earlier. I did shoot one more partridge on the way home.

I found tire tracks in and out of my road. My privacy had been violated. After pulling the breasts out of the partridges, I found a length of chain and cable to put up across the road. I gave the partridge remains to Royal. I put the cable across the Tote road right in the middle of the water hole in the alders. I figured that way if anyone drove up to the cable they wouldn't get out in the water to break the lock.

I wasn't any more than out of sight on my way back to the cabin when I could hear a pickup's motor. I circled through the trees up on the high side to see what they would do when they found the cable. I didn't have long to wait. Two older fellas in a jeep came into view and drove right up to the cable before stopping. The driver cursed profusely, but he had no choice but to back up and find a place to turn around.

"Maybe I should put a sign on the cable saying private property from here." I went back and made up a sign with hooks on top and grabbed my shotgun and went back out. After I fixed the sign I hunted along the alder filled Tote road to Turner Brook. Even though the road was grown in with alders, they were old enough so it was easy walking through them. It was excellent partridge habitat. I heard and saw many before I shot two with one shot. It was right at Turner Brook, near the old lumber camp; two partridges had walked towards each other and I waited until they were real close and I shot between them. I had my limit of birds for the day, so I was done. I saw five moose on the way back.

*　　*　　*　　*

I had partridge for supper that night. One breast was all I wanted. The white meat was juicy and filling. The other one I put in the gas refrigerator freezer, to keep for a winter day.

For the next several days I hunted the same routine and each day I shot my limit of partridge; four. The possession limit was eight. What I didn't eat I froze or canned. Every time I returned from a hunt Royal was always there in the yard to greet me and for his reward for staying home; he got the carcasses.

Before the end of October, I had had my fill of partridge breast for awhile. I had eaten two a day every day since the opening day. I had several frozen and several canned in pint canning jars. I knew I had more than my possession, but I had not taken more than my limit on any one day.

On October 16th it started to snow late in the afternoon and by the next morning there was fourteen inches on the ground. Winter was coming early this year. But in two days the snow was gone.

The weather turned wet and very cool towards the end of the month. There wasn't much to do except stay at home. It was too wet to ride the ATV and I had had enough of partridge hunting. With not much to do I suddenly found myself getting lonely. Jennifer never entered into my thoughts any longer, but Ronie was there more than I would have liked. You see, no matter how much I dreamed of being with her I knew it would never happen. I didn't know how to get in touch with her or her last name. So I spent the time, or at least some of it, doing little odd jobs around the cabin, garage and root cellar.

Through the years the windows had all loosened up. The glass panes as well as the casings. I found a can of glazing compound in the garage and window by window I dug out the old glazing and applied new compound.

I jacked the garage up out of the dirt and put new blocking under the sills. There wasn't much I could do to the root cellar, but I did clean out all the old cobwebs and hauled in clean sand for the floor.

With the obvious chores done and lacking for something to do I decided to take a walk back to the lake. The end of October was near and Don would have closed the gates in the dam and I wanted to see if the water had come up at all. Remembering the coyotes I had seen the last trip to the lake, I decided to take Uncle Royal's .22 mag. rifle. "Come on Royal, you want to go for a walk." Not far from the end of my road a fisher cat crossed the trail. Royal scented it and ran off the trail after it. The fisher is a gangly runner and this one must have known he couldn't outrun a coyote, so he chose a hemlock tree and literally ran up it away from danger. Royal circled and circled the tree but couldn't find the fisher. He could still smell it, cause twice he would put his nose up in the air and prance around on his hind legs.

I whistled to Royal and he came right back to me. "Good boy, good Royal." Not so much for treeing the fisher but because he came back when I whistled.

In all the trips I had made to the orchard hunting these last few weeks, I had seen the same partridge just around the bend from the river. He always managed to sneak off and disappear. Royal was ahead of me as I came to the bend by the river and he had his nose to the ground, smelling something that had already been through. I saw the partridge move, he was under the same tree. Royal was on his scent and he ran straight for the tree the partridge had been squatting under. I waited to see what would happen this time with something to chase the partridge. It wasn't long before there was a flutter of wings and the partridge flew up into a fir tree and perched on a limb. Royal saw which tree it was and he circled it like he had done with the fisher. The partridge sat there on that limb watching Royal below him.

I pulled the rifle up to my shoulder and leaned against a tree for support and took a fine bead with the iron sights, just below his head. But I couldn't do it. I just couldn't shoot this particular bird. No, he had tried so hard to stay alive, I wasn't going to eat it. I whistled for Royal and petted him on the head when he came back to the trail. "Maybe we'll find one at the orchard that'll tree for you."

Again Royal was ahead of me as I came near the orchard. The way he was reacting I knew he was on the scent of something. I thought another partridge, but when I heard him ky-yi, I knew it was something other than a partridge. I started to run and Royal met me at the bend with his tail between his legs running towards me. I looked up at the tree and saw why. There was a bear coming down in short order. I really didn't want to risk irritating that bear by shooting it with only a .22 mag. rifle, so I waited to see which direction he would take once on the ground. I breathed a sigh of relief when it went back into the woods and up the ridge. Apparently bear and coyotes don't get along together very well. "Just as well."

There were no birds at this end of the orchard, but at the east end Royal flushed three from underneath the last apple tree and they all perched at the top and watched as Royal circled at the bottom. I shot one and the remaining two continued watching Royal. I shot the second bird and then the third.

I really rewarded Royal this time. "I think we have something here fella. You're the best bird dog I have ever seen."

I was really surprised to see how much water was in the lake. The mud flats were all underwater again, and the rocked up boom anchors had disappeared. It wouldn't be long before the lake was full again.

That night for supper, I fried both partridges and let Royal have one. It was another reward; he deserved it. From that day on, every time I went bird hunting I took Royal with me, and more times than not the partridges would flush and land in the tree above him. And on an occasion I'd fry one of the breasts for him.

CHAPTER 4

Deer season arrived on a windy, rainy day. I was reminded of how the wind would blow the ocean spray inland out on the sound. I thought that was a little peculiar to be thinking of that out here in the woods, but all the same, I was thinking of that. Here though the trees swayed back and forth so violently I thought they would snap in two and fall.

I was sitting on the porch with Royal, eating a sandwich when I heard an ungodly roar. It was very similar to a freight train. But there were none here. There were no roads and the sound wasn't that of jets. And what surprised me most was that the roaring continued for several minutes before dying off.

The wind finally died enough so I thought it safe enough to venture outside to see how much damage had been done. I didn't have far to go. Standing next to the garage I counted six fir trees across the driveway. I sharpened my chainsaw and began work, cleaning the blow downs from the driveway.

After I had finished working up those six trees that I could see from the garage and throwing the wood and brush off to the side, I walked on towards the tote road. Around the first corner there was a solid wall of fir trees that had been up-rooted and fallen across the driveway. I began the endless task of clearing the driveway. I soon ran out of gas and walked back for more.

Next I ran the blade into a rock under the tree and sparks flew out from it. I was awhile filing the teeth; I hadn't yet become that proficient. Uncle Royal had said once and now I do believe and understand what he was saying, "Any man who can truly sharpen one of these beasts is truly an artist."

I did a satisfactory job and went back to work chunking up the trunks and liming the tops. I was soaking wet from sweat and my face and hands were black and sticky with pitch. I worked until it was too dark to see any longer. I could see the end of the driveway, but I had not yet cleared my way that far. I stumbled my way back to the cabin and locked the chain saw in the vice and said "To hell with it. I'll file it in the morning." I found a clean rag and soaked it in gas and cleaned the pitch from my hands and face.

*   *   *   *

I didn't have any trouble falling to sleep that night. Every muscle in my body was hurting and my back felt as if someone had hit me with a sledge hammer.

I was two days clearing the tote road from windblown trees. Most of them were fir trees. A few spruce and a couple of nice maple. Those I chunked up and piled close to the road. Next summer I'd haul them back to the cabin for firewood. I was still another day clearing the trees from the good gravel road, all the way to the four corners. No one was working out my way that year, so that meant if I wanted the road cleared, I had to do it.

The closer I got to the four corners, there were fewer trees across the road, and from the four corners out to the paved highway there were none. I needed a break from chain sawing and throwing brush, so I decided to drive out to the Matagamon store for lunch and coffee with Di and Don.

The store yard was empty except for Don and Di's vehicles. I guess that isn't to surprising considering this is the first week of deer season. When I stepped into the store Di was making a couple of Italian sandwiches, "Hi Thom, we've been worrying about you since that tornado blew through Saturday. You have got to get yourself a radio like ours. That way we can check on you, or you can call out if there is an emergency."

I promised to go to town tomorrow and get one, "What's this about a tornado?"

"Yeah, blew over here Saturday, just before noon. It came over the top of Horse Mountain, we never heard a roar like that before. Not from wind."

"It must have passed close to my cabin also," I said. "I heard the roar for several minutes. Trees were snapping and coming down all around the buildings. I was three days clearing the road out to the four corners."

"The boys in the park have been busy clearing roads too. That's all they have been doing since Saturday.

"The Savage boys were hunting up between Third Lake and Beatle Mountain when it went through there. I guess the tornado uprooted three hundred acres of trees there. The warden said he was up there and said huge rock maple and yellow birch were uprooted, and twisted and snarled, like a bomb had gone off.

"The Savage boys were hunting up there and got caught in that swirling mass of trees."

"Did they get hurt?" I asked.

"No, miraculously, they had enough savvy not to panic and they laid down in a hollow in the ground. The wind blew right over them.

"From what I've heard so far Beatle Mountain received the most damage." Di added.

"I know I have never heard anything like that roar before," I said. "At first I thought it sounded like a loaded freight train, then a low flying jet. I don't know yet how many trees are down across the Tote road to the lake. I'll have my work cut out for me there probably."

"You were lucky no trees blew down on your cabin."

Not to change the subject but I asked, "How many hunters do you have in this week?"

"The cabins are full. One of the hunters from Vermont shot an eight point buck the first morning, down river."

"Is Don here?"

"He's guiding a party for the rest of the week up the lake." Like I was suppose to know where up the lake was.

"Here, I've made two of these sandwiches, you might as well sit down and have lunch with me. Coffee is fresh too."

After I had finished my sandwich I said. "Di, this is the best Italian sandwich I have ever had."

"Thank you. Have you had a chance to hunt yet?"

"No, I've been real busy clearing the road of windblown trees. It's just as well, I'll have to wait until the weather cools first. If not the meat would just spoil."

"Did you put out any traps this year?" Di asked.

"I thought about it, but I decided against it. Maybe next year. If Don beaver traps this winter I'd like to go sometime and learn how."

"As far as I know he'll be trapping. He and Ted will be trapping together."

"What about snaring coyotes?"

"Oh yes, he and Ted set snares while they're tending beaver traps."

"If the price on beaver pelts drops, does he still trap?" I asked.

"Oh yeah, as soon as I skin each beaver, I roll them up and put'em in the freezer. That way if the price isn't good we tag them and hold them until the price goes back up."

"Trapping sounds like risky business to me. I mean if you had to depend on your proceeds for a living." I said.

"When Don and I and the kids came up here in '71, if it hadn't been for Don trapping beaver we never would have made it. Of course beaver fur was worth a good deal more than. It wasn't unusual to get upwards of seventy dollars for a good super blanket."

I thanked Di for the lunch and assured her that tomorrow I would go to town and get a base radio for the cabin. Providing there was daylight left, I wanted to check out the tote road below camp for blow downs.

I met Jim Randall on the Huber Road below the four corners. He was traveling faster than I would have thought anyone would have been. I waved and he waved and kept going. He probably got a call of some sort.

I left my truck at the turn where my driveway starts and walked down the tote road. Just as I had expected. The road was a solid wall of trees in places. There was no need of trying to climb my way through that mess. I went back to the cabin and filed my chainsaw and filled it with gas and oil. I'd get an early start in the morning. But I'd get me a snowmobile and a base radio first.

I got an early start the next morning. With the utility trailer hooked to my pickup I headed for Houlton. First I'd buy a snowmobile and then a base radio. I had noticed the snowmobiles in Don's yard were ski-doos, and decided he knew as well as anyone what make would best suit this area. I headed for the same dealer where I had bought my ATV. But when I left the sports shop on Route one, I had a year old polaris XLT long track, studded with carbide runners. Tidd assured me that this was a good bargain and the best sled for the conditions I would encounter.

It was a little before noon as I crossed the Sebosis Bridge on the CCC road and I decided to have lunch at Matagamon. This time I would insist on paying. Jim was just turning into the store yard from the other direction.

He looked my snowmobile over closely before commenting. I hoped I hadn't made a mistake. "Nice sled. This will certainly get you to where you'll want to go. Remember, it's a work horse not a damn pony and you'll have to be careful going around corners; especially at high speeds. That long track will tend to push you straight across the trail. You'll enjoy it though. Just another tip, find an old car jack somewhere and put it under your seat. You'll get stuck someday and when you do, there'll be so much snow up inside the track it'll be too heavy for two men to lift."

"I have one in the garage. Let me buy you lunch. I was about to get an Italian."

"Thanks."

As we ate lunch I asked Jim about the party he had checked on Hurricane Deck a month ago.

"I sat on'em that night and they didn't do anything. I came back the next evening just in time to see them bring out three partridges from behind the seat. But that wasn't the worst of their problems. It seems the moose permit holder was a convicted felon from Massachusetts. They didn't come back for the moose hunt.

"What have you been doing since then?" Jim asked.

I told him about the cable and I gave him a key to the lock. I told him about Royal treeing partridges; but I left out how many I had. And I told him about the wind damage. "I still have the Tote road to clear all the way to the lake."

"After deer season I'll help, if you don't already have it cleared.

"Look I've got to run. I'm supposed to meet Kirk Loring at the red gate on the B.S.A. road. Do you want to ride up?" "Sure."

It was a short ride to the B.S.A. road; just over the hill from the store. Kirk was already there. We got out and Jim started to introduce us until Kirk said, "We meet again Thom."

I shook his hand and asked, "How have you been Kirk?"

The niceties over, Kirk got right down to business. "Jim, some of the boys were hunting yesterday to the east of the B.S.A. road at mile three.

They found something I think you might want to look at."

"What is it Kirk?" Jim asked.

"They found a pair of old pants and someone had stuffed some bones inside. They said someone had put some moose bones inside of the pants for a trick."

"Sure I'll have a look. I don't have anything to do until tonight."

"I'll be in East Millinocket tonight with Alvin."

Kirk led the way up the B.S.A. road and Jim and I followed him just beyond a sign post that indicated three miles. Then we pulled off the road in an old log landing. "It's up this skidder trail for a ways."

We followed Kirk, I didn't know what to expect. Everything I had heard so far made absolutely no sense. But then it wasn't my place to question. There was a huge old maple log that had purposely been pushed across the skidder trail, maybe to stop ATV's from using the trail, as there were old ATV tracks running up the skidder trail. We followed this for about a hundred yards and came to a small run-off stream. Kirk stopped and said, "It's up here a little bit," then he took the lead again.

We had had a lot of rain and this stream was full, draining a low wet area between two knolls. There were a lot of hardwood trees, a few fir and some hemlock off to the left on top of a knoll. Jim stopped to look at something in the water. I wasn't sure what he had seen. Whatever it was he was rubbing it between his thumb and forefinger testing the texture. Still he said nothing.

Up ahead I noticed Kirk stop at an old pair of blue pants lying in the water. Jim knelt down to inspect the pair of pants. He pulled the top open and there, there were bones inside. Inside one of the pant legs was a bone. Jim pulled the pants top down, exposing more of the bone. It was coated with a white pasty substance. I was afraid of what that might be.

Jim touched the white pasty stuff and rubbed it between his fingers. Like he had done before. Then it occurred to me what he had seen in the water before. Then he knelt close and actually smelled of the mass. "This paste has human hair in it, he said. "These ain't moose bones. This is what's left of a dead body.

"Be careful, don't tread around." I suppose he was addressing Kirk and me. I understood what he was asking. This had to be treated as a murder scene and he didn't want any evidence destroyed. I stood in one place and didn't move.

Jim next pulled up the pant cuffs. There were no feet. He looked at Kirk and asked, "If I'm correct, this is on Tribal Land?"

"Yes it is," Kirk answered.

"Well I'll have to notify the State Police and secure the scene. Let's get out of here. Stay behind me and follow me up that knoll. We can circle around this stream so we don't disturb anything else."

We hadn't gone but about twenty feet towards the top of the knoll when Jim found an overshoe and a few feet from that was the second shoe. Half way up the knoll was a shirt lying on the ground and a dark blue windbreaker tangled up in the top of some bushes. "It would be my guess that the body was dragged through here by a bear." Jim said.

We came out on to a skidder road, the same one we had started in on only the road had veered to the right up the knoll. To the right was a large beach towel with brown stains that look very much like rust. "Those brown stains," Jim pointed not disturbing the towel, "is old blood. We'd better get back to my truck and I'll call this in on the radio."

We turned to walk back out the skidder road and Jim stopped underneath a hemlock tree and was examining a dark spot on the trunk. To me it looked like a grease spot on the bark.

Jim ran his hand up and down along the bark and said, "This darkened area was made by rotting meat. The bark has turned dark, the same as when bear bait is dumped at the base of a tree." Then he got down on his hands and knees and was smelling the bark and ground. He reached out in front of his face and picked something out of the dead leaves and stood up. Even from where I was standing I could see it was hair. "That guy was already dead when he got here. Someone carried him in and dumped him at the base of this tree."

"Are you saying this wasn't a hunting accident?" I asked.

"Exactly. Whoever he was he was killed somewhere else and brought here. Come on we've got to get back to my pickup."

When we were back out to the vehicles Kirk said, "You've got it from here Jim, I've got to leave."

"Ok, thanks. I owe you for this Kirk," Jim replied.

Kirk was gone and I didn't understand what he had said. "What did you mean Jim, Kirk owes you for this?"

"I'll have to notify the State Police, they are mandated by Legislature to investigate all homicides. The first officer on the scene, me, is responsible to secure the scene and keep an on-going time log about who arrives, who departs, who does what and so forth.

It involves a lot of writing and a lot of time in the middle of the deer season."

Jim radioed the police barracks in Houlton. "Houlton I have located an unattended death."

"Aye, stand-by 2247," the dispatcher said. Then there was a pause, "Would you repeat that 2247?"

"I have found an unattended death in T6-R8 in the woods off the B.S.A. road. By the looks of the body it has been here for awhile."

"Is the scene secured 2247?"

"Affirmative, it is."

"Stand-by 47 until I can contact one of the detectives."

"Aye, Houlton there's an individual coming out of the woods now carrying two rifles!" Jim was out of his truck and running towards the hunter who had just emerged from the skidder road behind the maple log. When he saw Jim running towards him he stopped with a bewildered expression on his face. I stayed next to Jim's pickup out of the way.

Jim escorted the hunter to the front of his pickup and asked him to wait there. Jim got back on the radio, "2247, Houlton, the individual had a .410 shotgun with the serial numbers removed that he found near the scene."

Jim handed the shotgun to me while he questioned the hunter and took a written statement from him.

When he was finished with the statement Jim said, "Carter is going to show me where he found the shotgun. You stay here and keep people from going in and if anyone else comes out make sure they don't leave until I can talk with them."

How was I going to stop people from going in or detain them? I didn't have his authority. In about twenty minutes Jim returned with Carter and then he let him go. "Where was the shotgun?" I asked.

"He found it yesterday and hid it under a rotten log. He came back today to get it. He had not seen the pants or the other clothing. You remember the beach towel," I nodded that I did. "The shotgun was in front of that behind that small mound of dirt. About twelve feet from the hemlock tree."

Jim picked the shotgun up and laid it sideways in his hands and said, "See those pit marks?" "Yeah." "Those were made with an arc welder."

"Why."

"Once serial numbers have been ground out like this the state police lab in Augusta have a technique where they can bring out the numbers in the metal below the grinding. But by attaching electrodes like an arc welder, will destroy those impressions deep in the metal."

"Then whoever killed this guy knew what he was doing."

The dispatcher called back and advised that Detective Havelock was on his way to T6-R8. "Now what do we do?" I asked.

"We wait. We can't let anyone contaminate the scene or disturb it. More than likely someone will have to stay the night."

It didn't take the curious onlookers long to hear about the unattended death. Every few minutes a vehicle would drive by and slow up, then go up the road and turn around and come back. Most not even wearing hunter orange. Occasionally one would stop and ask who the victim was and Jim would say, "There's not enough information to determine that."

"What happened?" was another frequently asked question.

"Can't say for sure," was Jim's only comment.

"Nothing has been determined yet." He was good, that's all I can say about him. He found the appropriate answers somewhere. Then why not, after almost twenty years experience.

Jim's radio broke the monotony of waiting. Detective Havelock was calling Jim for directions. "You'll have to come in almost to the bridge at Matagamon. There'll be a road on your right with a red iron gate. Stay on that road for three miles. "You'll see my pickup."

Havelock arrived ten minutes later. He brought his cruiser to a sliding stop and stepped out wearing casual clothes and low cut shoes. No orange. Havelock and Jim seemed to know each other by the casual conversation they were having. Something about Havelock wanting a red jacket and Jim responding by saying that he had given him several cases in the past and Havelock owed him.

"Where is the body?" Havelock asked.

"About three hundred yards out this skidder road. But there isn't much of a body left." Jim replied starting to walk towards the maple log.

"What do you mean, not much left?"

"Near as I can figure, a bear ate most of it. The only thing there is for sure is one leg bone with some flesh on it that has the consistency of lard, and human hair in that stuff. I didn't disturb the pants any further after I found that one bone."

"Where's the shotgun that someone walked out with?"

"That's in my pickup." Jim said.

Havelock stopped and looked at me and said, "Who are you and what are you doing here?"

"He's with me Merlin. Thom Wellington; attorney."

Again Havelock stopped and looked questioning at me, "Do you always ride around with an attorney in your pocket?"

"Thom is a friend."

We came to the run off stream and Jim led the way up along side of it, the same as we had originally done. Jim pointed to some of the white pasty stuff in the water and kept walking. "The pants are right up there about another twenty feet."

Havelock knelt down to examine the pants and he pulled the leg bone out just enough to see the pasty flesh and hair. "Yep, it's a human alright. Where are the feet?"

"As I said, I didn't disturb the pants anymore than I had to, but I didn't see any. I figured the bear ate'em."

While Havelock carefully examined inside of the pants, I noticed Jim was searching the stream bottom upstream from the pants. I would have thought that if there had been anymore bones or body parts laying near the pants that the bear didn't eat they would have washed downstream. "What are you looking for up there Jim?" I asked.

"We know where the body was when the bear found it, the shoes, pants and the general direction is up this way. I'm trying to find drag marks over some of these rotten logs."

Then he knelt down again to examine a log more closely. "Well look at this! Merlin, the bear dragged the rest of the body up this way to finish eating it."

"How do you know that?" Jim pointed to a single hair on the log.

"Here, mark it with this orange flagging and leave the hair there and don't disturb the scene anymore. Tomorrow we'll do a thorough search of this piece of the woods. You'll be in charge of that Jim. You were the first officer on the scene so that's your responsibility."

Jim laughed and said good naturedly, "You mean you don't want the paperwork." No comment.

Jim showed Havelock the overshoes then and Merlin tied another piece of orange flagging to a bush. Then he did the same to the shirt on the ground and the windbreaker hanging in the bushes. We all stepped into the skidder road then and I noticed that Jim had not said anything about the hemlock tree yet.

"The towel is right where it was when I found it." Havelock picked it up and examined it like Jim had done previously. "There's old blood on this. This case is getting interesting. Now where was the gun found?"

"Right there," Jim pointed. "It was lying behind this mound of dirt."

"What was the caliber?" Havelock asked looking at the towel again.

".410 shotgun with an empty seven and a half shot shell in the chamber."

"Umm, that's an odd shell to use to shoot yourself," Havelock replied.

"I don't think he did. I think he was already dead and carried in here wrapped up in that towel."

Both Jim and Havelock made a cursory look around the immediate area, and then I figured Jim had decided the Detective wasn't going to notice the dark colored bark on the hemlock, so he brought it to Havelock's attention.

"The body was dumped right here and laid up against this tree."

"How do you know that?"

"This darkened area on the bark was done by meat. The same as you'd see at any bear bait where the bait is dumped at the base of a tree. And there is human hair right there" and Jim pointed with his foot.

Havelock knelt to look at it, but unlike Jim he didn't smell the bark or the ground. He tied another orange flagging around the tree.

"Anything else?"

"That's all that we have found. About how long would you say that body or what's left of it has been in here?" Jim asked.

"Just a guess, but I'd say five to six months."

"Just when that car was torched?" There was an echo there somewhere, about a car being torched five or six months ago. I knew which car Jim was referring to, even if Detective Havelock didn't.

"What car are you two referring to?"

"Didn't your own people tell you about it? No, probably not because no one ever came out to look at it. Guess no one was interested."

"Back in June I found a car at the end of this road that had been torched and an accelerant had been used. The VIN plate and license plate had both been removed."

"I want to see that car." Havelock said.

"Okay, let's go."

We walked back out to the vehicles and we all got in with Jim. About half way there we came to a 'T' in the road and at the vortex of the 'T' was a large beech tree and a yellow sign attached to it and in black letters that said, "Beech Tree." Havelock started laughing and commented. "What do you have to do label your trees out here Jim?"

"That tree is used as a reference point when giving directions of how to get to the camps along Matagamon. Many flatlanders couldn't tell a beech tree from a white birch, so the sign was attached, so people couldn't misunderstand when they were told to turn left at the beech tree."

That sounds like something Uncle Royal would say and do. Simple logic, just like the character of those who have made this region what it is today. Was the sign ridiculous? No, it was put up simply to keep people from getting lost who couldn't recognize a beech tree.

We drove a little further and turned left. "I'm glad I decided to ride with you, instead of trying to follow directions to get out here."

The road was dry and there were no signs of recent vehicle traffic. That wasn't to surprising considering there was absolutely nothing out here to draw anyone's interest. Except that is for one torched car.

We all got out at the scene and Havelock walked around it three times before commenting. "No tags, no license plate. Did you check the trunk?"

"No," Jim answered, mopping sweat from his forehead and neck. I didn't think it was that warm.

"What do you have for tools with you Jim?"

"I've got an axe."

"That'll do." Detective Havelock went to work trying to pry the trunk open and when that failed, he stepped back and swung the axe head at the lock. The trunk door, popped opened. There was nothing in there either. No spare tire, no jack, even the matting had been removed. Probably in case the mat didn't fully incinerate.

"Whoever torched this certainly didn't want it traced. Too bad we didn't have the VIN numbers."

"We do," I said.

"We what?" Havelock and Jim said in unison.

"All vehicles after 1983, had the vehicle identification number stamped into the frame next to the transmission," I said.

"How do you know that?" Havelock asked.

"I'm a lawyer remember. Our firm handled a stolen vehicle case. The vehicle had been torched like this one. We had the vehicle taken to a maintenance garage and the mechanic turned the car over and showed us."

"Too bad we didn't have a wrecker or loader here to turn this over." Havelock said.

"I can do it with my truck," Jim said. "I have a long chain we can throw over the top and hook it to the frame and I'll roll it over."

"Okay but not all the way over. Just enough so I can crawl under it. Then we can set it back down. Forensics will have to do a thorough examination of the inside and the trunk."

Jim hooked the chain to the frame and over the top of the car to his bumper. He had no trouble rolling the car enough so Detective Havelock could slide under and get the identification number. "Okay, I have it. You can let it down now."

While Jim unhooked the chain Havelock used Jim's radio and called the dispatcher in Houlton. He already had tried his cell phone, but I guess he wasn't accustomed to using it in the big woods. He appeared to be having quite a conversation with whoever was on the other end. There was an exchange of words, regarding why Jim's initial call of finding a torched car had not been handled properly.

After several minutes Havelock came back over to the burned out car where Jim and I were talking. "This is an '85 maroon Oldsmobile registered to a James Lagasse from Bloomington, Illinois. Fifty nine years, gray hair, hazel eyes, five-seven. Apparently right after you made the initial radio call to the barracks reporting a dead body in T6-R8, Mr. Lagasse's daughter filed a missing person's complaint with the Sheriff's department there in Bloomington. Some coincidence isn't it."

"Maybe but I don't believe in coincidences," Jim said.

"There's more, Mr. Lagasse worked for an accounting firm and suddenly quit and left Bloomington. On June sixth he was at his brother's house in Salem, New Hampshire. He hasn't been seen since then. Reportedly."

"This is a strange place to shoot yourself. Burn your vehicle, remove and then throw the tags and walk five miles away from the car and shoot yourself. Strange."

"If this guy shot himself Merlin, then why is that beach towel soaked with blood? And why was the windbreaker hanging in the bushes and not on the ground like the shirt, if a bear had ripped it or tore it off? And why was the shotgun twelve feet away from the body?"

"As the bear dragged the body down the hill. Or why would the victim take the wind breaker off, throw it into the bushes and then shoot himself and then, then throw the shotgun twelve feet away?"

"I think he was dead inside this trunk, wrapped in that towel and carried to the base of that hemlock tree."

"I have to get back to my car and I'll have to get somewhere, where I can make some phone calls with my cell phone. Somebody will have to stay the night here and keep the scene secured."

"Don't look at me Merlin. That is your responsibility, not mine" Jim said.

"Okay, maybe I can get another detective or a trooper out here part of the night. But I want you here at 0600 tomorrow with a crew of wardens. This whole area around the body is going to have to be thoroughly searched. We, Doctor Rutledge, the medical examiner, is going to need more body parts to make an identification and cause of death."

"I'll be here with a crew. Do you want to help us?" Jim asked me.

"Sure, I find all this fascinating."

Jim and I got back in his pickup and started back towards the Matagamon Store. I had forgotten that I had left my pickup unlocked with the base radio and equipment sitting on the seat, to say nothing about my snowmobile on back and not locked. But, I really didn't worry about anyone stealing anything. That just didn't coincide with the character of this country.

"Jim, why does Detective Havelock want you to be in charge of the search and the searchers to be all wardens? I would think he would rather have his own people."

"He knows that wardens are more capable and better at searching the outdoors. The same as any police officer is better adapt at searching the inside of a building than wardens are. Out here police officers will overlook things, as simple as a turned leaf, or the dark color of tree bark or fail to look for drag marks over rotten wood. This is second nature to a game warden, we do it all the time without thinking.

"Can you be here at six tomorrow morning?"

"I'll be here." I assured him. I wouldn't miss this for the world.

* * * *

It was early evening by the time I got home and I still had to unload my snowmobile and take care of it. The base radio would have to wait.

I went to bed early and set the alarm for four. I was a long time going to sleep. The day's events kept racing through my mind and then I remembered that in June when I had first arrived at Matagamon I had been following two vehicles that had turned into the B.S.A. road and the vehicle directly in front of me had been an older model Oldsmobile and the driver had turned to look at me as I drove by. That had to be the same vehicle. I sure would like to have had a look in the trunk, knowing what I do now; who was in the front vehicle? Lagasse's brother from Salem, New Hampshire? A friend conspirator?

Then I started thinking about Jim Randall again; his ability to adapt from one situation to another. From chasing fisherman to night hunters and a murder investigation. And what surprised me the most was that nothing seemed to bother him. He always carried that self assured attitude.

I didn't sleep much that night and I was awake before four. I ate a big breakfast of ham and eggs. I was still hungry from the previous day. "I hate to leave you alone again today Royal, but I have got to go." It was just coming daylight when I turned the corner at four corners. I looked in the mirrors and saw an enormous log truck coming up fast behind me. Not wanting to antagonize the driver I found a wide spot in the road and pulled over. He rolled past me in a cloud of dust. The truck was purple and all I had time to read of the name on the door was something Brown something. He was loaded heavy with tree length hemlock. He wasn't long before he was out of sight, but I ate his dust all the way to the CCC road.

Detective Havelock was asleep in his vehicle when I arrived at three mile on the B.S.A. road. No one else had arrived yet. I was early. I heard vehicles approaching and figured it would be Jim and his crew. I was correct. By now Havelock's sleep had been disturbed and he was crawling out from under a blanket. He needed a shave, but out here there was no means to look presentable.

Along with Jim were only three other game wardens. Havelock was standing outside his car rubbing sleep from his eyes.

"Jim, the first thing I want you to do is lay out a six hundred foot square block around the remains. Try to have the remains near the center of the block. This will be the area that will have to be thoroughly searched. From here you're in charge of the search."

"Jim, Detective Havelock" I said as I walked over towards them, "before you leave Jim, I have some information about all this."

They both stood still looking at me, probably wondering if I was going to confess. "The night I arrived here at Matagamon, last June, as I was about half way across the long Tangent, two vehicles pulled onto the paved road from the right. They sped away, but I was already traveling rather fast and I wasn't long catching up to them. I followed them both to the B.S.A. road and when the vehicle directly in front of me turned I could see that it was an older model Oldsmobile. Maybe maroon, I couldn't be sure at that time. The driver looked over his shoulder at me as I drove by. In my headlights I could see the man had gray hair, thinning. Somewhere in his mid-fifties. And he was acting irritated that someone had been behind him."

"What was the date? That'll be important." Havelock asked.

"June ninth about eleven at night."

"According to Lagasse's daughter he was last seen at his brother's in Salem on June twenty-one. Of course, she could be lying as well as the brother.

"Get the area marked off Jim, by then Doctor Rutledge should be here. Our pilot is flying him up from Augusta."

"Alvin, I have to flag off a six hundred foot square block to search, I'll be about an hour. You might go out to Dudley's and have some Italian sandwiches made up for everyone and see if they have a large thermos for coffee. Ask Don or Di to keep a running tab and I'll pick up the bill when we're through here."

"John and Alan take a walk for about a half mile in both directions along the road and check both sides to see if anything might have been thrown. I wouldn't bother to get off the road unless you see something."

"What do you want me to do Jim?" I asked, not wanting to be left behind.

"You come with me and grab two rolls of that blue flagging. I'll set the corner markers and as I take a compass course and pace off six hundred feet I want you to walk behind me tying flagging to trees every twenty feet or so. Blue will be our outer perimeter. When we start the ground search we'll use orange flagging on the outside of each pass. That way we'll know what's been searched and what hasn't."

Jim marked the first corner and took a compass heading and started walking. And I following behind laying a blue line. Again I was surprised with Jim's ability in the woods with a compass. We were only about forty minutes and had the six hundred foot block all ribboned off. John and Alan were just getting back. Neither of them had found anything that might require a closer look later.

Alvin was back with the sandwiches and a large thermos of coffee and cups. We stood around sipping coffee and talking while we waited for the medical examiner. Before any of us finished our first cup the State Police Pilot radioed Detective Havelock that he would be landing behind the dam in five minutes. Alvin's pickup was the only vehicle here that wasn't blocked in. He left to pick up Doctor Rutledge. He returned in thirty minutes.

There was quite a bit of small talk between Doctor Rutledge and Detective Havelock and Rutledge wanted a cup of coffee before examining the remains.

"Which Game Warden was it that found that one hair on the log, Merlin?" Rutledge asked. Havelock pointed to Jim and said "Jim Randall."

"You have quite an eye. How in hell did you ever see one hair in the shadows like that? And what made you look at that particular piece of wood?"

"Well, it was obvious that the body had been dragged down to the gully where the remains are, inside the pants. And since the bear was going up the gully, I figured that it would continue in that relative direction, even if it had fed off the remains where we found the pants. I just started looking at the logs in the stream; the gully is full of water now. I was looking for signs that something had been dragged across the wood and blood or tissue left on the wood."

"Well, I'm glad you're here today. As I understand it we have only a leg bone. Unless there is a wallet in the pants; which is doubtful, or a name stitched in the inside the waist band, we don't stand a prayer in hell of discovering who it is or how the body died. What we need is the skull or the backbone and ribs would be good too, but the skull is the most important. From that we can determine whether it is male or female by the frontal bone and possibly the victim's identity by the dentures."

Detective Havelock escorted Doctor Rutledge up the skidder road to the remains. Jim, Alvin, John, Alan and myself went to the Northeast corner to start the search. Jim spread us out so we were only about four feet apart and he took the inside position to tie off orange flagging as we proceeded.

"Look at everything guys, keep the line straight and go slow. If you want to stop to look at something shout out to stop and we'll wait for you."

Everyone was eager to find the rest of the victim's body and at first the line was anything but straight. Finally, by the third pass we settled into a smooth routine. Then on the fourth pass, Jim was about thirty yards from the remains of the pants and he hollered, "stop!" There was obvious excitement in his voice. I knew he must have found something. "Doctor Rutledge! Doctor Rutledge I have found the skull!"

"Good. Great! Tie some flagging to the bushes and don't move it."

Jim started tying a whole bunch of flagging in the bushes. "There, they should be able to see that." Then he knelt down by the skull to tie a piece of flagging around the skull. Then he hollered out again, "Doctor Rutledge, there's half of the lower jaw here too."

"Good, flag it!"

This was going to be easier than I had first thought. Now all we have to do is find some ribs and backbone. What I really didn't want to find was a pile of rotting intestines. But then, those probably would have been eaten by the bear. "Jim, what makes you think it was a bear that ate that guy, instead of coyotes or some other animal?" I asked.

"Most animals will feed on a carcass where it lays, where the animal found it. A bear might feed a little from the rotting carcass, but it will drag it, or try, away from where it found it. Sometimes to feed cubs or to feed on it again at a later date. Cats, Fishers, Martins and Coyotes would have crapped all over the place, staking its claim to it. And there is no droppings anywhere." The State Police, without Jim's experience in the woods probably would not have ever have found the skull and lower jaw, let alone the one hair on the log. But as Jim said early, the detectives are just as sharp assessing an indoor crime scene as game wardens are in the out of doors.

As we were finishing with the first half of the six hundred foot block, a Park Ranger arrived that Jim had said would help with the search; Barry. He had another large thermos of fresh coffee. "Jim, you guys take a break and have some coffee." Havelock shouted from a distance.

We all gathered at the tailgate of Barry's pickup as he poured each of us a cup of coffee. When Havelock and Doctor Rutledge came over, everyone gathered around Havelock's vehicle, eager to hear what if anything Rutledge had for conclusions or assumptions. "The skull is definitely that of a male and my guess would be in the fifties. But, I won't be sure of that until I can thoroughly examine everything at the lab. I wish we had the jaw, so I'd know if he had dentures or not."

"What do you mean you wish you had the jaw?"

Jim's voice was raised slightly and I don't think from excitement. "I found half of the lower jaw three feet from the skull and I tied a piece of orange flagging around it." Then he was off running back to the scene, I could hear him muttering to himself, as well as all the others, in French I believe, but I wasn't familiar with that dialect or the terms he was using. He probably was cursing.

He returned in a few minutes with the lower jaw in his hand. "Someone trampled it into the ground." Then he placed it with the skull on Havelock's vehicle. Everyone could see he was irritated. No one said anything for a few minutes.

By noon we had finished searching the entire six hundred foot block without finding any more body parts or answers to who, what, why or when. The only things we found, were a few old bottles, an old pulp hook, a peavey end and a broken set of skidder chains. Doctor Rutledge and Havelock had taken soil samples from the base of the hemlock tree, where the pants were and again where the skull and jaw were found. The soil and leaves from each sight were put into separate plastic bags to be thoroughly examined at the forensic lab in Augusta.

After we had eaten, everyone was excused and could leave except for Jim and myself. "Jim, Doctor Rutledge has to leave, so I'll take him back to Matagamon, but I'll be right back and I want to go back where the car was burned. Houlton has dispatched a wrecker truck to pick it up and haul it to Augusta. Then we'll have to search the perimeter of that area. You and Thom can wait here."

Havelock had just disappeared around the bend in the B.S.A. road and a dark green pickup pulled up beside us and the driver got out and stood by Jim's door. "Are you in charge of the search?" the guy asked.

"Yes, what can I help you with Scott?" Jim inquired.

"This morning me and the boys," he pointed to the truck load, "were hunting between this road and the lake and I found something you might want to look at."

"What did you find?"

"Clean clothes sitting in the middle of a skidder road. They were folded and just laying there in the grass."

"Where is this?" Jim asked

"One mile and two tenths towards the beech tree on your left. There'll be an old log yard, at the back of this and on the left, you'll find the skidder road. The clothes are in there about a hundred and fifty feet."

"Is this road drivable?" Jim asked

"No, you'll have to walk it."

"Then whoever put the clothes there had to walk in."

"Well, there's a tree down across the road. I don't see how anyone could drive it."

"Okay thanks, as soon as Detective Havelock gets back we'll have a look at it."

After the pickup load of hunters left I asked, "Do you suppose those clothes have anything to do with this?"

"I'm not sure. But why would anyone walk up a skidder road to discard some clean-folded clothes? To hide them; and that is suspicious.

"I'd like to wrap this up. I've spent so much time on this, there isn't enough hours left to work night hunters."

"You make it sound as if you enjoy working night hunters," I said.

"That's the best part of this job."

"When you live in a small town like Patten and you arrest or summons so many local people, it would seem to me that you would soon be hated by most everyone." I inquired.

"Well the hardest part of it and the hate actually falls on your family. Your children are chided and teased at school and your wife will never have many close friends. And when she enters a store, all of a sudden the conversations stop and everyone looks at her. If there is something special going on for the weekend your wife takes the kids, but you're never there with your family. But I have always had my own rule."

"And what's that?"

"Every night hunter that I have ever arrested, if local, after everything is taken care of and the case is over I always make it a point to sit down with the individual and have a cup of coffee. That alone has earned me a lot of respect."

Havelock was driving into the old log yard then. He locked his cruiser and walked over to Jim's truck and got in. I never saw Jim lock his pickup. Did he command that much respect?

We started up the B.S.A. road towards the beech tree. "Before we go to the burned car we'll have to make a short detour. I received more information while you were gone. It may be nothing but we have to look at it."

On the way to this new information Jim told Havelock about the conversation we had with Scott. "This should be the log yard he was referring to, the mileage is right." He parked his pickup at the side of the B.S.A. road and I watched to see if he would lock it. No.

"The skidder road is supposed to be at the back on the left." We walked through a re-gen area of new spruce and fir trees. Who says lumbering isn't good for the ecology? Big trees have first to be small.

It wasn't difficult to find the skidder road Scott had described. We could even see old, I mean old, tire tracks through the new re-gen area. We walked up the skidder road, after first climbing over a blowdown, about one hundred and fifty feet and there smack-dab in the middle of the skidder road was clean folded clothes. Dark blue trousers and a light blue work shirt.

Havelock took photos of the skidder road. The clothes in the road and for some reason there were many small plastic bags scattered around, like baggies. Jim found a pair of rolled up socks that apparently were clean when they were thrown out here. Then Jim found an eight inch craftsman flathead screwdriver. He said "I'll bet a week's pay, that this screwdriver will end up being the murder weapon. Why else would it be thrown out with the clothing. The plastic handle would surely burn up in the fire but the metal shank would not. Forensic could have made a possible match to the entry wound if the body had been found while it was still intact. Whoever threw these out here probably was worried the clothes might not completely burn either. But who would have guessed that anyone would have found them this far off the road."

"You want to hear something else that doesn't fit. According to Lagasse's daughter the clothes her father should have been wearing matches the description of these, she said he always wore shirts like this," Havelock said as he unfolded the shirt and checked the pockets.

After all the articles were picked up, photographed and tagged, Jim and I made another quick search through the bushes on both sides of the skidder road.

"Well, let's take these back to the pickup and go look at the area where the car was burned," Havelock said.

When we got to the beech tree, Jim turned to the right and Detective Havelock made some sarcastic comment about the sign being ridiculous. Jim and I both ignored the comment. I could understand the logic behind the sign being there. I wondered how many had been helped from getting lost, throughout the years.

The incinerated car was gone. All that remained was a blackened spot on the gravel and bits of broken glass. "I want to see if anything was thrown over the banks, we won't have to go too deep in through the bushes." We separated about ten feet apart and worked our way around the circumference of the log landing and then back again. We didn't find anything at all.

"The only thing left to do now is run a dog through the scene; start at the hemlock tree and see if the dog can still pick up the scent where the bear took the rest of the remains. If we need anything else, I'll give you a call Jim."

"How soon do you want my report and the written statement?"

"Put'em in the mail Monday morning. I don't know if anything will come out of this or not. But thanks for your help Jim, and you too Thom."

Detective Havelock left, probably to start another investigation of who knows what crime. Jim and I sat in his pickup talking about the last two days. "What's your gut feeling here Jim?"

There was a long pause before Jim answered, then he said, "It's a damned shame the police didn't respond when I first called about the torched car. But I don't know if the dead body would have been found any sooner or not. But at an inquiry into Mr. Lagasse's whereabouts would have been initiated and possibly a lot more information could have been obtained. The body ----------- I think was probably killed elsewhere and brought here and made to look like a suicide. Whoever the killer or killers are went to great lengths to erase all evidence in the vehicle and then the clothes and screwdriver we found this afternoon. There is no logical reason why anyone would to go that extreme to hide those clothes and the screwdriver unless it could point to the murderer."

"But why go to the extent to bring a dead body all the way to Matagamon to dispose of it? I mean you could bury it in a shallow seashore grave and let the crabs have at it. Throw it in an abandoned quarry or there are forests elsewhere. Why Matagamon?" I asked.

"Well, suppose the individual or individuals were familiar with this area; had hunted, fished or vacationed here in the past and likely knew that where they had left the body was far enough off the beaten trail to go undiscovered until let's say the body had completely decomposed, leaving only a skeleton and shotgun with the serial numbers removed, or eaten by a bear. But in this case the bear didn't eat the skull.

"Let's take this a little further. Let's say the body was brought here in the trunk of the torched car. Burning it certainly removed all evidence. Let's say the owner, Mr. Lagasse faked his own death by picking up a street bum and fabricated the scene at the hemlock tree to look like a suicide. Then he would have to have a place somewhere to hide out.

"Remember Lagasse's daughter was filing a missing person's complaint six months after, supposedly, that he had last been seen at his brother's in Salem. This, only after my radio call of an unattended death in T6-R8. I don't believe in coincidences. I think whoever called Lagasse's daughter had heard the radio traffic and called to have the daughter file a complaint. That means he had to be close; East Millinocket to Fort Kent, a big area, but remember, the caller had to be familiar with Matagamon. So that narrows the logical places. My guess would be Upper or Lower Shin Pond. And I would also suspect that he might still be here, listening for more radio traffic."

"So what happens now?"

"It'll depend on what Doctor Rutledge discovers in the forensic lab. Or maybe when the technicians sift through the ashes and debris in the car, they'll find some answers. I know Rutledge was concerned about finding a pair of steel rim glasses and dentures. I saw a pair of rim glasses in the car. Maybe it'll be what Rutledge is looking for. As for the dentures, I don't believe there ever was any, connected to this victim."

Just then Jim received a radio call about an over due hunter behind Scraggley Lake and the complainant would wait for him at the Huber garage. "That's bad country to get lost in. Big woods and every lost hunter tends to walk north downhill. I'll probably be out all night. Thanks for your help here Thom. I'd better go meet the complainant."

CHAPTER 5

I didn't see or hear from Jim Randall for the rest of that deer season. I naturally assumed he had been kept busy between chasing night hunters, looking for lost hunters and looking for body parts. In fact I didn't see him again until the middle of January.

The week following the search for body parts on the B.S.A. road, it snowed for two days straight. There was twenty inches of snow in the camp yard. Too much snow to hunt through and too much to drive my pickup out to town, so I worked on the tote road, clearing it of trees that had blown down in the wind storm. It was grueling work. Snow to my knees and every time I disturbed the limbs of a standing tree I got snow down the back of my neck.

The weather turned warm again by the end of the weekend and I had to use the ATV instead of the snow sled to get back and forth on the tote road. I quit work each afternoon from exhaustion and I was wet to the bone; usually after the first half hour. I was beginning to understand how wood cutters felt after each day. But then they went to work before daylight each morning. I asked Uncle Royal once, 'why did the crews go to work so early?' In the winter the crews I learned were at the job sight long before daylight, so that meant they would have to get up at three. Uncle Royal had said that the early hours was more from tradition than anything else. It was simply something that never changed in the industry.

I had cleared the tote road as far as the orchard and the weather had turned cold. The dead water below the cabin had frozen over with a thin film of ice and Royal's water dish had frozen solid. It was time to hunt; to get winter's meat before the season was over.

That day I pulled the old aluminum canoe down to the deadwater so I could float across the next morning. I laid out my compass, lighter, knife, a flashlight, rifle and bullets, before going to bed that night.

I could feel the temperature dropping all that afternoon and by dark, it was really cold. By morning the temperature dropped to zero and there was three inches of new snow. It was dry and fluffy; good for hunting. After eating breakfast I packed a good lunch and a thermos of coffee. I put those in my pack and threw in a piece of rope, just in case. I left camp at eight. Uncle Royal had said five years ago that he had found long ago that it didn't pay to leave too early, "Unless that is if you intend to shoot the deer under a light."

Before I could cross the deadwater I had to break an inch of ice in front of the canoe. I had been so busy clearing the tote road that I forgot about clearing the hunting trail. But much to my surprise there were no blow downs on this side of the river. I followed the trail until I came to a well used deer crossing. I checked the tracks to see which way they were traveling. The tracks were all small, maybe six deer traveling a little North of West. There was blood in one of the tracks which meant that at least one of the does was in estrous. This would be a good place to sit and wait for a buck following her scent.

I sat down and made myself comfortable. I sat there and sat there, and all I saw all day were red squirrels chasing each other and scolding me. As the sun started to disappear down behind the tree tops the temperature fell as fast. I was shivering from the cold and my feet were almost numb with cold. There wasn't much daylight left and I had no choice but to leave. I stood up slowly, for I was so cold and stiff I couldn't have done anything but. I stood there feeling warm blood starting to circulate again. Just as I was about to leave, I saw a deer pick its head up from the doe's trail that it was following. He was looking up the trail ahead of him and not at me. Slowly I raised my rifle to my shoulder and sighted through the scope. He was so close all I could see was hair. I would have no idea where the bullet would impact the deer if I shot. And I didn't want to wound it and have it run off to die.

The scope was a high mount and I could use the open iron sights below the scope. I aimed for the brisket and pulled the trigger. The deer went down in a heap. I reloaded and walked slowly up to the deer. It was not as large as the deer I shot five years ago, but it will certainly be good eating. I set my rifle down, Uncle Royal's favorite; the infamous .38-55, against a tree and started to clean the deer.

My hands were so cold I had a difficult time holding onto my knife. Once I had the hide slit all the way up to the ribs I put both of my hands inside the stomach cavity. The hot blood felt like boiling water on my hands. It was so difficult working in the dark. I did have a flashlight, but in the excitement I forgot about it until I had finished.

By the time I had dragged the deer back to the deadwater I was soaking wet from my own sweat and the only way I knew I was near the canoe was the fact that I had followed my tracks back. It was totally dark, I was exhausted and wet. All I had was a pen-flashlight and the light has now almost non-existent. I decided to leave the deer there on the shore of the deadwater until morning, and daylight. Before leaving, I dropped my pants and cut off my shorts with my knife and then I tied the shorts to a low hanging tree limb, so my scent would ward off coyotes.

I had pulled the bow of my canoe up on land and tied it off, but the stern was still in the water. During the day the temperature had gotten colder than I had thought. The canoe was frozen solid now in the ice, and I didn't have an axe with me. "I bet Uncle Royal wouldn't be without an axe," I said out-loud. That was a good lesson. From then on wherever I would travel I'd always make sure I had an axe.

I really didn't feel like building a fire and spending the night on this side of the deadwater when my home was so close. I took the paddle from the canoe and tested the ice. It didn't break or even crack when I hit it. I tested it then with the weight of one foot, then the other. The ice held. I began to shuffle my way across, sliding my feet only inches at a time, after testing the ice ahead of me.

About four feet from the other shore the ice suddenly gave way and I went through. Not realizing what I was doing the moment the ice broke I threw my rifle ashore. I went down in the gawd awful cold water. The momentum of falling threw my torso forward so I went completely under water. I couldn't feel any bottom with my feet, but I knew it had to be there somewhere. I tried to push with my legs, but I just couldn't push against the black muck I was in. Reaching out in front of me I managed to grasp a hold of some bushes and managed to pull myself ashore. I remembered what Uncle Royal had said about falling through the ice in winter. "Roll in the snow immediately, so the snow will soak up the water from your clothes"

It was difficult to do. I had never been so cold, but I threw myself into the snow and rolled and rolled. My hands were like ice, but yes I was drier. After I found my rifle I started running for home. More to regain warm circulation than anything. I tripped and fell in the snow. My hands digging deep into the cold. I started running again, but in the dark without a light I kept running into overhanging tree limbs and into the butt ends of the trees I had cleared from the trail through the blow downs.

I was so exhausted now I could no longer run. I knew hypothermia was dangerously close. If I succumbed here I would die. Even though my feet were wet they were the only parts of my body that was not freezing. I lost my hat somewhere and my hair had turned to ice. My clothes had frozen making each move I made very painful and tiring. My feet slipped on the packed snow at the mouth of my driveway and I fell to the ground on my knees. That hurt, but I knew I had to get up and continue. I would not die like this. If it had not been for the snow outlining the road I would never have managed to find my way home in the condition that I was now in. Finally after what seemed to be hours, I could see the outline of the cabin. I pushed on the door and it opened and I fell forward onto the kitchen floor. Even then I had to struggle to kick it shut; then I just laid there on the floor in the relative warmth until the ice melted from my clothes so I could stand. I could hear Royal whining and barking outside, telling me he wanted to come in. I crawled on the floor over to the wood stove but it had long since gone out.

Before starting a fire in the stove I knew I had to get out of these wet clothes. I dropped everything on the floor and found a wool blanket and wrapped it around me; as coarse as it was, it felt comforting. It was still some time before I could rekindle the fire. The gas lights were a real problem though. My hands were still cold and I didn't have the strength to turn the handle or feel the match between my fingers. I found some candles after a while and managed to get one lit. I rubbed my hands together over the flame until the circulation had returned and they were sufficiently warm so I did eventually get a fire going in the stove and the gas lights lit. Royal was still whining but he would have to wait.

Little by little the cabin warmed up. I checked the thermometer once and it read 80 degrees. But I was still chilled through to the bones. I would sit in a chair beside the stove for a while, then I'd walk back and forth in the kitchen area. At ten o'clock I put on some dry clothes and took care of the wet ones on the floor and unhooked Royal from his run. He was indeed excited to see me.

I fixed a sandwich and washed that down with a cup of hot water, then I went to bed. I don't remember falling asleep, I was that exhausted. I awoke earlier the next morning than I had wanted to. Not relishing the task I had ahead of me this morning, I laid on my back staring at the roof. I had come very close to death last night. I tried to think if there was anything I should have done different. The ice on the deadwater was safe enough, until I reached the opposite shore. There must be a spring there. I was careful and I did as Uncle Royal had said about rolling in the snow to soak up the water from my clothes. If I had had a better flashlight I would not have been stumbling and falling so much. I decided right then that whenever I left the cabin during the cold months I would leave one gas light on and the oil heater on and set on low, so when the wood fire burned out the oil heater would automatically turn on.

I understand now how Chub Foster must have felt when he went through the ice on Snowshoe Lake. Except he had a backpack on and wearing snowshoes that he had to cut himself out of. As I laid there and seriously thought about my ordeal, I began to realize that I had not experienced anything that any woodsman had not at sometime in his life experienced. Then I laughed, "Except none of them were ever as close to home as I was when the ice broke."

My thoughts shifted in the direction of what I had to do now, to get that deer back home. I'd take the snowsled down, enough rope to reach across to the canoe, an axe to chop the canoe out of the ice. "I hope the coyotes haven't gotten it. Probably not with my scent in the air." I got out of bed, built a fire in the stove and had a big breakfast.

As I was closing the kitchen door I remembered my earlier proclamation about turning the oil heater on and one gas light. I doubted very much if I would be that late today, but now was a good time to start the routine.

The air was extremely cold and still the thermometer said it was -10°F. That's cold! I loaded everything that I would need and drove down to the deadwater. The air was cold enough, so ice was still making on the deadwater. Every once in a while I could hear the distinguishable sound of the ice groaning and snapping as it expanded. Today the ice was safe where I had fallen through the night before. I cut a hole with my axe and tested the ice. There was a good three inches. But still I was cautious as I crossed to the canoe. The deer was intact and no tracks, until I walked back on the trail and on top of the knoll there were three distinctive sets of coyote tracks. The scent in my shorts worked. They wouldn't come close. I loaded the deer into the canoe, then chopped the ice around the canoe, freeing it. I tied the rope to the stern and walked back across the dead water before pulling the canoe across behind me. It was an easy trip by snowsled to home. I hung it up in the garage and decided it might be a good idea to attach the tag portion of my hunting license; just in case.

The hide was going to come off with difficulty. Even if I had a wood stove in the garage it would take several days, two maybe, to warm the deer up enough so the hide would come off without much ado. But my first problem was to get it tagged properly. Then I remembered the base radio I had installed but had never used it.

I called the Matagamon store and Don came back, "This is Matagamon, go ahead with your traffic Thom."

"Don, I have a deer to register, but I'm locked in. Can't get out with the pickup – nor down the lake yet with the snow sled. What would you suggest?"

"I'll fill in the registration form and give you the tag serial number. You can pick the tag up sometime when you're out."

"When did you shoot the deer Thom?"

"Late, about four-fifteen, yesterday."

There was a long, long pause before Don came back on the radio, "Ah, don't you mean Saturday?"

Without thinking I replied. "Yeah, late Saturday afternoon." But what Don was trying so hard not to say, hadn't yet occurred to me.

Don gave me the serial number and said before signing off, "Check your calendar Thom."

Each day here was the same as the previous day and the day to come. I looked at the calendar, but in all honesty I didn't know what day it was. The only way to know for sure was to listen to the radio for a station break or news report. And then I understood when the radio DJ said, "There are now only twenty-three days before Christmas ----." There was more the DJ was saying but I wasn't listening. That meant today was Monday December first and yesterday when I shot the deer was Sunday in closed season. That's what Don was trying not to say.

Perhaps I've been in the woods too long already, I'm starting to live like Uncle Royal where the laws, from the outside as he'd say, never affected him. Wherever he was right now, I could see him laughing. This, had been a mistake. Now if I could only keep the truth from the warden. I didn't like deceiving him, but shooting that deer on Sunday was a mistake. Granted it was my mistake, but what harm would ever come from it?

CHAPTER 6

Deer hunting season was behind me and I had not yet seen or heard anything from Jim Randall. Perhaps he was taking some time off to spend with his wife.

I had hung the deer up in the root cellar. It was too cold and stiff to skin hanging in the cold garage. The temperature in the root cellar was about 40°F and I figured after a week in the cellar I should be able then to remove the hide.

There wasn't much to do, so I shoveled snow up against the cabin walls to insulate it from the cold. I hauled water and filled every pot, pitcher and bucked I could find. I stacked firewood in every accountable space. And I spent a lot of my time watching the newly arrived red squirrels torment and tease Royal. There were six of the rascals that descended on the cabin that afternoon that I brought the deer back. From that moment on, Royal hasn't had any peace or solitude. One would perch just out of reach and scold him, while another ran between him and the tree, the scolding squirrel was perched in. Sometimes one would be adventuresome and let Royal chase him for a short distance before disappearing in a snow bank.

There were no more chores that I could busy my time with, and there was not yet enough snow to ride the snow sled. The next day the weather took a surprising turn. The temperature outside was already $40°F$ when I got out of bed. By noon it was $50°F$, I hung the deer back in the garage and closed the door. "Another day like this one and I'll skin it."

And the next day was even warmer and by mid afternoon the snow was all melted. The deer was taken care of and the quarters and loins were hanging back in the root cellar. As soon as the temperature dropped again I would hang the meat in the garage until the meat was frozen solid and then back to the root cellar again. That night the temperature did drop again, and for the next two days and nights the temperature stayed below zero. Everything was frozen solid. I checked the ice in the deadwater, where I had fallen through and there was a foot of solid ice. Royal and I walked down to the lake and I cut several holes in the ice and there was between six and eight inches. The lake was full again and there was no sound or any disturbance, except for the groaning the ice was making, as it froze and expanded.

Before we got back to the cabin, it started to snow and it snowed and snowed. It never let up for forty hours. When it did stop there was thirty five inches of heavy snow. Rather than shoveling paths around the yard, I donned my snowshoes and packed the snow down. After a night of cold weather the packed snow would be like walking on concrete.

I needed something to do and I needed to get out for a while. I took a traveling pack of necessities and started down the tote road towards the lake and

Dudley's store. In places I was pushing snow over the windshield. That wide track Polaris was indeed some sled. I would never have thought that any snowmobile would have gone through that much snow. The ride wasn't fast, but it was enjoyable; seeing everything covered with the white stuff. The only tracks I saw were those of red squirrels.

The snow wasn't as deep out on the lake and the traveling was thus made easier. The snow covered ice was like riding a soft carpet. This was really a beautiful world. As I rode down the center of Second Lake I tried to remember what Uncle Royal and Don had said about the thoroughfare between the two lakes. "There could be good ice one day and the next, open water." I stayed to the right through the thoroughfare.

At Louse Island I went to the left so I'd be out in the center of the lake, so I'd have a better view of the snow covered mountains. They were exquisitely beautiful and everything was so still and quiet. What would it be like out there in a strong wind? I don't think I wanted to know.

There was still a lot of open water behind the dam and I had to pick my way through the dri-ki and rocks in order to avoid getting too close to the water on thin ice. The camp sites and cabins were all empty. It was a lonely feeling as I rode down the Dam road towards the bridge.

Only Don and Di were at the store. They were busy moving the shelves around making room for tables. "In the winter we do a good business with snowmobilers; lunch and hot coffee. We're just getting things set up. How have you been Thom?"

"Real busy since I was out here helping with the search out on the B.S.A. road." I didn't feel there was any need to bring up the deer.

"Oh! I'm awfully glad you came out. What did I tell you about that radio? Keep it on! Didn't I?" Before I could answer Di continued, "We have been trying for three days to reach you. Don forgot to tell you when you called to tag your deer" she handed me an envelope then and said, "This came addressed to you."

"Thank you," I looked at the return address. It was from Ronie. Addressed to me in care of Don Dudley at the Matagamon Store, T6-R8. It's a wonder I ever got it. But then everyone and including the postmaster in Patten, knew Don and Di Dudley in T6-R8, so no, now it wasn't quite so surprising.

Don came in carrying an arm load of firewood. "What brings you out Thom?"

"I was getting antsy at camp and needed to get out for a while."

"Before I forget it," and Don disappeared into the other room and then right back, he handed me a metal deer tag and said "you'll need this to put with your deer." That's all that was said and I was just as glad.

We talked of many varied subjects, of what they were I couldn't now tell you. I had Ronie's letter in my pocket. Di looked at the window and said "The wind is blowing. It'll be rough out on the lake Thom. I'm not trying to get rid of you but maybe you should leave before the wind starts to blow stronger."

"You know that would be a good idea I believe. Thank you for everything."

"Thom, keep your radio on! I mean it." Di said and I knew she meant it from the kindest of her heart. She and Don worried about me being all alone up there.

"Make sure to stay to the left of the islands through the thoroughfare. Don't ever suppose the thoroughfare is safe just because it is covered with ice and snow. The ice will be thin at any given time, no matter how cold the weather is."

Before leaving I filled my sled with gas, said thank you again. The wind was not that noticeable until I was out on the ice away from the protection of the tall spruce trees and the mountains. Then the wind blew so strong that I could only see about fifty feet ahead of me. The shoreline was obscured, as was the top of Horse Mountain. The opposite shore --- hell it wasn't even there!

The only way I had of knowing the direction I was traveling is the fact that when I came onto the ice behind the dam the wind hit me square in the face; so now I tried to keep the snow sled headed into the wind. I locked the handle bars against my knees so it would help keep me on a straight course. The going was rough. And my head speed was only ten miles an hour.

It donned on me that I was out here all by myself. I mean Chub and Fran were gone. The Martin camp was gone and Tom wouldn't be anywhere about. There wouldn't likely be anyone at any of the camps during the off-season time of year. Jim Randall wouldn't be at the Warden's camp, since that was scheduled to be burned. But Di and Don did know where I was. I should remember to call them on the radio to let them know that I had made it back.

The wind was driving the snow so hard that all around me looked like a blizzard. The icy pellets stung my face and eyes. I had to ride with the helmet visor up. I was close to Martin's Point, but all that was visible was a grayish shadow as I rode through the Devil's Throat.

As I turned more towards the West around the Throat the wind was ever the stronger. The snow was now like sharp needles piercing the now raw flesh of my face and my eyes were red hot and burned. The letter in my pocket was worth the trip, no matter how awful the return was, or was going to be.

The windshield offered some relief from the wind driven snow. That is if I kept my head down and my face turned towards the fuel tank. But in that position I couldn't see where I was going. Hell with my head stuck up above the edge of the windshield, I couldn't see anything either. I don't know how long I had been on the lake, but I was cold and if I didn't stop somewhere out of the wind and warm up, I'd never make it home.

Again Louse Island became my redoubt against the elements. How many times I and Uncle Royal had used the shelter of Louse Island to ward off the wind. How many times during the history of this region had Louse Island been used to shelter against the wind? This island had been purposely positioned here for a special reason, and that was obviously clear to me now.

There was a dark shadow ahead. Was it the island or just darkness setting in? I don't know how I had done it in these conditions, but as I neared the island the wind disappeared and the stinging snow. And I could see! Behind the island was like being in the eye of a hurricane. Complete calmness and all around me stood a solid wall of wind driven snow. I pulled up close to the shore. I opened the cowling and put my gloved hands on top of the engine. It was still running. It wasn't long before I could feel the engine heat coming through my gloves. One at a time I took my boots off and put my stockinged feet on the hot engine.

My hands and feet were warmed and I had to leave the protection of Louse Island once again. There were many more islands up through the thoroughfare making my progress even slower. As darkness settled in with my headlight off I could actually see better. I could see clear the shadows and shapes of islands ahead of me and the broken shoreline to my left. The worst wind on the lake hit me square in the face when I emerged from the protection of the islands in the thoroughfare. Now there was no more windbreak. Only the length of Second Lake. Three more miles and I'd be off this frozen piece of Siberia.

It was completely dark now and all I could see of either shoreline was the tree line where it met the sky horizon. I tried to keep in the middle of the lake, still with the wind whipping snow in my face. I was beyond Pine Point now and I was beginning to feel the cold again, but I would not stop. Not until I was safely home.

I pointed my sled in the direction of the trail that would take me off the lake to the tote road, but there was an island I'd have to go around first. If I didn't mistake it for the mainland and end up following the shore to open water where Webster Stream dumps into the lake. In the darkness everything had an eerie look about it, shadowed with the wind driven snow.

As I approached the island, it was acting as a wind break and I could see enough through the snow so I could safely make my way around the island to the trail on shore.

Once I was in the woods I turned my headlight back on. Here there was no wind, no stinging snow and from there, home the trip was uneventful.

As usual Royal was glad to have me home. I put the sled away, and unhooked him from his run. "Come on boy, let's go inside. I escaped the jaws of death again." I hadn't forgotten the letter in my pocket, but first I needed to get the fire going in the stove and turn the rest of the gas lights on. I was still cold but I couldn't hold back any longer. I had to read Ronie's letter, listen to her speak the words in my head. I pulled a chair up beside the stove and open her letter.

Oops, I forgot, I was going to call Don and Di on the radio and let them know I made it. I turned the radio on and waited for the static to clear. "Thom to Matagamon – Don, Di you there?"

"Go ahead Thom. Any problems?" Don asked.

"No problems. Just letting you know I made it back okay."

"Thanks Thom. How was the lake. Probably windy wasn't it?"

"Couldn't see anything. Fine now."

There it was again, these people never considered that going up the lake at night in wind driven snow might be just a little unsettling. It was something that was simply accepted and nothing extraordinary. What I accept as dangerous, Don, Di and those who have lived here before accept what I call dangerous as everyday events. "That's something I must learn and learn to grow from."

Radio call made, I went back to reading Ronie's letter. First though, I checked the return address. Ronie Ferris, Berlin New Hampshire. "There that's done." I laughed and added "you idiot." I sat down beside the stove again and I began to read.

*   *   *   *

Ronie asked if she could come up and stay over the Christmas holiday. If I wanted her, she said she would meet me at the Matagamon store on the twenty-second in the afternoon.

Before getting myself something to eat. I wrote a quick note and said I would meet her on the twenty-second.

After breakfast the next morning I rode back to Matagamon. Di said she would put my letter in with her outgoing mail. "Where is Don today?"

"Oh, he left early to check beaver traps. He won't be back until later this evening."

I thanked her and started my ride back. The air was still and cold but there was no wind today. Half way through the thoroughfare a large dark colored coyote ran onto the ice from one of the islands. When he saw me, he stopped and then changed direction and ran up the thoroughfare towards Second Lake. He was a curiosity and I decided to follow him.

The snow was wind packed from the previous day so the coyote had a hard surface to run on. But I never supposed that he would run as fast and as far as he did. I stayed about twenty feet directly behind him. When he passed the last island in the thoroughfare my speedometer read thirty miles an hour. He charged up the middle of Second Lake still maintaining thirty miles an hour.

I was finding the thrill of this chase exhilarating. Did I want to kill or injure the coyote? No, even after what I saw the coyotes do to the doe deer earlier this fall. But I did find myself wanting to ride beside it and tackle it and wrestle with it. Why? Just something to do. But I didn't. I stayed behind it and watched as the animal started to turn in the cove behind Pine Point and then thinking better of it, the coyote swung back out into the lake heading for the inlet. He had slowed to twenty miles an hour now, now after more than two miles. No wonder deer don't stand a chance against them.

He was running straight for open water at the inlet by Ledge Point. He never slowed as he neared the water. At twenty miles an hour he jumped in and started swimming for the opposite shore. I sat there on my snow sled in complete fascination. I shut the machine off and watched. After running nearly three miles at thirty miles an hour he had enough savoy to know that I would not be able to follow him into the open water. After he pulled himself out of the water onto the ice, he laid down facing me. I laughed and laughed until my gut hurt. That coyote knew what he was doing and he knew he was now safe. He was making no attempt to move. And neither did he look very menacing. Other coyotes began to howl, but this one made no attempt to answer. Perhaps he was as intrigued with me as I was with him.

I sat there for three hours as we watched each other. For no better reason than for something to do, I turned my face up into the air and howled as best as I could like another coyote. I started from the base of my stomach and started with a deep pitch howl and finished with a sharp, shrill pitch howl. My friend across the river stood up and lowered his head and looked intently at me, before lifting his head high into the air and answering my howl with his own.

"I'll be damned. Uncle Royal would roll over in his grave if he knew what I was doing." We howled back and forth a few more times and then the coyote walked off to the nearest bush and urinated on it and then he ran off. He marked his territory and then where? I doubted if he would join with others; I took him for a loner, like----yeah like me.

*   *   *   *

For the rest of my life I would always remember that incident with the coyote at the inlet to Matagamon Lake. Not chasing after him, but sitting there for hours as we watched each other and howled back and forth. Don't ever tell me animals and coyotes in particular can't think, because I'll tell you different from my own experiences. And I was glad that this particular coyote did not hunt me. But if he had the chance, I bet he would enjoy chasing me for three miles.

During the next few days I would ride my snow sled down to the lake. Sometimes I'd sit in the fir trees at Ledge Point waiting to see if the same coyote would return and then other times I'd ride the perimeter of the lake; always looking for that one particular coyote. I never saw him again, for sure. I saw coyotes at a distance, but I was never sure if it was the same one. Maybe when he heard my snow machine coming he'd lay low or run like hell off the ice. I never told anyone about that day with the coyote, except Ronie.

Ronie would be here tomorrow. I would certainly have a lot to tell her about what I have been doing with myself since she left last summer. To say nothing about the search for body parts on the B.S.A. road; almost drowning and twice almost freezing to death. I was hoping for good weather while she would be here, so I could show her some of this country from my snow sled.

Tomorrow finally arrived and I left in plenty of time so I wouldn't be late, for Dudley's Store. Near where Trout Brook puts into the lake I saw a flock of ravens take off from the ice. I had enough time so I went to investigate. It was a bloody tangled mess of deer sinew, guts, hide and bones. By the appearance of the blood it was probably killed about daylight. Up the brook a little farther, I saw another deer lying on the ice. I walked up the brook and this one too had been killed by coyotes, only nothing had been eating from it. This deer seemed somewhat smaller than the first, probably this years. There was nothing I could do now. But I began to wonder, if this killing kept up all winter would there be any deer left come spring. I know biologists all over would say that the coyote is only a natural part of the environment. That may well be in some places, like the west. But I don't and may never understand what the species is doing here in Northern Maine. Unless they were brought here on purpose. I remember Uncle Royal saying something about a biologist in the 50's studying the snowshoe rabbit population; seems as if in the 50's there was actually a problem with too many rabbits. Uncle Royal said he had heard stories that coyotes were brought in to control the rabbit population. If that is true, it would seem to me that the state would have been better served if the rabbits had been left to nature, as biologists are suggesting we should do with the coyote.

In this region with the expanding coyote population, it won't surprise me that if some day there isn't a deer left in all of Northern Maine. I walked back to my snow sled trying to forget about the two recent kills and coyotes. Ronie would be arriving soon and I didn't want anything distracting me.

I naturally arrived at the store before Ronie; actually I'd have another three hours to wait, Di asked me to have lunch with her and Don. The store wasn't opened yet. "We close generally in December. There aren't enough snowmobilers through to warrant keeping open."

As we ate, I told Don about the two dead deer I had seen on Trout Brook. "There's nothing I can do there. That's the park and the park director made it clear he doesn't want me snaring coyotes inside the park. After Christmas I was going to set snares at Dri-ki dam above your cabin."

"I'd like to go with you if I could."

"Tell you what, when you go back today, I'll give you my tote sled and you can haul up a deer carcass and a couple of beaver carcasses and freeze them in the ice on the deadwater just above the park line. That would save me some time and we'd get the coyotes coming to the bait sooner.

"Sometimes the bait will lay there for a month before the coyotes feel comfortable enough to feed on it. They'll come close, but not to it until they feel comfortable. I could never figure out if it is my scent they are afraid of or the disturbance at the sight.

"After you set the bait don't go near it for a week. Then check a couple of times each week and call me on the radio when the coyotes have established trails in the alders; then I'll bring my snares up and I'll show you how to set them without getting non-target animals."

"When do you expect Ronie? Don asked

"She said mid-afternoon. How many beaver have you and Ted trapped?"

"Oh, somewhere around a hundred and fifty."

"When do you find time to skin and stretch that many?"

"Di does all of the skinning and I flesh a few each week and put'em on the boards. When the snowmobile season gets busy I have to groom trails at night; that puts a damper on fleshing and stretching."

There were never a shortage of topics to discuss whenever I visited with Don and Di. They are the last; still living in this mysterious region and they have inherited the history of this region, passed down through the generations like Chub and Fran Foster and many others. And it will be their responsibility to pass it along to those who will follow.

*   *   *   *

Ronie was late. It was almost four before she drove in the driveway at the Matagamon Store. I went outside to meet her. "Sorry I'm late. I had to make a couple of stops." She closed her car door and ran into my arms. Wow! It was good to feel my arms around her.

"Hi, I'm sure glad to see you." We went inside and I introduced her to Don and Di.

"We'll have to visit another day. It's dark already and we really should be on our way; we have to haul a sled of coyote bait up with us too."

Don followed us behind the dam and while Ronie and I were loading her suitcase and backpack on the back of the tote sled, Don loaded the deer and beaver carcasses. We left her car there with mine and we started up across the lake. Ronie wrapped her arms around me and squeezed just enough to say 'Hi, I'm here.'

I was thankful the lake surface was still smooth. It made the trip easier and faster, especially since we were towing the loaded tote sled. "Hauling all this bait --- we'll probably attract all the coyotes around the lake and they'll follow us."

"Will that be a problem?" Ronie asked.

"I don't think they'll come into the camp yard." The moon was out full and the scenery up through the thoroughfare was beautifully eerie. I wondered if Ronie saw the same beauty that I saw.

There were fresh deer tracks on the sled trail and at the orchard. There was an old cow moose in the trail. As we approached her, the noise of the snow sled must have scared her, because she started to run off to the right and soon she was out of illumination of the headlight. When we turned the corner near the deadwater we saw several eyes reflecting in the light and then they disappeared as we turned the full corner.

Royal was glad to see us. It was almost as if he knew I was going after Ronie. It was a good idea to leave one gas light left on whenever I left. Even now in the full moon that one light help to illuminate some of the yard. Enough so we found our way, without stumbling to the door. "What will you do with that load of carcasses?"

"After we're settled I'll come back out and put the sled in the garage."

While I got us something to eat, Ronie unpacked and changed her clothes and put on one of my soft flannel shirts. That was all she had on except for a pair of slippers. The shirt was big enough so it covered most of her.

"I didn't bring many clothes. I hope your automatic washer works. I don't suppose you have an old gas operated wringer washer?"

"Nothing luxurious; I use the sink." I put the pot of simmering deer meat back on the stove and turned around and Ronie jumped into my arms and wrapped her legs around me and I could feel her warm bare skin under the shirt. We just hugged each other for the longest of moments and then we kissed. Each of us trying to fulfill a passionate hunger with the kiss. We searched each other's lips and mouth with our tongue. She tipped her head back and I kissed her neck. And the simmering pot was boiling over onto the stove top.

It sure did smell good. But our passionate hunger was a priority right at that moment.

Ronie unwrapped her legs and slid back to the cool cabin floor. Her flannel shirt was pulled up to her breast. She wasn't the least embarrassed. But I couldn't take my eyes away from her. "Perhaps you better go take care of that old coyote bait and I'll finish supper."

By now the entire cabin smelled like cooked venison. Which is a very pleasing smell in itself, but I would have preferred the sweet aroma of Ronie's natural essence. Once in a while the air would stir and I would just begin to detect her incense and it would be gone and replaced with the smell of cooked venison.

I changed into a pair of sweat pants and a clean t-shirt and washed my face and hands and then shaved.

"What will you do with all those carcasses?" Ronie asked.

"Don is planning to set snares for coyotes just out of reach of the park line and he asked if I would freeze these into the ice so the coyotes would start feeding on it, and establishing trails in the snow through the alders."

We ate, but I was somewhere else in my mind and thoughts. When we finished, we took care of the food and the dishes were stacked next to the sink. They could wait for morning. "I don't suppose that you'd have a bathtub kicking around here would you." She laughed.

"You know if I had thought about it I would have bought a portable tub before I was locked in here."

"Well I do need to wash up. I guess I'll have to do with a sponge bath. Will you put some water onto heat while I find something to lay on the floor so I don't freeze my feet while I'm washing."

I emptied the hot water tank that was behind the stove and that half filled the sink with very hot water. I refilled the water tank and put a bucket of cool water next to the sink, to mix with the hot water.

Ronie came out of the bedroom wearing nothing at all. She was carrying a towel, washcloth and the small rug I kept at my bedside. That she put on the floor to stand on. "Now you go sit down and let me wash up, you're next."

While Ronie washed up I sat in my chair in the, well one would have to call it, the living room. The cabin was warm, but because there wasn't yet sufficient snow to bank the cabin, the floor was cold. I watched Ronie, not ogling, but enjoying her grace and beauty. She had a tough sinewy body, slim and her butt was firm like a taut muscle.

"Will you wash my back, Thom?"

There was no need to answer; she knew I would. How could I pass up an invitation like that. She handed me her washcloth and I scooped it up and began to wash her back, gently. Savoring the moment. When I was finished she said, "Okay, your turn" she picked up another towel and began to dry off.

I hurried through my wash. Ronie had already disappeared into the bedroom. I finished, dried off, put more wood in both stoves, I'd have to do it again before we went to sleep, and turned all but one gas light off.

Ronie was in bed with the covers turned back waiting for me with a smile on her face. That smile was radiating her natural beauty. I lay there beside her and she turned so she could lay her head on my chest. I could smell sweet perfume in her hair. We cuddled and caressed each other. And oh yeah, we did make love.

*   *   *   *

The next morning Ronie and I lay in bed listening to the slight breeze blow through the frozen spruce trees. The icy snow on the boughs sounded like tiny ice crystals clinking together. The fires had gone out long ago and the cabin was a little cool. Finally I said "Come on we'd better get up. I've got to check the carcasses outside and after breakfast I've got to freeze them into the ice on the deadwater."

I got dressed and before I rekindled the fires I went outside to check on the carcasses and of course Royal had to follow me. The carcasses were all intact. Royal ran out the driveway with his nose held in the air. I followed him, curious as to what he was smelling. There was coyote crap piles and urine posts all up and down the snow sled trail, but not within fifty yards of the garage. They had been curious and cautious at the same time.

"Everything okay?" Ronie asked.

"Yes but they followed our sled trail to about fifty yards from the garage."

I helped Ronie with the dishes and cleaning the kitchen and when I started to put my outdoor clothing on she said. "Hey wait a minute, I'm going with you."

There were coyote tracks from the camp yard all the way to the deadwater. It was difficult to guess how many had followed the scent of the carcasses; each depositing their own scent on the sled trail. When I turned off the tote road onto the deadwater, Ronie held onto me even tighter. I guess she was uneasy about going out onto the river. There was only a skiff of snow on the ice and it was smooth riding. Here along the deadwater we saw more deer tracks then coyote. This was an ideal place for deer to feed. After a quarter of a mile we came to an orange painted line. I assumed this was the park boundary. "Don said to go only a short distance beyond the line."

I stopped at the first bend and shut the engine off. I could see yellow and orange ribbon tied to several alder bushes. And at close inspection I found wire wrapped around the bushes. "These wires must have something to do with his snares. I guess we're at the right location."

I took my axe out of the carrying compartment under the seat and began chopping a hole, one hell'va hole in the ice for all those carcasses. Even though it was cold, I was beginning to sweat. I stopped to wipe my forehead. "Here, let me do some chopping." I handed the axe to Ronie.

She was doing a good job, but her arms were getting tired. "Hey, I'll chop a while." When the hole was clear of ice except for the bottom I broke a hole through the thin layer of ice at the bottom and the hole began to fill with water. We put the deer carcasses in and the three beaver carcasses on top and made sure there was some water around each carcass.

"Why do you freeze them? Why not just throw them on the ice?" Ronie asked.

"I asked Don the same question. He said that if left on the ice the coyotes would clean it up soon and would be gone. This way they have to work at it and the bait will stay a lot longer and they'll stay in the area longer."

We rode up to Dri-ki dam. "I wanted you to see this so you'd understand where and what it is when you hear someone speak about Dri-ki dam. It's nothing more than dry wood that has floated down stream and fetched up here. There's so much wood piled in here now, no matter how much water is in the river, it won't break free."

"Is it any good fishing?"

"Only right after the ice goes out." We went back to the cabin and had a hot cup of coffee. "Why does Don snare coyotes?" Ronie asked.

"To remove them from the deer wintering areas. They kill a lot of deer."

"Isn't that only a part of nature?"

"It would be if man was taken out of the scheme of things."

"I would think the only deer they could catch or kill would be the sick."

"I think that is what the biologists would like us to believe. But I've seen for myself what damage they do. I have seen some strong healthy deer killed by coyotes. Uncle Royal was convinced that coyotes were brought in here to control the rabbit population back in the late 50's. If that's so, then this is a man made problem. Besides, the state stands to lose too much money if the coyotes are left uncheck; they could devastate the deer herd.

"There are millions of dollars spent every year by people who enjoy hunting them as well as those who enjoy taking pictures and just seeing them in their travels. People won't spend much money to hunt or take pictures of coyotes."

I don't know if she was satisfied with that answer or not. She never again inquired about why coyotes were being snared. We finished our coffee and left for snowmobiling. We went first to Third Lake. The bridge was out across Turner Brook so we had to snake through the trees and cross the deadwater and back onto the road. I was thankful Don had given me directions to the lake. I hadn't been on this road system much and the roads looked different now being snow covered.

I found the road on the left that I was looking for and I was amazed when I saw all the deer tracks crossing back and forth. I slowed the snow sled and showed Ronie the tracks. "Where are the coyotes?" she asked.

Good question, "I don't know." We continued on. At the end of the road, there was a trail, sort of, that wound its way through the raspberry bushes and small sapling bushes. We came to a tall pine tree and I just had to stop and take a good look. "Is this the same tree you showed me last summer?"

"No, this one isn't quite as big. Third Lake shouldn't be much further. At least that's what Don said."

We started up again and we found the lake only a hundred yards away. There hadn't been any deer tracks after we left the road. But here next to the lake, next to shore were several coyote tracks. There were three fairly recent beds. Remember the cold bath I took in the deadwater below the cabin. I decided to walk out on the ice first and chop a test hole or two. I went about one hundred feet out and after several minutes of chopping I hit water after fourteen inches of ice. That was plenty.

We turned to the right following the shoreline about two hundred feet out from shore. As we went around the point two coyotes took off running that had been feeding on an old deer kill. My first instinct was to chase after them, but I decided against it with Ronie on back.

There was part of one antler sticking out of the ice and coyotes had chewed on the points. No sense in chopping them out, I found one hind leg. The meat had all been eaten away, but the reason I picked it up was the size of the hoof. "This was a huge buck." Ronie didn't say anything, she sat on the seat and looked around the lake. "Look, those coyotes stopped out in the middle of the lake and they're watching us. They won't come after us will they Thom?"

"No, they're probably just waiting for us to leave so they can come and feed. What little there is. They must be really hungry. They might be this year's pups and too small to kill themselves. They have to scavenge."

We stopped and waded through the snow to the top of a knoll to look at an old cabin. It was in excellent shape and apparently used some. "How do the owners get in here Thom?"

"I'm not sure unless they fly in. There aren't any roads close by." It was a perfect setting for a camp. And the nice thing about it, it was the only one on the lake.

We continued our tour along the shoreline and we took a side trip up the inlet. Here there were hundreds of deer tracks again. Trails leading through the thick underbrush and cedar. We had gone up the inlet about as far as we were going to when two bald eagles flew up from underneath a spruce tree thicket near a set of small falls. I shut the sled off, I had to investigate. There was a real fresh deer kill there and the eagles had been feeding off the meat left by the coyotes. We continued on our trip around the lake and found evidence of a couple more old coyote kills but there was very little point in stopping to examine what little was left.

There was open water at the beginning of the outlet. The outlet was a wide shallow stream that narrowed to more like a brook about two hundred yards from the lake. The ice was safe along the edges and we walked along the alder shoreline. The middle of the stream was open water, even after all the cold weather. Behind the alder bushes was a small horseback that paralleled the stream. There were a few huge spruce trees, several smaller fir trees and alders. We found where several coyotes had been laying in the warm sunshine under the trees. By the looks of the beds, they were probably here when we motored onto the ice.

We walked along the horseback following the stream. The snow was up to my knees, but it was dry and fluffy and easy to walk through. At the end of the wide stretch of the stream Ronie stopped and said "Look at this Thom" and she pointed to an old roll-dam. "What is it Thom?"

"When Uncle Royal and I made our canoe trip and circled this whole region, we came back this way. This stream is the same one below the cabin. We took our canoe down here to camp. Uncle Royal said that during the river drive era all lakes, deadwaters and brooks had these wooden dams; called roll-dams, to hold a supply of water back , and then released when the drivers need more water."

About fifty yards back from the dam I found a huge apple tree. I walked around it, studying it. It was just odd to see an apple tree growing in the wild like this in a spruce and fir thicket. I began walking around some to see what else I could find "Hey Ronie, come here" She was still studying the old roll-dam.

"What is it?"

"Look at this" I pointed to the remains of a very old log cabin. A disintegrating stove pipe was sticking through part of the cabin roof that had collapsed onto the remaining wall and in that pile of rubble was still an old wood cook stove.

"You mean people once lived way out here?" Ronie asked.

"This was probably the dam tenders cabin. But somewhere around the lake we'd probably find a set of old lumber camps, where crews would live in during the winter, while they cut trees. And then in the spring when the water was high, they probably drove the logs downstream to Matagamon."

"I have a difficult time understanding how men could be shut away for so many months in the harsh elements of winter, how'd they do it?"

"I guess they didn't have much of a choice. But that's what this whole region is about."

On the way back to the snow sled we saw a red fox digging through the snow between the shore and the horseback. When he heard us coming he scurried off without even looking to see what was making the noise. Curiosity prevailed and I had to see what the fox was trying to dig up. Ronie and I on our hands and knees began to dig through the snow with our hands, we weren't long coming to the head of a small moose. "Do you suppose the coyotes killed this too?" Ronie asked.

"I wouldn't say so. I'd sooner think that it may have died from the moose disease or shot during the deer season. It's odd though how the coyotes have stayed away from it. There are no tracks at all. Only fox. I'll tell Jim about this when I see him again."

"Who's Jim?"

"The game warden. Maybe he'll send a coyote snarer up here."

We got back on the snow sled and finished our trip around the lake and headed back out along the trail pass the huge pine tree and back on the unplowed road. There were deer tracks crossing our snow sled track, I stopped to show Ronie. It was like that all the way back to the main road.

We crossed Turner Bog again and then turned left towards four corners, instead of going back to the cabin. Don had said that the road across at four corners wasn't plowed this winter and that would give us access to Millinocket and Millamagessett Lakes.

I wasn't exactly sure with Millamagessett Lake was and we rode every road until finally after we had given up and had decided to return home, I spotted a narrow trail through some small spruce and fir trees. This was a difficult trail that wound its way through an uncut old growth forest. Deer were everywhere along this trail. We saw somewhere between twenty-five and thirty. We came out to the lake behind what I later discovered was Green Island. This was a larger lake than Third Matagamon and many more islands.

We rode the shoreline again and there were deer tracks everywhere we went. We saw a lot of deer too and then down on the east end, we found several coyote killed deer. It was difficult to determine just how many had died because what was left for remains was usually scattered over a wide area on the ice. Along the north shore we found two freshly killed deer. The coyotes had eaten a small portion of the hind quarters. They were probably scared off by the noise of the snowmachine.

What a beautiful lake. So well secluded from any drivable road and there were only two cabins on the lake. One at the east end, Uncle Royal had said at one time had belonged to the Maine Forestry Service. The other camp belonged to someone down Portland way.

"Hey Thom, I'm getting cold, can we start back?" Ronie asked.

"Sure thing. I was getting a little cold myself." With a sled trail broken all the way back home the trip only took us twenty minutes but it was good to get in where it was warm and sit back in a comfortable chair. Of course Ronie was sitting in my lap.

*   *   *   *

Ronie and I enjoyed each other's company so much we forgot to celebrate Christmas. Actually the entire time we were together was the greatest celebration that I could have possibly imagined.

The day came though when we had our last ride together down the lake to her car behind the dam.

After we had started her car and packed away her traveling cases, we stood leaning against the hood of her car. "This has been the best week of my life Thom."

"Me too, when will I see you again?"

"Probably not until summer break. Maybe you can come see me."

"I wish, but I won't be able to get out of camp until the roads dry up, you'll be on summer break by then."

"Well, if you can."

As I watched her drive away I wondered how I could go back to the cabin alone and be alone with only thoughts of Ronie to keep me company all winter. It would be nearly six months before I saw her again. I wondered then if this life as an apprentice hermit was what it was cracked up to be.

The day after Ronie left, I went for a walk down to the deadwater to check the coyote bait. I took a rifle; just in case. It was a quiet morning and the snow squeaked under my boots. The temperature was dropping. "I guess it was a good thing that Ronie left yesterday. She would have been cold riding in this down the lake."

There were fresh deer and coyote tracks in the snow on the deadwater. But as I approached the frozen bait the deer tracks disappeared and there were so many coyote tracks, it looked like a sheep pasture.

About half of the carcasses had been dug out and eaten, but the coyotes had been actively trying to get at the rest. I walked up to the Dri-ki dam checking the runs through the alder bushes. There were many and they all were well traveled. And there were no signs of eagles or any other tracks. I spied a red fox on the way back to the cabin. I untied Royal and went inside to call Don on the radio to let him know what I had found.

He said he'd be up the next morning with more bait and snares. I checked the thermometer outside: -10^0F, the temperature had dropped ten degrees since I got up this morning. I brought in more firewood and stacked it beside and behind the stoves. Then I changed the broken mantles in the gas lights and replaced two old kerosene wicks. I banked snow around the cabin and hauled water from the spring. All this time Royal was trying to get me to play with him by nipping at my feet.

The temperature had dropped to -20°F by the next morning. I was sure that Don would wait for a better day. That he wouldn't venture up the lake in this cold. But just before nine that morning I heard the unmistakable noise of a snow machine. "Come in and warm up a bit Don, I just made a fresh pot of coffee."

He didn't answer, but he followed me into the cabin and started stripping his outer clothing. "I thought perhaps you might wait for a warmer day before traveling up the lake."

"If I did that I wouldn't ever set any traps, you get used to it, you've just got to dress for it. But this hot coffee sure feels good."

I gulped my coffee down and started to put on my extreme cold clothing. "You ready?" Don asked. "Are you going to leave that gas light on?"

"Yes. That's something I learned after I went through the ice after I shot my deer."

"You're learning." That's all he said, as he smiled.

I followed Don back to the deadwater and up towards Dri-ki dam. "Follow me, and watch how I set these. Then you can take a few and set on the other side of the stream."

He didn't walk up the coyote trails. Instead he came in at right angles to them. In many instances there was already a wire hanger attached to the alders in the trails. Don used these instead of hanging new ones. He made an eighteen inch loop with snare wire and hung it on the hanger wire so the bottom of the loop was about twelve inch from the snow. "Any closer and the coyote will step into it and then he stands a good chance of chewing out of it."

"Remember to tie orange flagging above your head after each set. That's the only way we have of finding each one when we tend."

I went back to his sled and grabbed a bunch of snares and wire and started on the other side trying to do everything exactly as I had watched Don do it. I was slower, of course, but I was enjoying myself so much, I forgot about being cold. Don finished his side and then helped me. When we were finished we had set thirty snares. Some were a hundred yards from the bait. Some were very close, which I had assumed that the closer the snares were set to the carcasses, the easier it would be to catch coyotes. But Don assured me that just the opposite was true. Don untied an ice chisel from his sled and chopped out another hole for new carcasses.

"When will you tend these next?"

"I like to give'em a week after we set snares; we have left a lot of our own scent here. It would be ideal if it snowed just enough to cover our tracks and scent. Otherwise it'll take several days before there's any activity back here."

"I'll be back in a week. If I can't for whatever reason, I'll call you on the radio."

We left and Don headed back towards the lake and I went home. The temperature stayed cold and each morning the thermometer read a little colder. It was rarely above zero now in the day, even though the sun would be out bright. On the third day it snowed three inches of real dry powdery snow. "This will be good for the snares, Royal."

The temperature the next morning was still zero, but I'd been shut-up inside long enough. I got dressed for snowmobiling and headed for the deadwater. Don said coyotes weren't bothered much by snow machines, so I took a ride up to Dri-ki dam. There had been some activity at the frozen carcasses but not much, and only a few old tracks in the snow.

I rode down to the lake then. In the woods the wind hadn't blown the snow much. But out on the lake, well the ice surface was something else. The wind had blown the snow into hard pack drifts and it was so rough I couldn't go over ten mph. I made a short loop and went back to camp.

The cold weather continued and only occasional snow squalls. Don called on the radio one evening and said he couldn't make it in the morning, he had a meeting in Augusta; to go ahead and check the snares and re-set if necessary. The next morning the temperature had dropped to -32°F. I had never seen that kind of cold. Remembering what Don had said and knowing he'd be here in the cold if he had not had to go to Augusta, I got dressed for the outside and I pulled on an extra sweater, I would not shame myself.

Riding at slow speeds in the woods, wasn't too bad, but I'd hate to have to go out on the lake. The snow was so cold it squeaked beneath the snow sled. I wouldn't have supposed that any animal would be out and about this morning. But to my surprise I saw several hearty red squirrels.

There had been very little activity at the bait. But when I started checking snares I understood why. Don had three snared on his side of the stream. The cables were so twisted and kinked that I couldn't get the snares off around the necks of the coyotes. I had to take coyote and snare. It was just as well because those snares certainly couldn't be used again.

I had two coyotes on the side that I had set and I saw where a coyote had walked up to one snare and then backed-up and went around the snare through the bushes. Some smart coyote. My hands were getting cold, the rest of me was ok.

I hauled the coyotes back to camp and hung them up in the garage and put the sled away. Trapper or not and cold or not, I was going to stay inside for the rest of the day.

At noon I called Di on the radio and told her about the five coyotes, "and Don will have to bring more snares when he comes with the bait?"

It snowed that night and the temperature rose above zero, but by morning it had dropped to -35°F. That's some damned cold temperatures. At mid-morning I heard a snow machine outside and surprised when Jim Randall walked through the door. He didn't knock, he just walked in. He must have been cold, because he stood beside the fire for half an hour before sitting.

"I haven't seen or heard from you since we were looking for body parts on the BSA road. Then on the coldest day of the year you show up as if this frigid weather is nothing at all," I said.

"Well, I had a busy fall. Between lost hunters and special details and night hunting, there wasn't much time left for anything else."

"I heard you shot a buck. Was it a trophy?"

"No, just a small buck. But good eating. I told him the story of falling through the ice and almost not making it home and then lying on the floor with hypothermia. I didn't tell him that it was after the season had ended and just a little beyond sunset. I figured I had earned that deer.

While the coffee was making. "Hey, come out to the garage. I've got something out there to show you."

Jim didn't say much at first. He hand inspected each coyote. It was obvious that they had been snared. "Did you get these on your own?"

"Oh no, I wouldn't have known how if it hadn't been for Don. I went with him when he set the snares and he showed me how it was done. I hung a few, but I'm not as fast at it as he is. He called by radio two days ago and said he had to be in Augusta for a meeting and asked if I would tend for him. Two of 'em were caught in the snares I set."

"What you going to do with these?" Jim asked

"Leave 'em hanging until Don comes back and he'll take 'em back with him."

"Is he paying you to help him?" I didn't know where Jim was going with this but it donned on me that in his subtle way I was being interrogated.

He ran his fingers through the fur again and said, "These are fine hides. It'll be interesting to see how much they weigh."

Jim saw the questioning look on my face and added, "Don weights every coyote. You know Thom, when trapping – snaring, the activity requires a Trapping License. Even if you're only helping another trapper. And to snare coyotes requires a special certification from the Department. Let's go back to the cabin. The coffee must be hot by now."

He was going to make me suffer. He wasn't going to finish what he had started to say until – well probably not until he had a cup of hot coffee.

While I fixed both cups, Jim shed his coat and sweater and left his boots by the door. Then he stood by the kitchen woodstove rubbing his hands together over the top of the stove. I handed him his cup and without yet saying a word, he began to sip. I sat at the table and waited for the axe to fall. My gut was beginning to tie itself in knots. Now I knew how his victims felt when he toyed with them.

Then he spoke, "You know, if you were interested I could use another predator control officer out here in the middle of the woods. Don and Ted are spread out pretty much and really can't take on much more. But there's another snarer that I'm going to send to Third Lake and Millamagessett Lake." I told him about the dead deer Ronie and I had found a week ago.

"I'd like you to work with him. Third Lake is isolated from everything and I'd just feel more comfortable knowing Ray had help, two men can usually get themselves out of trouble, but one man alone sometimes doesn't have a prayer. You work with him. You're not to tend any sets without him. As far as down here at Dri-ki dam, well I'm the only Game Warden who hasn't retired that knows where Dri-ki dam is. Enough said?" And he looked square at me to see if I understood what he was saying.

"Understood."

"I'll write out a special permit authorizing you to work with Ray Gallagher. I'll give it to him to give to you when he comes in. Do you keep your radio on all the time?"

"Yes"

"I'll talk with Ray and call you."

I was only hearing about half of what Jim was saying. Apparently he didn't think it was safe or proper to travel in this country alone, but he did every day; and no one knew where to look if he should not happen to show up at home. He might be at the bottom of a beaver flowage, curled up in a snow bank or watching some poacher, who would ever know if he needed help. If he ever did I doubted very much if he'd ever call out for help if'n he could.

Jim was never concerned about his own safety. But he worried about others. To him the cold was perhaps only an inconvenience. "What's the coldest you have ever seen the temperature?" I asked.

"In '56, '79 and '82 I saw the thermometer drop to -62°F. That's cold. People have to work then in order to stay warm."

"What will you do after you leave here?"

"I'll sled over to Grand Lake Sebosis and see if there are any dead dear there. The coyotes usually kill eight or ten on the ice every year. Trouble over there is that last year, Ray found cat tracks near the bait, so he had to pull his snares."

*   *   *   *

Two days later I got a radio call from Jim in the evening to meet Ray the next morning at ten o'clock at the four corners. The temperatures had risen slightly. In the morning it was -15°F to -20°F and it warmed up to zero during the day. Zero doesn't sound warm but the difference was considerably noticeable.

Not knowing what to expect working with Ray, I ate a good breakfast and made sure the oil stove was set to come on when the wood stoves burned low. I hooked Royal and loaded my pack and axe onto the sled and headed towards four corners on the Huber road. The trail was good and I was there early. Just when I thought I'd have to wait I saw a blue Ford coming around the corner.

The driver was wiry and he jumped from the cab of his pickup and extended his hand towards me before his feet hit the ground. "You must be Thom, I'm Ray Gallagher.

"When Jim called me last night he said the road had just been plowed beyond here. The crews are cutting on Caribou Ridge and the other side of Brayley Brook."

"We can put your sled with mine. It's easier if we don't have to double up.

"I didn't know your Uncle. What brings you up in the middle of nowhere from New York? You running away from something?"

"I needed to straighten out Uncle Royal's affairs after he died and I need to change my life around." Running away? Perhaps; the memory of a woman?

"I guess we've all been there. Jim said you've already worked with Don?"

"Yeah, a couple of days. First tend we had five coyotes."

That's about how the conversations went all the while to the Third Lake Road. By the time we arrived I had learned Ray had recently retired from potato farming and his wife Jeannette retired from bank management so the two could enjoy life together.

We unloaded the sleds from his trailer and Ray loaded his snares and threw four beaver carcasses onto the back of my sled and he put four more on his. "That's a nice sled, you must have bought it over in Houlton."

"How did you know where I bought it?"

"That was my sled. I thought I had to have a new one just like it. You won't find a better sled for this terrain."

I let Ray lead the way. He knew what he was doing and where he wanted to go. Every once in a while we'd stop and look at the deer tracks. He was also checking for coyote tracks. Strange how the coyotes stayed mostly around the lake and the majority of the deer stayed in these cuts away from the lake.

Before going out on the ice we stopped and turned the machines off. What I didn't know then was that Ray was looking for a coyote running across the lake in hopes that he might overtake.

I told Ray where I had seen the dead deer the previous week and he said, "Jim and I tried setting up in the inlet once but that winter we had a hell of a time with open water. So I stay away from there now. We'll sled around the shore and see if there are any recent kills.

The dead deer that Ronie and I had found were gone. There was no evidence at all that deer had been killed by coyotes until we got to the mouth of Sly

Brook. There wasn't much left but the coyotes had made a couple of easy trails to set up.

Ray handed me a bunch of snares and he took one trail and I the other. I watched as he walked in the coyote trail itself. We were close enough so we could carry on a conversation as we worked.

"I know working with Don, he doesn't walk up the trails like I do; instead he comes in from the sides, never crossing the trail. My theory is to disturb as little as possible. Your scent is going to be here regardless where you work. But as I work out a trail, I'll try to brush out my tracks as much as I can. Don catches coyotes his way and so do I. Go figure."

I was working with Ray so I switched over to his method of walking the already made trails and disturbing as little as possible. We only set a few snares on these two trails and then we moved on, along the shoreline.

We didn't see anything else of interest until we came to an old camp sight. The coyotes had a well used trail and as near as we could tell there wasn't anything dead. After hanging a few snares Ray wired two beaver carcasses to the base of a spruce tree. "This will keep 'em coming back. The best place to set is down the outlet."

"Jeannette and I came in one day to tend and we noticed where Jim had left his sled and walked down the outlet. I had snowshoes on and was following his tracks across to the other side. The ice broke and I went in. Damned cold I was. I pulled those snares. And we'll stay away from that shore. That outlet is too unsafe."

I showed Ray where I had found the dead moose and we went to work hanging snares and tying orange flagging. There was plenty of the moose left so there was no need to leave any more bait. "A dead moose makes for the best coyote bait."

"Why is that?" I asked.

"The smell and mass of meat. If left alone the same coyotes will keep coming back to a moose carcass all winter."

We left Third Lake and followed the plowed road to Brayley Brook. "One of the crew told me yesterday that coyotes had killed a small deer here. He said they chased it into a fir thicket before killing it."

Once we waded through the snow bank it became obvious that a deer had died. There was blood and hair all over the snow. Ray found the remains of the deer, which wasn't much, and he put them in a depression amongst several small fir trees. There wasn't any real designated trails, but we set snares everywhere where a coyote had walked.

From Brayley we went towards Caribou Ridge and stopped at an old beaver flowage. "Anytime I was ever through here, there were always coyote tracks across this flowage. All we can do today is set out some beaver carcasses and get the coyotes coming."

The snow was deeper here and we had to put our snowshoes on. We crossed the flowage and found a cove hidden from the road and Ray broke out some shell ice along the shore and we dropped the beaver carcasses in and packed snow around them to freeze them in.

"What if we made a snowshoe trail through the trees? Won't the coyotes follow that like they do snowmobile tracks?"

"Let's try it and see what happens." We made a trail up the bank and back towards the road. For whatever reason I got the impression that Ray had already tried this and didn't have much success with getting coyotes to follow his track. Instead of saying "It won't work", he was willing to try and let me see for myself. I liked that.

*   *   *   *

The next day and as it seemed every other day afterwards for two weeks, it would snow. Sometimes only a dusting, which was beneficial and then sometimes there'd be several inches. But when the wind blew strong the bushes that held the snares up off the snow would move just enough to drop the snare wire and it would have to be reset. The first week went by and I met Ray again at Four Corners. It was a bright sunny day, but cold.

We had three coyotes on Third Lake and we found another coyote killed deer in the inlet. But because of the many deer tracks and trails there, Ray decided against setting any snares because he was afraid of so many deer, one might wander into one of the snares and then, it would in itself become coyote bait.

At Brayley we had two coyotes and at the beaver flowage no coyotes had used our snowshoe trail. "I didn't think they would. But it was worth a try." Ray said.

We did set snares and Ray even put one in the snowshoe trail. On the way back across the flowage we spotted a bald eagle perched in a dead pine stub. I asked "Any chance of that eagle getting caught in one of our snares?"

"No, all the snares are up on the bank and set far enough away from the bait so it would be unlikely as any threat."

We tended the snares each week. Sometimes we'd only have one coyote and other weeks we'd catch three or four. "This makes thirty-eight for the winter. I have snares back at home too."

"That represents a lot of deer," I said. As it happened when I was helping Ray at Third Lake, Don and Ted had twice tended the snares on the deadwater. The first tend they had two and the second tend, they had three. That made ten so far from that one area. I wondered then just how many coyotes were there in 'my woods'.

I began to look forward to each trip to Third Lake. This was the closest that I was ever going to be to experiencing the life of a trapper. I wasn't necessarily enjoying the destruction of an animal, but I was helping to remove an awful predator from the deer yards. I was enjoying the thrill of the hunt and the chase. Trying to outwit a very cunning adversary of the deer.

March was here before I had realized the end of February and with it the cold temperatures again and wind. For five days the thermometer never rose above -5°F even in the daylight. At night the temperature dropped once to -27°F but it usually stayed between -15° and -20°F. The wind made it feel colder though. Even with both woodstoves burning, I sometimes was cool. When the cold and wind subsided, it began to snow. Twenty inches more on top of what we already had. All the snares would have to be readjusted and dug out of the snow. Don and Ted had taken a total of fifteen coyotes from the deadwater. And Ray and I had caught twelve at Third Lake, Brayley and the flowage.

With the new snow I assumed that coyotes would be lured more easily to the bait, and it would be easier to snare them. But I was going to learn another lesson about coyotes. The morning following the snowstorm Don called on the radio and said he would be busy for the next several days melting ice from around the gates at the Dam so he could open them and start draining the lake in anticipation of the spring run-off. And he asked if I'd pull all the snares on the deadwater. He said that there were thirty snares still set.

There were no tracks at all around the bait. Some snares were buried under the snow and others had slipped the lock and hanging cockeyed in the coyote trail. When I finished I counted the number of snares and I had only twenty-nine; I was lacking one, but where was it?

I retraced my steps and double checked again at each hanger wire. I had pulled off every piece of orange flagging. I circled each side twice and I still couldn't find that last snare.

I started walking parallel with the deadwater through the alder bushes setting over only three feet each pass. I finally found it when I stumbled over an alder bush that had been bent over by the weight of the snow and the top had frozen into the snow burying the orange flag and snare.

Satisfied, I went home and called Don on the radio that I had found all thirty snares. "Thom, when traveling down the lake now, stay all the way on the west side of the thoroughfare. I'm having to drop a lot of water through the dam and the thoroughfare will open."

When I met Ray next at the Four Corners, he too said they had probably better pull their snares. "I don't want the outlet of Third Lake to open up with snares still hanging in the bushes. Besides, if we get any rain now we won't be able to cross the lake."

We had one coyote at Sly Brook, one at the picnic spot and one had chewed itself out of a bad fix at the outlet. The coyotes were already showing signs of being mangy. "Isn't this early for coyotes to be shedding?" I asked.

"They usually start right after the females come out of heat. It'll be a slow process before all the old hair is gone."

I had learned a great deal that winter about coyotes, surviving in the cold and learning to rely more on my own resources. I said good-bye to Ray at the Four Corners and I returned home.

Spring would be here soon, at least I thought, and I would be locked in again until either the ice was gone in the lake or the frost from the roads. So before that happened I took inventory of all my food stores. I had all of the necessities but I made up a list of ice cream, pies, chocolate bars and some orange juice.

I radioed Di at the Matagamon store and she said she was going to town in the morning and if I wanted to ride in, to be at the store at seven-thirty.

It was cold again the next morning. Nothing like the day Jim came to visit, but to me the temperature was cold. And to make matters worse the snow was blown into hard packed drifts. The drifts made it very difficult sledding, and staying up-right. I was a long time getting to the thoroughfare and it was as Don had said, wide open.

The return trip back up the lake was even worse. Now I was going into the leeward side of the drifts. It was as if I was trying to ride up an eighteen inch square wall. By the time I arrived home I was exhausted. The ice cream I left in the garage where it would stay frozen and the pies I put in the root cellar.

That was the last of the frigid weather, and the snow on the cabin roof began to melt and my sled trails melted and settled. The weather was so nice now, I tried to take advantage of it and rode my snow sled as much as possible. When bare gravel started to show in the road beds I knew it was time to store it until next year.

Royal and I did a lot of walking. If we went early in the mornings the snow was firm enough in the snow sled trails to hold us. Only occasionally did I break through. But warmer days were coming and eventually we had to stop hiking. The snow was like mush.

I was lonely and I needed someone to talk to, anyone would be fine. I sat on the porch and daydreamed of Ronie and when I would get to see her again.

The snow was finally gone from the driveway and the road that goes to Four Corners and there was only patches of snow left in shady spots in the woods. It was time to go fishing. I got my gear together and put it on my four-wheeler and headed for Third Lake. I wanted to fish off the point that juts out into the center of the lake and then I wanted to hike down to the Roll dam on the outlet.

There was still a lot of mud in the old winter road that goes to Third Lake, but I eventually made it to the path through the raspberries. From there I decided it would be easier if I walked.

It wasn't easy getting out to the point. The peninsula was covered with thick brush, which was very difficult to crawl through. But I was determined and when I did reach the very point of the peninsula I was disappointed to find that the bushes grew right out to the water. There was no place to stand on dry land. I had come this far and crawled through the bushes; I guess I could wade out to fish.

I waded out as far as my knees. The water was cold. There was still a little ice in shady coves. When the breeze stirred the ice crystals they sounded like a faint wind chime. With my first cast I hooked a sixteen inch brook trout. I cast another hundred times and didn't get as much as a nibble. It was time to leave, I had lost all feeling in my legs from the knees down.

The fishing at the roll dam was so good, I could have filled a pack basket full. I threw back everything that wasn't over twelve inches. I would like to have taken more, but what would I do with more than my legal limit? I cleaned each one and wrapped them in green grass and then put them in my pack. Now to get the hell out of here. "There is no easy way back."

As I was securing my pack and fish rod to my four wheeler, Jim stepped out from behind a blow down. Boy was I glad I didn't take any more trout. "I wondered who was down here. Our pilot flew over and said someone on an ATV was heading for Third Lake, any luck?"

"Actually the fishing was quite good." He didn't ask to see them, but I pulled the bundle of trout out of my pack to show him anyhow.

"Those are nice trout. You were either at the falls on the inlet or at the roll dam. And since you'd have to have a boat to fish the inlet, you must have fought your way through that dangled hell hole."

"Roll dam," I said. "I guess it doesn't get fished that often."

"There's a couple of parties that fly in from down below, and someday I'll be here when they are here. Their overdue, I've had too many complaints about them flying out of here with hundreds of trout."

I offered Jim a ride out, but "Thanks, I'll walk."

*   *   *   *

The ice had been out of Second Lake for two weeks but I was just now able to get to Webster Stream on my four-wheeler. I cleared the trail and then brought my canoe down. Royal ran along behind me. After storing the canoe I took Royal down to Second Lake.

People were fishing from a boat, trolling from the ledges to Little East and back again. I walked on not really paying too much attention to them. I followed the tote road to the old boy scout campsite and Royal and I sat on the grass watching tranquility. From here I couldn't hear or see those trolling in the boat and there were no more sounds at all, except for nature.

I had to ask myself though "Is this all I ever wanted out of life? Will this life, living with no more worries than survival, become so complacent that life then becomes a bore?"

I looked in the inner then at Jim Randall's life. He never knew from one moment to the next what was in store for him. There was always something new and different around each corner. The beginning; the middle and even at the end of each day. And there is no one who knows more about survival in these harsh elements than he does. I laughed out loud then with my next thought, "What would Uncle Royal have said if I became a Game Warden?"

I jumped up suddenly and spooked Royal. I knew now what I must do. Tomorrow I'll motor down to the dam, and go to town with my car and find Jim and find out what I will have to do to become a game warden. My car needed to be registered also. On my way back along the tote road I met a lone bear sauntering along the trail near the old orchard. The wind was in my face and I saw him before he knew I was on his trail. Royal must have smelled him cause he went charging up the road with his nose to the ground. Right then I remembered Brian's encounter with his bear. I didn't have anything to defend myself with.

There was no sense in chasing after Royal, he'd come back when he figured he had chased the bear far enough. There was no doubt he'd follow my scent home. I kept thinking about the possibility of me becoming a game warden.

By the time I got back home Royal had caught up with me. His tongue hanging low and he was obviously pleased with himself. I praised him and patted his head "good boy."

CHAPTER 7

I was up early the next morning. Anticipation was growing with the idea of becoming a game warden, my eggs were all gone. The last three I had to throw out. So I had a deer steak and biscuits for breakfast. I cleaned up and hooked Royal and drove down to my canoe.

The lake was still calm and I could see fish breaking the surface all around. So could the many fishermen that were gathered near Ledge Point. I raised my paddle to say hello and motored passed. There were people camped at Pine Point. Probably some of the same fishermen that were at Ledge Point. No matter how long I stay in this region or how old I get, I'll never get used to seeing the Davignon camp gone, the coyote den and I bet every time Jim Randall even thinks about it, he gets a naught in his gut. "Yeah, the park director left him in -20^{0}F weather and if not for that camp he would never have made it." I shook my head in disbelief and motored on; down Second Lake, through the thoroughfare towards Matagamon Dam.

I was about one half mile from the dam when I noticed something very peculiar towards the east shore.

Someone was in the water and waving their hands. My first thought was an overturned boat. I changed direction towards the person in the water. As I came closer I could see it was a woman and she didn't have anything on. She was also screaming hysterically for help. The water was cold and she couldn't have been in the water for long or she would have drowned because of hypothermia.

I had no idea at all how I was going to get her into my canoe without capsizing. Just then I noticed two men in a boat pulling away from shore. They were coming this way. I shut my motor off and eased to a stop near the woman. She was still screaming and flailing her arms. I brought my canoe over until I just bumped into her, then I reached down and took hold of her arms. All I could do was steady her until the other boat arrived.

They pulled up next to me and the operator said, "We'd better pull her into my boat, or you'll capsize." The fight had drained from the woman, she was cold and if we didn't warm her up soon, she would die. "We'd better take her to my camp. There on the point and warm her up. My wife has clothes she can put on."

I followed them to the camp. Once inside the camp, Mr. Phillips laid the woman on the couch next to the woodstove and put a blanket over her. "When she warms up a bit, I'll give her some hot soup that'll warm her insides." He extended his hand and said, "I'm John Phillips and this is my friend, Bill."

"Hi, I'm Thom from up above Second Lake"

"Uncle Royal's nephew, right?" John said, "I've heard a lot about you."

It wasn't long before the woman thawed out some and started talking. But she wasn't very coherent. John gave her some of his wife's clothes and while she dressed we went into the other room. When she had finished, she came out and tried to thank us, but she still wasn't very coherent. The soup was hot and John gave her a cup full.

I was going to Matagamon, so it was decided amongst the three of us that it would be best if I took the woman with me and call the authorities. Without any doubt, probably Jim Randall would be sent out here to take care of this also. The woman said her name was Jane, but wouldn't say what her last name was. She did agree to go with me to the Dudley Store.

All while I motored from the Phillips' camp to the dam, I kept wondering if she would try to get out of the canoe. She had a starry-eyed far-off expression on her face.

"Where are you from Jane?" I was trying to keep her mind off whatever it was that led her into the water.

"Down by the coast, Belfast."

"I have never been there, what is near Belfast?"

"Lobsters."

That answer was puzzling to say the least. "Where is your vehicle Jane?"

"By the water."

"How did you get on this side of the lake? There are no roads that come close."

"I walk around shore," and she began pointing. As if retracing her trip, she stopped pointing at a peninsula between the dam and what Di calls Blueberry Island. That's probably where she left her vehicle.

"Okay, Jane I understand, do you work?"

"No, but I'll have to soon. He quit and went away." She started staring at the shoreline again.

"Are you cold Jane?" no answer.

"Where are your mother and father, Jane?"

"Florida."

"Have you been to Baxter Park before or the Matagamon region?"

"No."

There were people fishing behind the dam and after I helped Jane out of the canoe I asked an older gentlemen, "Would you watch this woman for me while I unlock my car and get it started, she has had quite an ordeal this morning."

"Sure, no problem."

I wasn't sure if my car would start or not. It had been sitting out back here for ten months; much to my surprise it started very easily. The gentlemen walked with Jane over to the car and before she got in she turned and looked at him and said "God bless you."

During the short drive to Dudley's store, Jane was quiet. I thought she had gone to sleep. I let her be and went inside. I told Di and Don what I knew and Di said she'd call Jim. Just in case it was a boating accident. "We probably should bring her in here where it's warm and see if she'll eat some hot soup."

"Maybe I'd better do this myself. I think she trusts me." I went out and opened her door. She was asleep. I hadn't noticed it before but she smelled very strongly of wood smoke. She must have had a fire going wherever she had spent the night. I got her inside and helped her to sit down at the table.

"Don got a hold of Jim. He'll be here soon. Now you two go out in the store and have your coffee. I think Jane would be more comfortable talking to me alone" Di said.

Don and I left and Di closed the door. There were a lot of people coming and going. Fisherman and apparently some of the wood crews were going back to work, now that the frost had left the gravel roads and the wood roads had dried out some.

It wasn't long before Jim arrived. Don and I told him as much as we could. "She never said anything about a boat. I understand that she had walked away from her vehicle, around the shoreline where I found her this morning. And I think she's been alone all this time. She smells strongly of wood smoke so at sometime she had a fire going."

"Is she alright here for a while Don? I'd like Thom to take me back where he found her and then see if we can find her car," Jim said.

"She'll be fine. Best thing for her now is to get some rest."

Di came out to join us then, "She left her car at the end of the Dyke road, she's a manic depressant and left her medication in her car. She's sleeping right now and she'll be fine for a while. When you and Thom get back there's more to her story, but I'll wait until you get back."

"Is your canoe and motor behind the dam, Thom?"

"Yeah"

"Okay, if we take that, it'll save some time."

"Sure, not a problem."

Jim threw his pack in the canoe and held onto the bow while I climbed in. The wind was blowing some, but not bad yet. "It's odd, when Di called I was on my way to Tilly Palmer's funeral. I was to be one of the pallbearers."

I pointed towards a point of land just out of sight of the Phillips' Camp. "She was in the water off that point."

"Let's go have a look." Jim said.

She had a fire alright. She had burned all the dry wood that had been on the little peninsula. "She must have been cold after the dry wood was gone." There were tiny pieces of paper scattered everywhere. Something she probably had torn up.

"Look at this Thom" she had placed a dime, a penny and a costume jewelry ring together on a rock "that's peculiar isn't it?" Jim put those in his pocket. "Let's have a look at her car."

We motored over to the Dykes and had a difficult time trying to find a place to put in. Finally I brought the canoe alongside a rock and Jim jumped out and secured the canoe. Jane had driven her car just as far as she could on the Dyke road. It wasn't locked and there didn't seem to be much there that would offer any answers. Jim did find an empty prescription bottle. "This must be the medication Di was asking about."

There was nothing in the trunk, under the seats or in the glove box. "It looks like another case of someone driving to the end of the earth, looking to end their life. I think mentally ill people associate the wilderness park with the end of the world and it becomes an appropriate place to end their own life here. That's the only explanation that I can find why so many strange and bizarre things occur here. Let's get back to the store." Jim said, "I could use some coffee."

While we were gone Di had telephoned the health center and they were sending an ambulance and a practitioner out. "It seems as though her boyfriend broke off their relations. This was quite a while ago, but she's been in and out of mental hospitals for depression, without her medication she becomes disoriented, confused and maybe she wanted to end it all; when she took off her clothes and waded out into the lake. She telephoned her folks in Florida, they weren't much comfort, I'm afraid. Jane said they were flying up but she didn't seem happy that they were coming."

The ambulance and practitioner arrived and I went into the kitchen to see how Jane was doing. She looked frightened, "These people are going to help you Jane, you need the medication that you were taking."

She relaxed then and I walked with her out to the ambulance. Before getting in she turned to look at me and she said "Bless you."

*   *   *   *

After everything was settled I sat with Jim in his pickup and talked with him about becoming a game warden and what I should be studying for the test.

"There is a new test for applicants in Augusta. The filing deadline is June 30th. You know I've been thinking lately, maybe it's time I retired. If you were to pass the tests and lucky enough to be hired the first time around, it just might be the Department would leave you right here in Matagamon. You have a big plus, you own property here and you live here. That is something no other warden has been able to do, because all the land is either owned by large woodland owners, paper companies or the park. The fact that you already live here would give you an open door. But you'd have to get to the hiring board."

"Okay, what do I need to study for preparations for the written test?"

"All of the laws outlined in Title Twelve, I can give you a copy of that." And he reached behind his seat and pulled out a recent copy. "Know this book from cover to cover. The opening dates of fishing and hunting, the history of the department, who the present

Commissioner and Chief Warden are. Go to the library in town and get all the back issues of the Fish and Wildlife magazines. You could also use the computer to research the department and laws."

"How do I get an application?"

"Just so happens each warden received those last week," and he reached behind his seat again and brought out an application.

"After the written test; that is if you pass, is the physical agility test. This usually eliminates about sixty percent of the candidates. Then there's the oral boards. They'll have twenty five minutes to make up their minds about you. Then the polygraph."

"What's the reason for the polygraph?"

"They're looking for drug use, criminal activity and anything in your past that if discovered might be used against you in a trail to persuade you to change your testimony. Oh, and then there's a background investigation. This usually takes several days to complete."

"They're real thorough I see."

"We have to be. We have more responsibility than any other law enforcement out here."

* * * *

I went to town and registered my car and then I went to the library. Filled out the application; I decided to use the library's typewriter, for neatness and I signed out all the back issues of The Fish and Wildlife magazines that Mrs. Shorey would let me take. "When you've read these, you can exchange them for more."

I thanked her, mailed my application and then went to the Ellis Family Market for supplies. The thought of fresh eggs made my mouth water. I talked with Jon and Peter and asked how their father was. "He's fishing on the river today; he and mother just got back from Florida two weeks ago."

Before leaving town I stopped at Raymond's ice cream place for a butterscotch sundae. That was one of my weaknesses.

That evening after supper and everything had been cleaned up, I began studying all those magazines. I made notes of everything of importance. This was like cramming for a final exam weeks ahead. By midnight I had read through them all and had rewritten the notes so they were more legible.

The weather turned off unseasonably warm and I walked out to the tote road to see if it was drivable yet. If I had had a four wheel drive I would have tried it. I needed more magazines so I made the trip down the lake again and into town. "Are you back already? If you're going to read them that fast I see no reason why you can't take the rest. I'll get a couple of boxes to put them in," Mrs. Shorey said.

For that night and for the next several nights I read and outlined information I found that I supposed would be important. The only time I took a break was, one evening I took Royal for a walk to the deadwater looking for fiddleheads. I wanted enough to can like Uncle Royal had shown me and enough for a couple of meals with fresh trout.

I waited until after Memorial weekend to return the magazines and I spent the entire day at the library working with the computer researching the department's history, personnel and up-coming law changes. I printed everything off so I wouldn't take up any more time than was necessary. When the printer was finished I had a stack of paper about an inch thick.

That night I studied the history of the department. My outline in itself was beginning to read like a manuscript. Each night I would read, outline and re-read until I had thoroughly understood the material. Then the next night I would move on to another topic. Title Twelve I had to study a little at a time. By the time I had finished with that, I was thoroughly disgusted with whoever had authorized such a mess. There was nothing consistent with it and it was a wonder that some five hundred dollar an hour attorney had not ripped it apart and totally embarrassed the department.

I tried sitting on the porch while I studied but the seasonal black flies and mosquitoes drove me indoors. I had reduced everything to an outline and side notes; points of interest.

Jim Randall stopped by one evening in late June while I was going over my outline. "Thought I would stop and see how you were doing with your study material. I talked with Christine at the library and she said you had taken enough research material back with you to write your own book. How's the studying going?"

"It's coming along very well. I've learned some interesting things about the department. And I don't know how you Wardens can interpret and understand Title Twelve as disorganized as it is."

"You memorize it, so you don't' have to use it!" he laughed and I understood what he was saying and I laughed with him.

"What's a dipsy-doodle?"

"Woodcock"

"You have been studying. I'm impressed, what about map reading and compass work?"

"Uncle Royal taught me."

The next day I was at Dudley's store and Don said, "This came for you in the mail yesterday."

It was a written test schedule. "August first"

"What's that?" Don asked.

"August first, that's when I take the written test."

The weather turned dry and very hot. I wrote to Ronie and told her about the test. She was ecstatic with happiness for me. "I hope you make it, I know you will." She wrote a lot more but I'd savor that while sitting on my porch at night.

*   *   *   *

The written test began at ten o'clock and there were many people already seated. Afterwards I learned that there were four hundred there that day for the test and over the four days of testing there were somewhere over fourteen hundred applicants in all, hoping to fill fifteen positions.

While I sat and waited for the exams to be passed out, I look about me at the others. Some I could tell were here simply for something to do. Some to make a statement, some needing a job and some who really wanted to be a game warden.

The exam papers were finally passed around and everything became very subdued and quiet. I found the format of the multiple choice very easy. But, before finishing, I was glad I had done the research into the department. When I had completed, I went back and checked each answer. I wanted to be sure.

I had done the best that I could and as I dropped off the answer sheet and exam papers, I asked the attendant, "How long will it be before we are notified of the results?"

"One week from today the results will be mailed to you."

"Thank you."

* * * *

The next week, while I waited for my results was --- well it was hell. Total anxiety. The day came finally and I drove around to Dudley's store with my pickup. "Hello Thom, Don should be back from town anytime now. You must be looking for your test results," Di said.

"Yes, I've made up my mind and this is what I want."

I was only there for nineteen minutes, but it seemed as if it was a life time. Don handed me the envelope. As I opened it, I noticed that everyone was watching. I unfolded the cover sheet and silently read down through the short paragraph. "Well, I'll be damned! I aced it and I am to be in Augusta Friday morning! That only gives me two days to get in shape. They sure don't give you much notice."

* * * *

As I try to look back at that moment on that day in August, there wasn't much I could remember other than opening the letter from Warden Service. The rest of that day was a total blank. I couldn't even remember motoring back up the lake or whether I walked home from Little East or rode my ATV.

Not wanting to wait until Friday morning or the 24th to drive to Augusta for my physical agility test, I decided to drive down Thursday and have a restful night before the physical testing. I hooked Royal on his run and left plenty of food and water and just for the exercise I walked the two miles to my canoe at Little East and carrying an overnight bag. Even though it was early morning and the temperature was still cool. I soon worked up a sweat. I enjoyed the walk along the old tote road and I had wished I had been living-working in this region when the Eagle Lake tote road was such an important road system. How much wood had been hauled out along this road? How many men lost their life working on the road? To say nothing about the audacity of those early lumbermen who opened up this country.

The water level in Webster stream was too shallow to use the motor, so I drifted with the current until I came to the point-of-ledge. It was a peaceful trip down the lake this morning. There were no boats or canoes out and the only campsites that were being used were at Boody Brook and Togue Ledge.

As I motored around Martin's Point. I shook my head in disgust. Why in the world did the park take this beautiful camp down and burn the warden's camp on Second Lake? And why in hell did the commissioner of Fisheries and Wildlife let the park do it? I'll never understand that for as long as I live. Even Uncle Royal would have found the park's actions contemptible.

I pulled my canoe ashore behind the dam. As I drove down the dam road towards the store. I met two men dressed in bib-coveralls, walking on the road. The older gentlemen was taller and wore a graying beard. As I drove across the bridge I noticed other men folk, dressed in the same attire, at a campsite downstream from the bridge. There were also a couple of women who were wearing old style grayish, long length gowns.

These people caught my attention because their dress was out of the norm for this region and for those I had seen who came here to enjoy the out-of-doors.

They waved as I drove by. They seemed pleasant enough.

I was only going to stop at the store long enough to say goodbye to Don and Di. Inside the store there were another man and woman dressed the same as those I had seen on the road and there were two small children with them who displayed exceptional manners and politeness. And something else I noticed about the two children, unlike other kids who play with everything in the store, these two simply wandered around looking and never touching anything. This was certainly a credit to their upbringing.

I never like listening-in to other conversations but I couldn't help myself in this instance. The young couple was talking to Don about how something, one of the members of the group had received leadings from the Lord to come to Maine and make this the new Jerusalem, the True Holy Land, and how the Lord had been leading them to shun society and government, medicine, the television and radio, newspapers and most books that were not directly related to the Bible or their way of life. Boy! Would I hate to be a kid growing up in that society. Cult!

When the two adults and their children left the store, I looked at Don and he just shrugged and said, "They came in this morning from Seekonk, Massachusetts."

"They appear to be friendly enough. And the kids have been well mannered," I said. "I'm on my way to Augusta and I stopped just to say good-bye."

"Good luck Thom," Don said.

*　　*　　*　　*

I telephoned Ronie from the motel room that evening. It had been several weeks since I had written and I had a lot of news to tell her. I told her about the people I had seen at the Matagamon campground and how well mannered the children were.

She wanted to know when training would start at the Academy, if I was hired. "The new class is scheduled for January Third. Twelve weeks of basic police training and then eighteen weeks of warden training."

Ronie asked me to spend Christmas with her and her family this year and I thought that was a terrific idea. After two hours on the phone I decided I'd better say good-bye. I needed a goodnight's sleep before tomorrow.

I don't know why, but I wasn't at all nervous about the testing tomorrow. In fact I don't remember much of anything after I turned the light off.

The next morning I was up early and went for a walk before eating a good breakfast of bacon, eggs and home fries. At nine o'clock I reported at the Armory on Western Avenue in Augusta.

There were twenty of us being tested. In the afternoon the last twenty on the list would be tested. I wasn't having any difficulty at all but there were a couple that had real difficulty with the sit-ups and running. There was no score; only pass or fail. "If you pass, you'll receive a notice for a scheduled interview next month. If you fail, you'll be notified before leaving here today." I was surprised to learn that only seven of the twenty had passed.

During the trip back to Matagamon I kept thinking about Uncle Royal. How I wished he was still alive today. I wished I could have spent more time with him before he died. During his life he had certainly witnessed many changes in the Matagamon region; cultural as well as technological. Some changes being for the betterment and some not so good. I wasn't sure how he would have responded about me becoming a game warden; but because I was his nephew I'm sure he would have accepted it. I also would have liked Uncle Royal to have met Ronie. I know he would have liked her instantly.

The next phase of the testing was the interview. I wasn't sure just how I felt about that. Jim had said that seven interviewers had, usually, about twenty-five minutes to make up their opinions about someone. What kind of questions would they ask? Would they get into my personal life? Would me being from New York City make a difference to them?

I stopped at the Napa Store for gas before driving on to Matagamon. Mrs. Gallagher came outside to pump the gas. "Hello Thom", she said, "fill it?"

"Yes, please."

"I heard you went to Augusta today for your physical agility test. How did you do?"

I was surprised she knew what I had been doing before I even had returned. But such is life in a small town. "I passed. Some didn't do so well though."

"When is your interview?" Sonya asked.

Again I was surprised that she knew about that. "It'll be next month, sometime."

"I hope you do okay on that. I hear it's a tough interview." Thanks, I thought to myself.

I paid for the gas, purchased some work gloves and said good-bye.

I thought about eating supper at the deli, but decided against it. I wanted to get home and see Royal and relax on my porch.

Don and Di were busy at the store so I didn't stop. The sky to the West was looking like rain and I wanted to get up the lake without getting caught in it.

I parked my car out behind the dam and there were five men standing together in conversation near my canoe. They were all dressed in the same attire as those I had seen just the other day at the store.

As I was getting out of my car, the group started to move away. I said, "Hello," they ignored me and kept walking. Unfriendly sorts.

But I soon forgot about the men as I motored up the lake. As usual the wind started to blow and the lake got rough as I motored through the devil's throat at the Martin Point. I was still ecstatic after passing the physical agility test and I wasn't at all concerned about the rough water.

By the time I pulled my canoe ashore at the tote road, across from the Little East campsite the sun had already set below the tree tops. It would soon be dark and I would have to walk the two miles home in the dark because I didn't have a flashlight. There would have been a time when walking in the woods in the dark would have made me feel uncomfortable. But tonight I look at it only as an inconvenience.

Royal, as usual was glad to see me. I unhooked him from his run and he followed me inside. After supper Royal and I sat for a long time on the porch listening to the stillness and enjoying the loneliness; a welcomed companion, Uncle Royal had said "Gives a man a quiet moment to reflect and think."

The next day I started working on the winter's supply of firewood. When I needed a rest from that I'd sit down and make out a list of supplies I would need before the first snow. Heating oil and cooking gas was at the top of the list. If I did make it into the Warden

Service this time around, I of course wouldn't need as many supplies. But I decided to stock up all the same, just in case.

Jim Randall stopped by one day while I was splitting wood. This allowed for a convenient break. "I heard you did okay at the physical agility test. Have you received your letter yet and your appointment for the interview?"

"No, not yet."

"You should have it by the end of the week. I heard the letters have been sent out."

"Any advice about the interview?" I asked.

"It won't be like a social gathering. There'll be seven people, they'll be very professional and to the point. They'll have twenty-five minutes to get to know you. A bit more if they like you. You'll be asked a variety of questions. The only advice I can give you is the same advice I was given. Be completely honest. If you aren't sure about your answer, tell them. Don't bluff, but above all, be honest."

We finished our coffee and Jim said he had to leave and I went back to my woodpile. In another two days I was done with the firewood for this year. It was split, piled and a tarp thrown over the top. Di called on the radio and said I had a letter from the Warden Service. "I'll be down this afternoon, thanks Di."

I went to town first to get supplies then back to Matagamon. The back of my pickup was full. As I was driving into the store driveway I saw a group of people crossing the far end of the bridge. They were wearing the same attire as those I'd seen before at the store and behind the dam. They must really enjoy this area I thought.

I hadn't anymore than walked through the door and Di handed me the letter from the Warden Service.

"Well, aren't you going to open it?" she asked. She was as excited as I was. I smiled, "October 8th," I said, "My interview is October 8th."

"Come in and have a glass of ice tea. It's too warm to drink hot coffee."

"Where's Don?"

"Out with the bear hunters. They won't be back until after dark."

"The group camped out below the bridge have been here for a while?" I asked.

"They're leaving tomorrow, the 30th, Corneau just came in to settle up with me. When he pulled a roll of bills out of his pocket, he saw me looking at it and made the statement, "The group doesn't believe in using checks or the financial system; that was alright with me."

"Are they a religious group?" I asked

"Yes, but I'm not sure what they call themselves other than the Body. Mr. Corneau and an older gentlemen Roland Robidoux; those two seem to be the spokesman for the group. Don't get me wrong, they were no trouble, they shunned the other campers and people in general. Some of the other campers seemed to think they were somewhat aloof."

I thanked Di and drove back out to the Huber road and then I turned left at the four corners. The people camping at Matagamon did not exist in my conscious mind now; nor would they for the next couple of weeks. I was too excited thinking about the interview on the eighth, to be thinking of anything else. That night and for several nights to come I would lay awake on my bed or sit out on the porch until after midnight trying to guess what I would be asked at the interview.

I was so consumed about what the interview might entail or how personal their questions would be, that I overlooked the fact that the annual moose hunt "started today!" and I'd missed the first two days of bird season. I donned my hunting apparel, my shotgun and four shells. "Hey Royal, you want to go get some birds for supper?"

I missed the first bird and when it flew off Royal sat down in the middle of the tote road and turned his head toward me, as if to say "well, what happened?"

Royal was ahead of me when we came to the orchard and he flushed a whole family that roosted at the top of an apple tree. I shot two before the others flew off. I found another partridge sitting in the middle of the tote road where the old bridge once crossed Webster Stream to the Little East side. As I was picking this bird up I counted seven more fly off. But I was out of shells. Besides three was all I wanted for now. The excursion enabled me finally to stop worrying about the interview. The next day I took Royal hunting up along the tote road to the old McDonald camp site on Turner Brook. I shot four birds on that trip and saw several more.

On the way back to camp Royal was out in front like he always was and a coyote came running up the road towards him. He stopped and the hair on his neck stood up in warning. I stepped behind a small fir tree to watch and see what would happen. Royal stood his ground as the other coyote slowed to a walk and approached him. They sniffed noses then they began to circle each other, smelling the other's butt. When they had decided that the other was of the opposite sex the female urinated in the road and ran off.

Royal rolled in the fresh scent making sure there was enough of the perfume on his neck and shoulders and then he urinated in the same spot. He started to follow the female but he stopped and came running back to me. But his attention was with the young female. I knew then that I would have to give him up; let him go back to his own kind. Especially since it was looking tentatively as if I might be in the Warden School this winter. That gave me something else to think about, parting with the best friend I had.

*   *   *   *

My interview wasn't until one in the afternoon on the eighth of October. I had stopped being nervous and I felt very comfortable during the drive South on I-95. I left Matagamon early so to allow myself plenty of time and a small lunch before the interview.

I don't know why it was, but I started thinking about the group that has been camped out at Matagamon; that called themselves The Body. What is it that would make anyone refuse to acknowledge everything in today's society, medicine, education, government, books, the television, radio and other forms of entertainment. I couldn't understand.

I couldn't find an answer to that and I suddenly realized I was approaching Augusta.

It wasn't difficult to locate the Department's Headquarters at 284 State Street once I was able to wedge my way through the traffic rotary at the end of Western Avenue. I found a sandwich shop not far from the main building. I kept lunch light, coffee and sandwich.

Promptly at five minutes before one, I introduced myself to the receptionist. "Yes,

Mr. Wellington, they are expecting you. Upstairs, go through the doors and the first room on your right."

"Thank you." As I walked up the stairs I adjusted my tie and buttoned my sport coat. I was still a minute early when I walked in the room.

Much to my surprise everyone stood up and introduced themselves. I was offered a cushioned seat directly in front of the interviewers. Now I was beginning to feel somewhat uncomfortable.

The game warden on my left said, "Have a seat Mr. Wellington, I'm Lieutenant Bill ------"I never heard what his last name was. I was that nervous. He was a distinguished looking older warden; gray hair and wearing glasses. I just never heard what his last name was.

"Just Thom please," I said

"Thom, I see you have a degree in law."

"Yes Sir."

"Where did you go to College?"

"Oxford, England sir."

"You mean, you're telling me that you have a degree in law from Oxford and now you want to be a Maine Game Warden?"

"Yes sir, more than anything."

"Why did you go to Oxford? You are from New York, correct" the Lieutenant asked.

"It was a promise I had made to my father. He is from England and he went to Oxford."

"I would think Thom that your financial possibilities would be far greater as a New York attorney, than a Maine Game Warden."

"Yes sir, that would be true."

"Why?" the Lieutenant asked.

"I have spent some time in the Maine wilderness and I love it. I also got acquainted with Warden Jim

Randall and I am impressed with his dedication and ability. He has inspired me."

"How long have you lived in Maine?" the Lieutenant asked.

"Two and a half years all total. I spent a year with my uncle before I went to Oxford. I have been here now for the last year and a half."

"How do you feel about working alone in the woods?"

"I don't see any problem. I have lived alone in the woods during the past year and a half. I feel very comfortable alone."

"Don't you ever get lonely?"

"At times, but loneliness can also be a companion."

"That's strange coming from someone so young. That's a statement more typical coming from an old hermit."

The Lieutenant's next question caught me off guard. "Have you ever smoked dope?"

Instantly I remembered what Jim had said about being honest. "I have tried it. But I don't smoke and can't inhale. The smoke hurts my lungs."

"Feels a little like barbed wire being pulled back up your throat, huh?" The lieutenant said.

"Yes sir."

It was the next interviewer's turn, Lieutenant Dan.

"Mr. Wellington – Thom, have you ever shot a dog?"

I immediately thought this question was just a bit strange, "No sir."

"Have you ever violated any law?"

"Yes sir, I suppose I have."

"If you were hired where would you least want to go?"

"Near any city."

"You don't like people then?" Lieutenant Dan asked.

"I have spent most of my entire life in cities. I don't like the crowding effect they have on me now."

"Do you like people --- are you a people person?"

"Yes I would say so. I enjoy conversing with people."

"Have you ever filed a workman compensation claim?"

"No sir."

"If you were to become a Game Warden, what would be the most difficult thing for you to do?"

That I had to think about. "It would have to be terminating a search for a lost child."

"Could you give your best friend a summons for too many fish?"

"Yes sir , I could."

"Would you arrest that same friend for night hunting?"

"It would all depend on the situation. But probably not."

"And why not!" Lieutenant Dan glared at me.

"An arrest is to ensure one's appearance in court. If I could issue a summons instead of arresting a friend, then I probably would."

"That was a good answer. Somewhat prejudice because you have a degree in law. But I like your honesty."

It was Sgt. Appletree's turn now. He sat there looking at me before saying anything. I knew he was going to give me an over-hauling.

"You said earlier that you supposed you have violated a law along the way somewhere. Let's clarify that understanding a little. Have you ever violated a Fish and Game Law?"

I could see my immediate future sinking before me. How did he know about that deer last fall? Or about my trip with Uncle Royal? "Yes sir, I have." I could feel their eyes staring at me. Probably because the temperature was rising and my face was getting red.

"Have you ever night hunted?" Sgt. Appletree asked.

"I don't believe so sir."

Before I could continue Appletree interrupted, "What do you mean you don't believe so? Don't you know if it was night or not!" he was getting excited now.

"At the time I didn't think anything of it. But later when I got to thinking it over, I questioned the time myself. I was so excited, now that I look back on the event it may well have been after sunset."

Before I could continue he interrupted me again, "It sounds to me that the time may have been twilight and not actually night hunting. Sgt. Appletree was about to ask another question and I interrupted him this time, "There's more."

He looked over his glasses at me and dropped his pen on the desk. "Explain!"

I swallowed hard. Tried, but my mouth was too dry. "It was on Sunday." I paused and looked at everyone; they were looking at me. "Sunday following the last day of open season."

I waited for the explosion. But all was quiet. Appletree just glared at me, so I supposed they were waiting for an explanation. "The only excuse I have is an honest one." "I bet," Appletree said.

"I live in the woods. I have a log cabin. Sometimes days blend into the next. I had lost track what day it actually was and when I went hunting on Sunday I really believed it was Saturday." I looked at the clock on the wall behind Appletree. My twenty-five minutes were up, but I didn't think they were through with me yet. And I was correct. Sgt. Appletree came back at me.

"You sit there and you expect me to believe that the deer you shot, let's say was only as late as twilight hunting and not actually night hunting. Was shot on Sunday! When you thought it was Saturday?! It was closed season to boot! I have a good mind to arrest you now instead of wasting any more of our time."

"Sir, I don't mean to be disrespectful or impertinent, but you do not have any corpus and you cannot convict me on just what I have said. You can't prove that a crime was committed even though I have told you that I violated the hunting laws." I noticed Lieutenant Bill whatever and Dan were smiling. I didn't know if that was a good sign or not. But they weren't going to let me off that easy either.

The next interviewer Warden Lewis asked, "You do understand law and courtroom procedure, that's quite evident and I believe you are being honest with us. Besides this deer you shot on Sunday is there anything else that perhaps you think that we should know about?"

"There are a couple of other incidents. I was there but I didn't do any of the shooting." Appletree's pen went up and hit the ceiling.

Lewis said to continue, "Six years ago my Uncle took me on a canoe trip up Webster Stream as far as Churchill Depot and back via Third Lake." Warden

Lewis' eyes opened and he straightened his back. He was smiling too. That bothered me.

"You're Thomas Wellington the Third! Well, I'll be damned." The others looked at Warden Lewis and then back at me. "It seems there was a deer near Hudson Pond and another on the Deadwater above Third Lake and you asked the Wardens if they'd like to stay for a venison supper!" He laughed and rocked back in his chair. But he was the only one laughing.

"My Uncle was the one that invited the Wardens to stay for supper."

Appletree asked, "Just who in the hell is your Uncle?"

"Royal Lysander," I replied.

"Uncle Royal was your Uncle!" Appletree exclaimed. "That explains a lot." Then he laughed, "I wonder what the old reprobate would say if he knew his nephew wanted to be a game warden?"

"Didn't Uncle Royal have a brother that was a game warden a long time ago? Rufus Lysander," Lewis asked.

"Yes sir, but I wasn't as well acquainted with Rufus."

"You chose, instead of the law abiding side of the family, for the poaching side," Appletree interrupted again.

Before I could comment to that Lewis asked, "Why do you want to be a game warden?"

"I never thought much about it until I started working with Jim Randall. I saw how he was required, by different situations to be more than a game warden. There were times when he was Deputy Sheriff, Homicide Detective or Drug Enforcement. And I observed how people respected him for his abilities.

"I like living in Maine and as a game warden I could enjoy the lifestyle afforded by the position and I believe I have something to offer."

"What would that be Thom? What could you offer?" Lewis asked.

"My dedication to the job, my knowledge of law, and my honesty."

"That's quite a resume."

It was the next interviewer's turn now. A State Police Trooper, John Wittmore. His posture was altogether different from the Wardens. He sat with his back straight, never leaning back in his seat and very straight forward.

"Mr. Wellington, you say you have a degree in law. With that kind of education I would think you would set higher goals than wanting to spend your career traipsing through the woods."

"That's exactly why I want to be a Game Warden," I replied.

"Do you drink, Mr. Wellington?'

"On occasion, yes."

"Do you drink while driving?"

"No sir."

"Have you ever been stopped for O.U.I.?"

"No sir."

"Any traffic violations?"

"None."

"Not even a stop sign?" Trooper Wittmore asked.

"No sir."

"Have you ever been charged with anything?"

"Well I got a warning once from a park ranger, because I didn't have a life preserver with me in the canoe. He gave me a written warning and his life preserver to use."

"So Mr. Wellington, you have never been to court?"

"Yes I have, before coming to Maine. I was a member in a family law firm and I represented several clients in court." That was all from Trooper Wittmore.

"Hello Thom, I'm Ben Chistle from the Guide's Association. How do you feel about game wardens being allowed to wear facial ornaments?"

"I think a well trimmed beard on a Warden in the wilds would look fine. But there would always be a few that would be unkempt, so I'd have to say not at all."

"Do you think wardens should be given complementary licenses to fish and hunt?"

"It would be a nice gesture."

"What about guiding? Do you think Wardens should be allowed to guide?"

"Yes, what better guide could you ask for."

I could tell by the reactions of the committee that I had hit upon a sore point with Chistle.

"Do you think sporting camp owners should be required to turn in their sports people who violate the fish and game laws?"

"That's already a law and I approve of it."

"Do you have a Guides License, Thom?"

"No I do not."

"Do you trap?"

"I have some; for beaver and coyotes."

"If you were guiding a party of fishermen Thom, on your day off and at the end of the day you discovered that one of your people had kept too many fish, what would you do?"

I didn't like this question, "That would be a difficult position to be in. I'll have to think on it a moment." Without a doubt Wardens in the past have probably found themselves in this position. I tried to visualize in my mind how Jim Randall would handle it. "I'd wait until just before I was going to leave and make sure that I was paid for the day and then as politely and amicably as I could, I'd hand him a summons."

They all laughed, except Mr. Chistle.

Sally Crandle was the last interviewer. She was from personnel.

"Thom, do you snowmobile or ride an ATV?"

"Yes, I have both machines and I do a lot of riding."

"Do you work well with other people?"

"Yes I do."

"When two wardens team up together for fall activities, they are apt to develop a close intimate working relationship that might not always be able to be shared with a spouse. Do you think that might become a problem for you?"

"I'm not married and even if I were I don't believe there would be a problem."

"Many wardens before you have said the same thing and the divorce rate among Game Wardens is one of the highest. What if your partner was a woman would that change your opinion?"

I thought about that before answering and I could see the trained looks from all the interviewers. Finally, I replied, "If I become a game warden that is what I'll do foremost in everything I do. My personal life will have to be separated from my professional life and if I ever get married I hope that my future wife could understand that."

"I'm not sure if you understand the question I put before you Mr. Wellington. Do you feel that women should be game wardens?"

I had a feeling that was what she was beating around the bush trying to get at. "I'm sure there are some phases of the job or some areas that women could perform the duties of a game warden as well as men. But from what I have seen of Jim Randall's work, and I'm sure there are many more who work as he does, that I don't believe women would do what I have seen him do, or put themselves in perilous situations to apprehend someone. I cannot see a woman knowingly walking into a bunch of felons and informing them that she was going to take their fish, partridge or deer and was going to arrest one or more of them. I don't believe any woman would put herself in that position, alone and in the wilds of Maine."

"And there are probably some male wardens already out there who wouldn't put themselves in a similar position," she replied.

"If that is the case ma am, then they too should not be out there."

"The times have changed Mr. Wellington where the Warden Service is no longer strictly men."

"I am aware of that ma'am, but it has come to my knowledge that Warden Service had to change some operating policies and entry requirements to accommodate women."

I decided I had said enough, probably too much. Ms. Crandle was frowning and apparently she was through. The others I noticed were smiling.

"Does anyone else have anything they'd like to ask Mr. Wellington." No one did. "If not, do you have anything you'd like to ask Thom?" Lieutenant Bill asked.

"No sir, I think I have said enough." I noticed the Lieutenant smiled.

"Then you are free to leave and you'll hear from the panel soon."

I stood up and looked at the clock at the same time. An hour and a half had passed. "Thank you" and I left the room. I was sure I had said too much to Ms. Crandle.

*   *   *   *

The drive back to Matagamon was a short one. At least what I can remember of it. I can remember taking the exit off Western Avenue and driving toward I-95, but I don't remember much of the drive from there until I pulled into the driveway at the Matagamon Store. I don't know if it is possible to be out of your body and still drive an automobile safely and know where you are going or not. Or perhaps my conscious mind was still back in that interview room. I felt if I had just been through an extensive interrogation. "Well! How did it go?" Di asked.

"I'm not sure. I was in there for an hour and a half."

"They must have been impressed," Di said.

"I don't know if I'd go so far as to say impressed. A lot came out about my activities with Uncle Royal on our canoe trip and the deer I shot last year."

"What's this about a deer you shot last year?" Di looked at Don questioningly, "I'll tell you later," he said.

"There was a woman there from personnel and when she asked me what I thought about women game wardens, I was honest about my reply. She didn't like that."

The sun had set before I got to Webster Stream. I was familiar enough with the lake and channels by now, that darkness didn't bother me. And neither did the walk along the tote road to home. Only I've got to remember to carry a small flashlight.

I didn't sleep much that first night after the interview. I was sure I had said too much to Ms. Crandle. Although she asked for my honest opinion and what must the committee think about me as a potential game warden after I admitted to violating the hunting laws and my participation with Uncle Royal at Hudson Point and on the deadwater above Third Lake. I was only too glad to see that Warden Farrar and the pilot, young Rider were not with the interview committee. I was so afraid I had blown my chances of ever becoming a game warden.

Royal and I went hunting the next day, after missing two easy shots, I soon forgot about Augusta and the interview.

The weather had turned cool and all weekend the clouds had a gray threatening look about them. I finished banking the cabin with fir boughs on Sunday and finished up the little seasonal chores before real cold temperatures started to set-in.

I was up early Monday morning. I wanted to go for an early hunt down the tote road. I had been lucky this year. I hadn't seen any other bird hunters at all between the cabin and the lake. I changed my mind about the walk to the lake this morning when I saw snow on the ground. I decided then that it was time to bring my canoe and motor back and store them for the winter. It was getting to cold now anyhow to continue motoring on the open lake.

After breakfast I hooked the small trailer to the ATV and drove to Webster Stream. Royal ran ahead of me and flushed many partridges and looked at me as if to say, "Well what are you waiting for?" "Not today Royal." As I stopped and shut off the ATV at my canoe, I looked across Webster Stream where the foot path goes to the stream from the Little East Campsite. There were two men standing there, maybe having a conversation, but when they noticed that I was looking towards them, they moved out of sight back towards the camping area. They were dressed the same as the people in The Body, the group that had been camped at the Matagamon campground a couple of weeks ago. They seemed a bit concerned about my presence there.

After I had loaded my canoe and motor, I walked down opposite the campsite, near the old bridge that wasn't there anymore. I didn't want my presence to upset the campers anymore than they already were, so I stayed concealed behind some small fir trees. I couldn't see too much. Movement mostly. It looked as though people were setting up tents. If they were talking, they were keeping their voices low.

I decided to make it appear as I was leaving but not really. Just to see what they would do then. I started the ATV and drove out of sight and hearing, then I turned it off and hiked back through the woods to the bridge; sat down and waited. There seemed to be a lot of discussion but it wasn't clear what they were talking about. Two left and walked along the trail that followed Webster Stream towards Grand Pitch and two stayed behind. From the activity there I thought they were probably setting up tents.

There didn't appear to be anything here particularly interesting, so I decided to walk down to the lake. Along the way I thought about my camping experience at Little East and how I had discovered my Uncle. I silently hoped that those setting up camp there now would find as much solace in this region as I had through the years. I walked down to the old Boy Scout campsite. The one the scouts didn't use anymore. That would be an enjoyable spot to sit and enjoy the view of the Katahdin Mountains across the lake.

Much to my surprise when I stepped out through the spruce trees at the top of a knoll I was certainly surprised to see an orange colored airplane tied up at shore and the pilot lounging in a lawn chair on the bank.

"Hello there." I said as I walked down the knoll towards the pilot.

He was somewhat startled, then he relaxed. "Well hello, I didn't know anyone else was on this side of the lake." He eyed Royal then coming down the hill behind me. "That's some dog you have there. He looks a lot like a coyote."

"He is. A coyote I mean. I found him on the tote road a year ago last spring. He's really a great bird dog."

"What are you doing here today? You obviously aren't hunting."

"What makes you say that? I asked.

"You don't have a shotgun."

"I could have left it on top of the hill leaning against one of the spruce trees."

"No I don't think so, you don't have any shells in your pockets."

"Why do you say that?"

"You have both hands in your pockets and you aren't playing with – most people would be fumbling the shells in their fingers and you could hear the brass clink together."

"You're very astute"

"It's a habit. I'm a retired Game Warden Pilot."

"No, I'm not hunting. I leave my canoe and motor in the bushes above the Little East campsite and I brought my ATV and trailer down to take them back home."

"You must have come down the Old Eagle Lake tote road," Jack said.

"Yes, my cabin is about two miles up the road. Uncle Royal was my Uncle."

"I knew a lot about him; I guess everyone from around here knew Uncle Royal one way or another. But I had only met him once."

"You are from around here then?" I asked.

"Born and brought up in Patten. You must be young Thomas. I've heard a lot about you from Tom Chase and Ted Hansen."

"I'm trying to be a game warden. I had my interview last week."

Jack started laughing and after a while he composed himself enough to say, "You better not say that so loud or your Uncle will hear and he would turn over in his grave. From what I've heard from Jim Randall, you'll make a good warden. I hope you succeed."

"Thank you. I'm Thom Wellington," and I reached out to shake hands.

"I'm Jack McPhee."

"So what are you doing now, that you have retired?" I asked.

"I own sporting camps on Haymock Lake in T8-R11. I'm waiting to meet two bird hunters that I dropped off at the Old Hana farm. They were going to hunt the orchard and then hunt along the old tote road to here.

"What happened to the warden camp?"

"The park burned it. They also removed the old Martin camp on the point."

"Why in the world did the park do that for?"

"I'm not sure."

"I used to use that camp to work out of on occasions when I was in the area. Especially when I was flying in and out of Frost Pond checking fishermen. When the fisherman first discovered we were stocking the pond and the fishing was excellent there was a lot of activity on the pond. I used to hold up at the Warden camp instead of flying back to Shin Pond or wasting flying time. There were times when the weather turned sour and I'd hold up at the camp for a while."

"The biggest shame is that more history of this area is now gone."

"When does the new warden school begin?"

"Right after January first."

"If I had the time and wasn't waiting for my hunters to come back, I'd take you up and show you some of the region from the air. Things look a lot different from the air."

"Thanks, I certainly appreciate the thought but I do have to be going." We said goodbye and I left Jack McPhee sitting in his lawn chair at the old Boy Scout Campsite.

* * * *

Two days later I received a radio call from Di saying that a letter had just arrived from the Warden Service. "I'll be there as soon as I can drive around from the Huber road." Butterflies started churning in my stomach again, as I raced out the old road towards four corners. As anxious as I was to learn how I did at the interview I was glad I didn't have to motor down the lake.

Di handed me the letter as I walked through the door into the store. I ripped open the envelope and began to scan down through it. "Well, what does it say?" Di asked.

"Ah, I passed --- and with high regards to my honesty it appears, by all except for Ms. Crandle." As I read down further I became a bit more excited. "Because of my written test score and the recommendations from the interview committee as a whole, my name has been placed at the top of the hiring list. I have a polygraph appointment in Augusta, at the State Police barracks on October 22nd. I'll be to go to hell! I made it."

I looked up from the letter at Don and Di, they were both smiling. "Congratulations Thom."

"This reminds me of the day Alan got his letter," Di said. "Damn, we're going to miss you."

* * * *

At mid morning the next day I was sitting at the table drinking coffee and someone knocked on the door and before I could say to come in, Jim Randall opened the door and walked in. "Congratulations, I heard the good news from my sergeant. He said you made quite an impression on the committee. I have never heard of an interview lasting an hour and a half. An hour but no more."

"I just took your advice and was completely honest. There were times when I thought perhaps I might have been too honest.

"Can you fill me in about this polygraph test?"

"There are several different categories of questions. They're designed to see if there is any criminal history, drug activity or anything in a personal nature that if discovered might be used against you to change your testimony during a trial. You haven't robbed a bank or anything like that?"

He laughed, "You wouldn't believe how many people try to lie their way through the questioning and when you lie once, you have to continue."

"Well, there shouldn't be any problem there. I have already admitted to my worst dastardly deed in front of the interview committee."

There wasn't much Jim could say to help prepare me for the polygraph other than again to be completely honest.

We talked through a pot of coffee. Jim was looking forward to the deer season starting in a couple of weeks. The deer herd was looking good and there was an abundance of beechnuts this year. The bucks would be running the ridges and feeding late. But the beechnuts would also delay when the bucks would start following the does.

After Jim left, I took Royal for a walk down to the lake. I already had quite a few partridges so I left my shotgun in the cabin. The leaves were in full foliage and the air was cool. There were no partridges this trip, only a red fox who didn't hesitate to leave the tote road once it saw Royal. He wasn't at all afraid of me.

I stopped for a minute at the old bridge abutment at Little East. Everything was quite. Only the gentle sound of the water current as it flowed through shallow rips. I stood there in the stillness thinking about the people that I had seen here on the eleventh. Then I thought about my stay at the Little

East sight and my meeting with Uncle Royal. My thoughts didn't stay there for long. Many images, scenes of the past started crossing my inner vision as I could see the old tired, worn out men, at least they appeared to be old and worn out, building the old bridge. Cribbing the abutments and the center pier and filling it with rocks. The team of horses pulling supply wagons full of timber. Smoke rising from the cook tent as cookee was preparing lunch and hot black coffee. Spruce logs being driven down the river in the spring freshet; the men all lean and muscular after the winters work, locked away in a lumbering camp. A week from here they would all stop off at Louse Island before going to their homes at Matagamon, to get deloused. I saw the giant steam lombard log haulers crawling at a snail's pace, towing twenty-nine sleds of spruce and fir logs.

Then suddenly a shiver went through me that started at the soles of my feet and up my back and shoulders. It felt like an electric shock. Realizing that everything I had just experienced on the inner was now in the past. Some of the events a long time ago. And the faces I saw were now all gone; I translated to another level of being. That left me with an overwhelming sense of loneliness. A loneliness that was neither a companion nor comforting. Another shiver went through me.

I moved on to escape the forbidding loneliness. I strolled on to the old Boy Scout campsite and sat down at the top of the knoll with Royal by my side. There was a gentle breeze blowing through the tops of the tall spruce and fir trees. Almost a whisper.

Uncle Royal had tried to explain once what he had meant when he said, "Loneliness can be a welcomed companion." I didn't know then just what he was saying and he couldn't explain exactly what he meant or felt. But there had been times during this past year that I think I had experienced the same sense of loneliness. The sensation wasn't so much of being lonely and depressed, but rather a feeling of well being, of being alone. Comfortable.

But the loneliness that I had experienced back at the old bridge was not the same. There was no sense of well being or comfort. It was more a sense of sadness because of all those who helped to build this frontier, they became a part of it and no one had made any attempt to preserve the history of their memories. This was an important era in the history of the State of Maine and it's a damn shame that so much of it has been burned and covered over; like, "let us pretend it never existed."

I chuckled out loud and Royal looked up at me. I was thinking about those few early lumbermen that had declared war on the entire British Kingdom. What a stalwart bunch of people they must have been. That kind of attitude is exactly what this country is lacking today.

All of a sudden this whole region seemed so empty. Jim Drake at Telos dam was gone, Chub and Fran were both gone and Uncle Royal. The last of that forgotten era. The Martin camp and the Davignon camp, the ole coyote den and its many memories. Ronie didn't come back to the Scout base this summer, although I knew that ahead of time. Maybe it's time for me to move on also. Take another district instead of Matagamon.

I was still feeling empty and wistful. Wanting something but not quite sure where to reach for it. I scratched Royals belly and his head, then got up and headed for home.

*　　*　　*　　*

On the twenty-second of October I was up early and decided to have an early breakfast at the restaurant in Patten before starting the long drive to Augusta for my polygraph test. It was still dark when I got to the restaurant and I was surprised to see how busy the town was even this early. Yeah, people around here really do get up before breakfast. I was soon to learn that these people were regulars on their way to work. Some to the far end of the Huber Road cutting wood, some operating equipment, putting in a septic system or building woods roads and one trucker on his way back from his first load in Millinocket.

When I arrived at the State Police Headquarters in Augusta the receptionist said that there was another applicant ahead of me and she would be finished shortly. I waited an hour before the female applicant came upstairs from the testing room. Her face was red and tear streaked. She obviously had had a difficult time. Behind her was a uniformed officer "Mr. Wellington, you're next. Follow me please." I followed him downstairs to a small windowless room.

"Have a seat please," and he started writing in what looked like a questionnaire booklet. "My name is Captain Smith and I'll be your examiner during the polygraph testing. Before we get started I must inform you of your Miranda Rights," and he handed me a type written paragraph.

"Why is Miranda necessary, Captain?"

"These questions are designed to see if there might be any criminal activity in your past that would prevent you from doing or interfering with your duties as a law enforcement officer. If I discover any serious criminal activity anything you say or disclose could be used against you. Miranda is to inform you of your constitutional rights."

I read the paragraph to myself as Captain Smith recited Miranda from memory. "Knowing your rights do you wish to continue with the polygraph test?"

"Yes."

"Is there anything in your past that you would like to discuss before we start?"

"Not that I can think of Captain," I replied.

"If there is these questions are structured to find it. And believe me, I will find it."

"Let's get started." It took him ten minutes to attach all the sensing equipment to me. It was very uncomfortable sitting there strapped to all those senses and not being able to move or cross my legs.

The first few questions were simple; my name, do I drink milk, "have you always lived in Maine?"

"No," I noticed Captain Smith made a check on the roll of graph paper. There were a few more odd but simple questions.

"Okay, when you respond to the next question I want you to purposely lie. This will create a base line for me to compare the rest of the testing with. "Have you ever or contemplated having a sex change?"

"Yes"

"I want to go back to a previous question. You said you have not always lived in Maine. Is that a correct answer?"

"Yes Sir, I am originally from New York. I have only been in Maine for about a year and a half."

Smith continued with the questions. Had I ever stolen anything? Had I ever been charged with a criminal offense? Had I ever used drugs? "How often?"

"I tried marijuana twice, but I don't smoke and I can't inhale. Oh yeah, I do smoke a cigar sometimes to keep the mosquitoes away."

"Other than what you have already told me about trying marijuana twice have you ever tried smoking since then or used any other drug?"

"No."

Once Captain Smith was finished with the drug questions he returned to criminal offenses and behavior again. Then about twenty minutes into the testing, he shut the machine down and said, "Let's take a break. I'll remove the pressure cuff from your arm but remain seated. I'm going out to have a smoke." He left.

The air was stuffy in that small room. I wished I could have gone outside too for fresh air. I rested my head back against the back rest and looked up at the ceiling. Directly above me was a small camera lens. I was being watched. The smoke break was only an excuse.

Captain Smith came back into the room after five minutes and reattached the pressure cuff and sat back down at his desk before saying anything. "While I was out what were you thinking.

"I was wondering why the excuse of needing a smoke when you don't smoke. You do not have the burnt tobacco smell on your clothes and nothing but car keys and change in your pockets. Then I noticed the camera lens directly above me. Then it occurred to me that not everyone who passes through here might be as honest as I am."

"You're correct on all points," Smith replied.

During the next twenty five minutes the questions were of a personal nature. I figured they were designed to see if I had a skeleton in my closet.

There were questions about my sexuality. Had I ever had homosexual tendencies. Had I ever dressed in women's clothing. Do young boys and girls turn me on. And then Smith asked, and why, I was never to understand, "Have you ever had sex with a fish?"

"No," and I looked at him and lowered my eyebrows. He shrugged his shoulders.

"Have you answered all these questions truthfully?"

"Yes"

Smith studied the graph paper momentarily, made some notes on the side and then turned the machine off. "This test isn't designed to see how well you'll do. You either pass or fail. You passed Mr. Wellington." He removed the senses from my arm, leg and fingers. "Oh, you have a message here. You are to go directly to Fish and Wildlife Headquarters as soon as you have finished here."

*   *   *   *

On the way to the Fish and Wildlife Headquarters I kept wondering what they could possibly want with me. Did I have to go through the oral exam again?

I was directed to the Chief Warden's office. "Colonel, Mr. Wellington is here sir." The receptionist said and left before the Colonel could answer.

"Have a seat Thom. I'll get right to the point. Your name is at the top of the hiring list Thom. You are so far ahead of all the other applicants, it isn't funny. The Department would like you to come to work November 1st as a temporary Warden. Normally you would have to attend a short version of the Training Course at the Academy. But considering your background in law and the recommendations from the oral board, this training can be over looked for a short period. Unless there is something serious in your background, which I doubt if there is, you'll be permanently hired on January 1st. We would like you to assist Jim Randall this fall. There is a vacant district bordering his and the warden in the next district will be taking some sick leave. We would like you to assist Warden Jim Randall working night hunters and lost hunters."

"Yes sir!" I couldn't think of anything else to say. Apparently from the expression on my face the Colonel understood exactly how I was feeling. He smiled too and shook my hand, "Congratulations."

I was issued two winter uniforms, one green jacket, a pair of leather boots and a pair of insulated rubber boots. A .38 caliber revolver, gun belt and accessories and a wool blanket. When Linda at the storehouse handed me the blanket, she noticed the puzzled look on my face and said, "You'll need this to keep warm working night hunters with Jim Randall. He doesn't sit in his pickup. I don't have one to give you, but you'll need raingear also working with Jim."

This entire day had to be the most exciting that I could remember in my whole life. As I was leaving the storehouse I was thinking of Uncle Royal when I experienced a lightning sharp pain in my left shoulder. It felt exactly like an electric shock. Maybe Uncle Royal was observing from his world and the shock, just when I was thinking about him, was his way of saying that he was proud of me for becoming a game warden. I laughed out loud then and other people in the parking lot turned and looked towards me. I'm glad I didn't have to chase him through the woods, and lay awake at night wondering what devilish prank he would execute next.

I wore my new uniform home. Stopping first at The Matagamon store. I had to tell someone and Don and Di were the only family I had.

The next day Jim stopped at the cabin early in the morning. We had many things to discuss before I started work on November 1st. "First, I'll call you on the radio or have Di relay a message for me when I need your help. Don't call me asking to work."

Deer season started a week from today but the Colonel said I wasn't to go to work until the first.

"Have you given it much thought about staying right here and taking this district?"

"Actually I have given it a lot of thought. I don't think so. I want to go out to the settlement where people live. I want to get my feet wet first before settling here."

"That's a smart decision. Although this is by far the best district in the state; there is only Don and Di who live here year round. No phones, not many complaints and a new turn around of people every few days, and there are still spots in this district where the State Police radio dispatcher or the Warden Service repeater can't get me on the radio. But you'll never use search warrants or warrants of arrest here. You wouldn't get much of any opportunity to assist other law enforcement. And if you're looking to promote --- well the Division Lieutenant and Augusta don't know much about this little corner of the state."

"No, I think you have made a smart choice."

*　　*　　*　　*

I was ecstatic to say the least. Circumstances would have been better for me, if instead of working part time with Jim starting the first of November, the warden school had started. As it would be now I would have a lot of traveling to do. But what worried me the most, what if we got a freak snowstorm in November that dumped a couple of feet? There would be no possible way of driving out of here with the pickup. I would worry about that later.

November 1st finally arrived. The opening day for non-resident hunters. I didn't hear from Jim until Tuesday evening. I was just beginning to fix supper when Di called on the radio and advised, Jim had a lost hunter in behind Scraggley Lake in T7-R8. "Jim is going to stop first and talk to the guy's friends at Shin Pond Village. Then he'll meet you at the Huber garage at seven."

I had been in that country behind Scraggley on a snowsled and my ATV and it wouldn't be an easy terrain to walk over in the dark with only a flashlight. There were steep cliffs and drop-offs. This would be a long night, I could tell.

The hunter was from Connecticut and had never been in the area before. I got in with Jim when he arrived. "Whenever someone gets lost behind Scraggley they go north, knowing damn well they're going in the wrong direction. We might as well drive around Snowshoe Mountain and fire a short on that side of Soul Ridge. Maybe we'll be lucky and he'll answer back. Before these new roads were built lost hunters would come down off the ridge and go past Soul and hit Millimagassett Lake and follow the shoreline around the tip and hit the old fire trail and walk that out to Fournier's road that goes to Oxbow."

"What if we don't get an answer when you fire a shot?" I asked.

"His buddies fired shots where he was last seen and didn't get an answer. As dark as it is now he won't move much without a flashlight. So it's a pretty safe bet he wasn't going south up the ridge. If he does move he'll come down hill towards Soul Ridge. If he answers we take a compass course and go in after him."

On the backside of Snowshoe Mountain fog blanketed the ground. "It'll rain before we get him out," Jim said matter of factly.

"Why do you say that?"

"It always happens. No one gets lost on a clear, dry night. This probably won't be more than a drizzle."

We soon came to the end of the road near Soul Ridge. Jim shut the truck off and we got out. The air was still and quiet. Only a loon on Millimagassett Lake. Jim walked away from the truck and cupped his hands around his mouth and hollered. No answer. He hollered again and a third time. Still no answer. "Thom get my rifle out from behind the seat."

It was a .30-06 "nice rifle."

"Fire a shot in the air. Point the muzzle southerly. It's loaded; just pull the bolt back."

I pulled the trigger and it sounded like a cannon. "Now listen," Jim said. We waited and waited. Then about four minutes later there was a faint reply. Jim checked his compass. "269 degrees West. That figures. That jerk is down on the inlet of the lake. He went in the wrong direction off Soul Ridge. Probably doesn't even have a compass with him. If he does he doesn't know how to use it. Fire another shot Thom and let's make sure before we walk our asses off."

I fired again but this time there was no reply. "Maybe he didn't hear that shot," I said.

"Oh, he heard it alright. He probably shot up all his bullets early. Now he can't answer back again. But I'll guarantee when we get to him he'll have saved one bullet."

"Why would he save one bullet?"

"For that big bear or himself. They always do. I have never seen a lost hunter but what will have one bullet left when you find him. He wastes all the others early, but he'll save that one. Just in case."

It was 8:15 when we left his truck. I followed behind Jim. The first hour was difficult walking. This ridge had been cut over a couple of years ago and we had to walk though the slash and raspberry bushes. We could have followed old skidder trails to the back of the cut, but Jim preferred to follow his compass across the semi-clearing so we wouldn't get off course. Once we were through the old cut the walking was easier, but we couldn't see as far ahead of us.

I noticed the bushes were wet. It had started to drizzle. Once we were on the Westside of Soul Ridge the landscape was rougher. We had to skirt around ledges and tangles of blowdowns. I looked at my watch 9:50. We stopped and Jim hollered. We waited but there was no reply. "What if you fire a shot from your revolver?" I ask.

"That would only get him to move and leave our compass bearing. Better if he just stays wherever he is."

"We've traveled a long ways from the truck; do you suppose we might have walked by him?"

"I don't think so. He'll probably be close to the shore of Beaver Brook. That's still a mile ahead of us."

At 11:00 we could smell smoke and ten minutes later we saw the first flicker of flames through the underbrush. Jim slowed his pace and was very careful about making noise. To me he was acting like he was sneaking up on a poacher. About two hundred feet back from the fire Jim stopped. "Turn your flashlight off." Then he hollered. And this time a reply.

"This is Game Warden, Jim Randall. Are you Richard Peduto?"

"Yes."

"Are you okay?"

"Yeah, hungry and tired."

"Okay Richard before we come any closer, make sure your rifle is unloaded."

I heard the action being pulled back and the metallic clinking of a live round being ejected. "Okay, it's empty." Jim was right he saved his last bullet.

"Now Richard set your rifle down against a tree and stand near the fire."

"Okay." Through the trees we could see him standing in the firelight.

As we approached the fire, Jim carried on a conversation with Richard and I walked over to the spruce tree and picked up his rifle and cleared the action. His face was black from the wood smoke and ashes. I sat down on the ground and leaned up against the spruce tree.

"What happened?" Jim asked.

"I jumped a deer about 3:00 and started running after it. I got down in this hell hole and didn't know how to get out."

"Where's your compass?"

"Back at camp, I forgot to bring it."

"You should have made a trip out to get it before coming into these woods. Is this your first time here?"

"Yeah, and I ain't coming back. Not after this experience."

"Well Mr. Peduto, you have nobody to blame but yourself."

"How are we going to get out?" Peduto asked.

Jim replied. "The same way Thom and I got here. We walk. It took three hours of walking to find you. It'll take four, four and a half to get back."

"I'm not walking out of here in the dark, in the middle of the night."

"Well suit yourself Mr. Peduto. Thom and I are leaving. The shortest compass course out of here is 180 degrees South. That'll probably take you back to the road where you left your pickup."

Jim started to leave. "Wait, maybe I'll go out with you."

"Thom carry his rifle and Richard you stay behind me and our lights should give you plenty of light to see by."

I was somewhat dubious now about finding our way back to the pickup. But I knew Jim knew what he was doing. In fact we had to walk around the same blow-down tangles and ledges as before. The trip out was slower of-course because we had to keep waiting for Richard. I knew he was tired; he kept stumbling and falling. But as Jim had said, four hours later we came right out to his pickup. I was impressed.

In the light of the pickup I noticed Peduto's boots and pants were wet, more so than Jim or me, and covered with black mud. Apparently he hadn't been as cool headed from being lost as he tried to have us believe.

I was tired and I was having a difficult time trying to stay awake. When we finally got to the Shin Pond Village and Mr. Peduto discovered we weren't going to ferry him behind Scraggley so he could bring his pickup out, he became very angry. "How am I supposed to get my pickup now? Your Superiors are going to hear about this! I'll stop at Augusta on my way home!"

"That's fine with me Mr. Peduto. Just make sure you put it in writing and spell my name correctly. It's Jim Randall."

I couldn't help it. I started laughing and that made Peduto even angrier. I was surprised to hear Jim respond like that. But he was polite about it.

It was now four in the morning. "We might as well catch a night hunter now. It's too late to go home and sleep." I didn't say anything. I was trying to find some rationale in that last statement.

At The Crommet Field we turned right onto the Snowshoe road. A gravel woods road. About a mile in, there was a grassy spot off the apex of a corner. We set up Jim's decoy deer off this corner in the grass so just the eyes would reflect as a vehicle started around the corner. "If they're interested, a night hunter will stop and back up and turn the vehicle so the headlights will illuminate the whole deer. If someone shoots we both step out of the bushes and arrest them. Normally my Sergeant would be waiting in his vehicle at the bottom of the hill to stop the vehicle if they try to run on us, but he isn't here, so if they run, we're out of luck."

Jim hid his truck quite a-ways off the road on a snowmobile trail. He no more than had the truck tuck away behind a thicket and we could see headlights coming around the corner at the top of the hill. Jim took up position on one side of the road nearest the driver and I on the other side. The vehicle wasn't coming very fast. It went by us and at first I thought they had not seen the eyes, but the brake lights came on and the jeep SUV came to a sudden stop and started up again. Ten minutes later there came another vehicle and when this one saw the eyes it skidded to a stop and came to rest in the ditch. They backed up and sat there for a moment. I could see the decoy illuminated. They were probably discussing whether to shoot or not. They finally drove off.

No sooner were their taillights out of sight and a third vehicle came around the corner at the top of the hill. This one was traveling slower; as it went by me I noticed it was another jeep SUV, just like the first vehicle. The brake lights came on and the vehicle jigged to the left, illuminating the decoy and Bang! The passenger fired from inside the SUV before it had come to a complete stop. My heart was suddenly in my throat. What a rush. Jim beat me to the vehicle by one stride and I heard him say rather loudly and sternly, "You are under arrest for night hunting!" I grabbed the rifle by the barrel, it was warm, and I took possession of it. I removed a clip holding two loaded shells and a live round from the chamber of a Winchester .30-06 rifle. I placed that on the hood and asked the passenger to step out. I opened his door. "Step out and turn around and put your hands on the roof." I frisked him and removed a pocket knife and another loaded clip. I checked under his seat, the dash and glove box, looking for any handguns. I noticed Jim looking in the backseat.

Neither of the two looked to be over twenty. "Where are you boys from?" Jim asked.

"Fall River, Massachusetts," the driver replied. His name was Dick Avery, twenty-one and the passenger shooter, was Romeo Justin, nineteen.

"Are you two up here hunting alone?" Jim asked.

"No, our fathers are a few minutes ahead of us."

"Did they have an SUV just like this one?"

"Yeah."

"When you saw the eyes of that decoy you should have driven on like your fathers. Now you both are going to jail. Have a seat inside." After the doors were closed, "I'll go get my truck, you stay here with these two and don't let them get out."

When Jim was back with his pickup, he walked down and got the decoy and put it in the back of his truck and pulled a piece of canvas over it. Another vehicle was coming up the hill. We could see the headlights illuminating the trees. When it got near us, it slowed and then stopped. It was the boy's fathers and the passenger, Mr. Justin seemed just a bit irritated. "What's going on here?" he was standing directly in front of me.

"They are under arrest for night hunting and we are taking them to jail at East Millinocket," I said and then looked at Jim. He nodded his head and said nothing.

"I want to talk with my son."

"Sorry sir, they are in our custody now. If you wish to follow us to the police headquarters then you can speak to him after we have processed them both." Still Jim stood there not saying a word.

"I want his rifle back! That belongs to his grandfather."

"Sorry again. That is evidence in a crime now and will be held as evidence. When they are convicted the rifle becomes property of the state by statutory law."

This made Mr. Justin even angrier. "We'll have to stop at our cabin first to change clothes and get some money. Will you wait for us, so we can follow you in?'

"No, we are going to the police headquarters directly." Jim gave him directions.

"How much is this going to cost?"

"Thousand dollars each, plus the victims fund and the cost of court, and oh yeah, three days in jail."

"What!"

"Come on it's time we left, you drive their SUV and take the shooter, Romeo with you and I'll take Avery." We left and Mr. Justin was still screaming. Avery's father was pretty decent.

On the way to East Millinocket I thought to myself that Mr. Justin was really going to be upset when he learned his son just shot at a decoy. It was breaking daylight and I was tired, but there was so much adrenaline surging through me that I couldn't have slept if I wanted to.

I tried to engage Romeo in conversation, but the only thing he said was something about he was really going to get it from his father. I had the impression that he was more afraid of his father than of going to jail.

At the police headquarters Jim said, "Make sure you lock the car doors and grab the rifle from behind my seat. I'll take these two inside."

The boys fathers had arrived and rudely stepped in front of me as I was about to go inside. "Is that my boy's rifle? There had better not be any scratches on it." Mr. Justin said.

Once inside Mr. Justin was obnoxious. He was really irate that the boys had stopped and shot the decoy when he and Mr. Avery had driven on. He was looking at me again, "You probably feel like a big shot arresting two boys for shooting that damn target decoy. We spent good money to come up here to hunt and I don't like being harassed by you. This is god damn entrapment!"

"Mr. Justin, it is my firm opinion that your son's rifle was loaded inside the vehicle long before he ever saw the eyes of the decoy. I can prove that in court. Second, he would not have fired from inside the vehicle before it came to a full stop, if he did not believe that he was seeing and shooting at a real deer. The use of decoys, Mr. Justin, has been tried and tested in the Supreme Court," I said. I looked at Jim. He was smiling.

"I still think there are more important things you could be doing than trying to catch young boys."

Jim stepped up then, "Mr. Justin before we set that decoy up, Thom and I spent nine hours walking in the woods to bring out a lost hunter. If you want to file a complaint, it'll have to be in writing. Who do you want to address it to? My Sergeant, Lieutenant. How about the Chief Warden? If you'd like I can give you a toll free number to the Commissioner's office. Now if you don't want me to take these boys to the county jail in Bangor, I suggest you shut up and let us and the bail commissioner do our job. Bail is going to cost each eleven hundred and twenty-five dollars to get bailed out of jail now. If you do not have that much I suggest you go down to the Western Union office and call home and have the money wired up. While you're doing that Thom and I will finish processing them."

The fathers left without saying anything else. Romeo and Dick were looking pretty sick. While I recorded the make, model and serial number from the rifle and inventorying the evidence we had confiscated Jim wrote out two summons for night hunting and a second summons to Romeo for hunting from a motor vehicle.

"Are you through Jim?" Bill asked the police officer on duty.

"We have everything we need. These two are yours until their fathers come back with the money."

"Okay boys I'm going to put you in the holding cells until your fathers return."

During the drive home there wasn't much conversation between Jim and me. We were both exhausted, but still too excited to relax and sleep. When Jim dropped me off at my pickup at the Huber garage he said, "Get some rest Thom, we'll take the rest of the day and tonight too, off. I'll be in touch."

*   *   *   *

This was the year of the lost hunters. Between the two districts we had four lost hunters a week. Sometimes two in one night. We didn't catch anymore night hunters that fall. We were too busy finding lost hunters and dead bodies.

On the afternoon of November 18th I received a radio call from Jim asking me to meet him at his house as soon as possible. "Okay, I'll be about forty minutes. What's up?"

"I can't say over the air," he replied.

I changed into my uniform as fast as I could, hooked Royal to his run. There was two inches of snow in the road which made negotiating corners a bit hazardous, by the time I got to the Four Corners the snow was gone and the gravel road, dry and dusty. I drove faster and faster, wondering what Jim had encountered now that he couldn't say anything about it over the radio. I even passed a heavily loaded log truck. I bet that surprised the driver in the purple Freightliner. To get to Jim's house on time I had to break a few speed laws.

Jim was in his garage when I arrived. "Hi Thom. Come on in, my wife put a pot of coffee on before she went to work." He poured two cups and sat down at the bar.

I waited for him to tell me what was so urgent. "I got a phone call today from the Greenville Headquarters. Sergeant Roger Guay. He has requested that you and I, with other wardens, assist him tomorrow searching a big piece of real estate in Baxter Park."

We sipped at our coffee for a bit then I asked "What will we be looking for?"

"Two bodies. Two dead bodies that are supposed to be buried somewhere in the park. No one is really sure just where. Roger has called in other search dogs and handlers. Roger said he was more interested with the Freeze-Out Trail from Trout Brook Farm to the Blackwater Brook Trail."

"Do you remember the people who stayed at Don's campground the end of September? The religious group?"

"You mean the ones dressed in bib-coveralls?"

"Yes, they're the ones. I don't have the names yet, but a man and his wife starved a young baby to death and another baby was supposedly still born, to another couple. They buried the two bodies in the park while staying at Don's."

"Why the Freeze-Out Trail?" I asked.

"Apparently they were seen at Trout Brook Farm down by the foot bridge and according to the gate records, out the next day."

"The mother and father starved to death their own baby?" I couldn't believe it.

"They are part of a cult. Why did they starve their baby? I don't know. Roger should be able to explain a lot more tomorrow."

"Why Matagamon? Why take the chance of transporting two dead bodies five hundred miles and stay at a campground where there is bound to be other people? Why here?"

"Why does strange things always seem to happen at Matagamon? A dead body dropped off in the woods, a naked woman wading in the icy water in May. Some guy in a canoe that thinks he's the Lord, another guy that has a slip of paper that says he is sane. I could go on and on about the strange happenings at Matagamon. Why does this region draw these weirdoes like a magnet? I can't tell you. I'm just waiting for someone to come up missing only to show up later claiming to have been abducted by aliens," Jim said.

I started to laugh, "Mysteries at Matagamon, as strange as the occurrences in the Bermuda Triangle."

"So what time do you want me tomorrow?" I asked.

"Roger and his dog Reba are flying in from Greenville and he said he would meet us at the Matagamon Store at six. Detectives from Attleboro Massachusetts are coming up today and will be at the store tomorrow morning."

"There must be more to it. I mean why take the risk of being caught traveling that distance to dispose of two really small bodies," I said.

"I've told you everything I know. Hopefully Roger can enlighten us more tomorrow."

"Are you working tonight?"

"No, Dave and Richard are covering for me tonight. So get a good night sleep. You can count on doing a lot of walking tomorrow."

I was listening to the radio on the way home and the weather report was calling for an unusually warm day tomorrow, for the middle of November; low 70's.

What Jim had said about the occult group staying at the Matagamon Campground, being seen at the foot bridge that crosses Trout Brook to the Freeze-Out Trail jogged or shook my brain and I saw in my inner vision the two individuals standing on the shore of Webster Stream and backing off out of sight when they had noticed me walking on the Eagle Lake tote road, at the Little East Campsite. I tried to remember the date. I had taken the ATV down to bring back my canoe and motor from the water. It was the Monday following my interview at Augusta which was on the 8th of October. So it had to have been the 11th when I saw the two men at the Little East Campsite. I remembered how they had seemed concerned about my presence there that morning. I wished now I could have seen more clearly through the bushes to know what was going on at the campsite. I wished I had crossed the streams to investigate more closely. But hind sight won't help much now.

I don't know why but I started thinking about when I was going to set Royal free. He might get shot by deer hunters if I turned him loose now. I'll wait until after the hunters are all out of the woods and I'll take him on the Snow sled with me up near Brayley Pond.

*   *   *   *

I was up early the next morning in order to be at the store at six. The weather report had been correct, the temperature was already unseasonably warm. On top of the hill before Four Corners, two bucks were fighting in the road. I stopped and they didn't pay any attention to my presence. Somewhere there would be a doe deer that they were fighting over. Finally, one of them ran off and the other walked out of sight and then I saw three flags go up as they ran off.

Jim was already at the store and much to my surprise so were the two Massachusetts Detectives. Di had the coffee all made and was filling cups. "Don is guiding this morning but he'll be back at noon."

Jim had his portable radio sitting on the counter and the Warden Pilot was advising Jim that he and Sergeant Guay would be landing in five minutes behind the dam. While Jim drove up to the dam to get Roger and his dog Reba, the rest of the searchers and dog handlers arrived. They all looked at me questioningly. I was the new Warden. The new kid on the block, and no one knew me. "Hi," I said "I'm Thom Wellington, I'm working with Jim this Fall and going to Warden School in January." That seemed to break the ice.

After Jim had returned with Roger and Reba, Di said, "Why don't you use the large cabin today."

Her son Alan, now a game warden in Eastern was one of the searchers. He would be as familiar with the woods and trail systems here as anyone, probably more so, having grown-up in the region.

"Apparently Jacques and Karen Robidoux from Seekonk Massachusetts starved to death their ten month old son Samuel; he died April 26, 1999. Then in August Jeremiah was still born to Michelle and David Corneau. Why did the Robidouxs starve their son?" Sergeant Guay shrugged his shoulders and added, "The Detectives aren't going to say. They are still interviewing people in the group."

The information that led the Detectives Brennan and Brillon to Matagamon was also sketchy. Apparently another member of the group had had a falling out about the time the others were planning their trip to Matagamon. He had gone to the authorities with what information he had and apparently a ten page diary written by one of the members describing the slow death of Samuel and later Jeremiah being still born, but neither body being properly buried. And this informant only knew that the rest of the group had traveled to Maine; to Baxter State Park and the Matagamon Area. And that they had taken the two bodies with them. But he had no idea where the group was planning to bury the two infants. Since the group had been staying at the Matagamon Wilderness Campground and some of the group had been seen crossing the foot bridge across Troutbrook; access to the Freeze-Out Trail, this is where the search would start. This region was so huge that it would be like looking for a needle in a haystack.

I interrupted Sergeant Guay, "Excuse me for interrupting Sergeant, but did you say they were seen early on the morning of October eleventh crossing Troutbrook?"

"Yes."

"That same day, around noon I was on the Eagle Lake tote road across the stream from the Little East Campsite and saw several of these people, men, at the site. When two of them noticed I was watching them they backed away from the stream out of sight. A bit later these two went for a walk up the trail towards Grand Pitch but there was still someone at the site, because I could see movement."

"How did you happen to be across the stream from the campsite?" Guay asked.

"I live two miles above there," I replied.

"You live just two miles from the campsite at Little East in the middle of nowhere?" he sounded somewhat doubtful.

"Yes, I do."

Each of the dog handlers paired off with another Warden, I went with Guay, while Jim and Alan ran some base lines with orange flagging, since they were more familiar with the region than anyone else. One team worked the perimeter of Troutbrook Farm, another walked the brook banks, another walked the Freeze-Out Trail towards the Little East Campsite and Sergeant Guay and I went directly to the campsite and after checking there we were going to work our way back to the farm.

When we got to the sawdust pile, the old mill sight, Roger asked, "What's this?"

"There used to be a mill here back in the fifties. The Diamond Match Company," I replied.

"This pile of sawdust will have to be looked over thoroughly. String some of this police security tape across the trail."

A short distance beyond the sawdust we came to another trail off to the left, marked with orange flagging. "Where does this trail go Thom?" Roger asked.

"Frost Pond, about two miles."

"Better flag this one also."

Then we came to another slightly used trail beside Hinckley Brook "How about this trail?"

"Just a hunting trail." I flagged that also with the security tape.

Beyond Hinckley we came to a beaver flowage and on the far shore there was another trail up along the edge of the flowage. "And this?" Roger asked.

"Now it's only a hunting trail. At one time this was part of the old road system that went up along Webster Stream to the lake. The trail is easy to follow until you get about two hundred yards from the Freeze-Out Trail, near the Webster Stream campsite." Roger wanted that flagged also.

We rested at the Northwest Cove campsite. We sat at the picnic table while Reba drank from the lake and sniffed around the site opening. "There is more country here to search than I first realized. Unless the Detectives come up with some more information we could be here for eternity and not find where the bodies are buried. They could be out there," he waved his hand indicating the lake, "on bottom, or set adrift in the river below Matagamon."

"What is the soil composition like around here?"

"From what I've seen, mostly shale and dirt."

"All they had to dig with was a trenching tool."

"It would be real difficult to dig much of a hole in this ground using trenching tools unless they found a gravel bar somewhere," I replied.

"Or a sawdust pile," Roger said. "We might as well look this sight over closely while we're here and then we can exclude this, for now."

I stayed on the picnic table and watched as Roger and Reba worked as a team inspecting every nook and under every piece of dri-ki along the shore.

At the Little East Campsite we stopped briefly again for Reba to relax before she went to work, "Where were you when you saw them here?"

I pointed to a tall pine tree across the Little East Branch of the Penobscot, on the opposite shore, "I had just come into view of the campsite here and the two guys were down over this bank near the water having a conversation when they noticed me."

"What were you doing again? What brought you here on that day?"

"During open water I keep my canoe and motor cached near that pine tree. I came down that day to haul it back to my cabin, about two miles up the old tote road."

"Could you describe them?"

"Not really. The sun was in my eyes. I could see the two next to the water were wearing bib-coveralls and both men had beards. That's all I can describe."

"And you aren't sure whether or not they camped here that night?"

"No, it appeared to me as if someone was setting up camp, but it was several days before I got back here again." Roger took his hat off and wiped the sweat from his forehead. The temperature was too warm for the third week of November.

"According to my conversation with the Detectives no one has stayed here at the sight since the four men crossed the foot bridge at Troutbrook. While Reba and I are searching, I'd like you to sift through the ashes and see if you find anything. After Reba sniffs out the outhouse, pull the boards off the back and have a look. Don't go pawing through it with your hands. Then the same with the lean-to and check the framework for names and the picnic tables." He handed me a list of several names to compare with anything that might be engraved into the wood.

My hands were black by the time I finished with the fireplace and ashes. I pawed through the dung pile using a stick; nothing. The lean-to produced nothing, and no names. I did find some names that matched two of the first names that were on the list, but they were older and filled with that awful brown stain.

I walked out to this end of the bridge abutment that at one time crossed over to the Eagle Lake tote road. I was trying to visualize how the bridge was constructed and how it looked, when Roger walked up behind me. "We're finished here."

"There used to be a bridge across here that connected this side to the Eagle Lake tote road," I said.

"I wonder if it went all the way to Eagle Lake?" Roger said.

"Oh yeah, I've walked along much of it and Uncle Royal showed me the rest on one of our trips."

"Nothing here?" I asked.

"Now tie off the entrance trail with that security flagging. Where does this other trail go?" He was looking at the one that ran alongside Webster Stream.

"It follows the stream to Grand Pitch. It isn't far."

"I'm sure we'll have to search that also, but for now we have got to work our way back to the farm."

The hunting trails and the Frost Pond trail were left for another day. Roger was more interested with the sawdust pile. He worked Reba around the perimeter first, then he worked a grid pattern across the pile. I over turned abandon roof pieces to the mill. The sheet metal piping and odds and ends of equipment left behind.

Again we found nothing; only bits of trash buried in the sawdust by hikers. "I think Reba has had enough for one day. We'll take a break and I'll let her work her way back towards the Farm. We'll hike out a little slower. This search will probably take up the rest of the fall."

It was past five when we got back to the farm at Troutbrook. The other handlers and searchers were already there. Roger told the Detectives they would be back in two days. The dogs needed a day to rest. "Perhaps the weather will cool off some after tomorrow. Right now they aren't much good."

* * * *

I spent the rest of November searching for the grave site in the Park. At times I was sent to walk out a trail, brook and once up along the outlet of Hudson Pond and around the pond. That trip awakened some fond memories of the trip Uncle Royal had taken me on when we stopped at Hudson and smoked some venison. Jim and I searched both sides of Boody Brook to Wadleigh Mountain and criss-crossed the North side of Wadleigh-------. I lost count how many times we traversed the North Slope. It was dark before we got out, that much I do remember.

There was only one more lost hunter during this time, but we didn't work any more night hunters either. Locating the two bodies was a priority and that was understandable. Come Spring a bear just out of hibernation would be able to smell the decaying bodies and would dig them out and devour them. And as soon as we get snow the searching would have to cease. More game wardens were called in to assist and more dog handlers from all corners of the state.

November thirtieth arrived and this was my last day of being an assistant game warden. I was told to hang onto my uniform and gear as I would be needing them at Warden School in January. The weather was still unusually warm for the end of November and the ground was still bare. Dressed in civilian clothes I continued to help with the search in the Park. All the trails had by now been walked over and sniffed out by dogs; six times, but we expanded the searches on each trail widening the parameters.

December was half over and the ground was finally covered with six inches of new snow and the search for a grave came to an end until Spring, or unless one of the members, who had been incarcerated for contempt of court for refusing to disclose the location of the two bodies, decides to cooperate with the authorities and discloses more information about the burial.

My time here at Matagamon was being cut short also. I had promised Ronie that I would spend Christmas with her and her family this year and on January third of the New Year I had to be at the Police Academy in Waterville to start my training. And it was time that I set Royal free; to be a coyote. I couldn't just let him go here. Not with Don snaring coyotes on the deadwater or Ray Gallagher snaring at Third Lake. I studied my maps and decided the next morning to take Royal out on my snow sled beyond Brayley Brook, as far as I could go; towards the arm of Chamberlain Lake. A good distance away. Then the next day I was leaving to be with Ronie for Christmas.

I was up early the next morning and called Royal inside while I fixed breakfast. I gave him a plate of bacon and eggs also. When breakfast was finished I loaded up the snow sled and Royal jumped on in front of me and put his paws on the handle bars. I had a difficult time seeing: not because Royal was blocking my view, but because of the tears in my eyes. That was a solemn trip.

I continued on beyond Brayley. Past the turn that would have taken me to Sly Brook and Third Lake. I went as far West as I could go with the snow sled "Come on Royal. We'll walk from here." We crossed the North Branch of Brayley and continued on towards the West and the Arm of Chamberlain Lake. I crossed the town line into T7-R11. I followed a natural ravine downhill to a low lying cedar marsh. Here there were plenty of deer, rabbit and coyote tracks. Royal was really enjoying sniffing each track. Particularly the coyote tracks. Probably a female. I found a spruce that had blown over and sat down. Royal kept running around sniffing all the different scents. He would be okay, I knew. But I sure hated to walk off and leave him.

"Come here Royal." He came over and laid at my feet and rolled on his back so I could scratch his belly. I took a small rope out of my coat pocket and tied it around his neck and the other end to a four inch cedar tree. It would keep him from following me back and in a few hours he'd have chewed out of it, but by then I will be far away.

He knew something was wrong. He sat up on his haunches and rested his head on my knee. I pet his head and scratched behind his ears. "I'm sorry boy, it has to be this way." I stood up and started following my tracks back. Royal fought against the rope. He barked and whined. The more distance I put between us the loader he barked. He was out of sight now and I began to run. To run away from the sadness.

I stopped to catch my breath and I heard a long deep throated howl and I knew it was Royal saying goodbye.

EPILOGUE

It is important to remember that Thomas Wellington is a fictional character, as well as his experiences. He was created as a modem to tell the story of Matagamon.

Jim Randall is also fictional. Although his stories and experiences in the book are mine. Except for his work searching for the two buried bodies. I had already retired before this event.

I actually did find a decomposed body in T6-R8 and the name in the book, Lagasse, I got from the phone book. As far as I know the forensic lab determined that the skeletal remains that I found were not those of the registered owner of the torched vehicle I found five miles away. The skeletal structure of these remains were too small for the torched vehicle owner. I was also advised that no missing male of the age and size matching that of these remains was unaccounted for in Maine. I don't know if the investigating officer ever pursued the case beyond this or not.

*   *   *   *

Jeremiah Corneau is allegedly to have been still born and his cousin Samuel Robidoux, ten months old died a horrible and painful death from starvation. As his parents Jacques and Karen Robidoux and the entire religious group stood by and listened to his crying and screams. Yet no one did anything.

Both bodies were wrapped in cloth and put in a wicker basket and placed inside the cool bulkhead at 415 Central Avenue Seekonk, Massachusetts. Roland had declared his son Jacques an elder and Jacques had stated to the rest of the members of the body that he was one of two of the witnesses in Revelations; Chapter Eleven and he assured the Body that by laying on of his hands to the now cold and rigid body of Samuel that by the following morning Samuel would be alive.

*   *   *   *

Roland Robidoux was the backbone of the group. They preferred to be identified as The Body. During the seventies Roland had been active in a California based religious sect; The Worldwide Church of God. After becoming discouraged with the sect he dropped out and started, innocently enough a bible study group. He introduced many of the same ideas and believes as the former sect such as: Revelations or leadings, faith healings, home births. The observance of Tabernacle, Passover and Pentecost Celebration and they did not celebrate Christmas, Easter or holidays. Music was forbidden, and recognition of government and law, the media and modern medicines. Saturdays were usually spent reading from the bible. The Old Testament being the structural backbone of the pillar for The Body. For answers to everyday problems The

Body members would read through the Old Testament until they found a scripture with a line or two that supported their purpose.

All jewelry, books and even family photos were thrown away. They began to isolate themselves from their neighbors and the world. The members were instructed not to have dealings with banks.

Jacques' wife Karen was a very attractive petite woman. After reading the journals kept by unnamed members it might appear that Jacques' sister Michelle Mingo, wife to Dennis Mingo, might have been just a bit jealous of Karen. In early March of 1999 Michelle claimed she had had a Leading from The Lord, that because of Karen's vanity she was to put on weight and should drink a substantial amount of almond milk every day. And that her ten month old son should be taken off solid food and only given breast milk. This way the son would grow to become more dependent on his mother. But Karen was pregnant and she soon stopped producing enough breast milk to nourish Samuel.

Samuel began to cry and scream from hunger and Karen wanted to stop this diet and give Samuel solid food once again. Or at least water so his stomach would be full. She found a scripture in the Old Testament in Lamentations to support her view, ("children who faint from hunger"). She was admonished by her Sister-in-law Michelle and her own husband Jacques, and The Body elders convinced her to continue only giving Samuel breast milk. That Satan had put these ideas into her head to confuse her. Jacques asked, "Who do you trust more, God or Satan?"

Samuel became so weak from malnutrition that when he tried to suckle he could no longer hang on to the nipple. According to the journals there was a lot of discussion about Samuel's health and the weight he had lost. But members had convinced themselves that they were doing God's will.

For fifty one days Samuel was denied food. Then on April 26, 1999 he died. Just three days from being a year old. When Samuel began to cry and scream because he was hungry and the pain he must have felt, Karen locked herself in her bedroom, she could not endure his screams any longer. Before his death Samuel was only a skeleton with a pale chalky appearance. A decaying vegetable.

Jacques, the father wrapped the baby in cloth and put him in a wicker basket and put him in the bulkhead enclosure where it was cool.

*   *   *   *

In August of that same year Samuel's would be cousin, died in child birth. The mother Rebecca Corneau refusing modern medical services of a doctor or hospital, chose instead to have the birth at home. Which today a lot of women are choosing to do. But even when the birth became apparent that there were difficulties, outside professional help was not an option. Jeremiah died in child birth.

Jeremiah's body like his cousin Samuel's was wrapped in cloth and placed alongside Samuel's body in the cool bulkhead. To be resurrected at a later date.

*   *   *   *

Dennis Mingo husband to Michelle had spent twelve years with The Body; Bible studies and trying to observe the strict restrictions on their personal life. But he noticed that the members were going astray from their original study groups. He enjoyed music and music was not allowed. There were times when he would sneak off so he could enjoy listening to some secular music and enjoy an occasional soft drink. But after a while The Body elders realized what he was doing and he was punished by being ostracized from The Body.

In November of 1998, Dennis Mingo decided to leave the religious group. The practices had strayed too far. It was a difficult decision to make. In his own words when he first started studying with The Group and learning about God 'it was like living with the Walton's.' He tried to convince his wife Michelle to leave with him, but she would not separate herself and their five children from The Body.

During the next ten months Dennis would visit his children to make sure they were okay. He kept trying to no avail. He had noticed that Rebecca Corneau was pregnant and then on one of his visits when he noticed Rebecca was no longer pregnant he asked about the birth and was told that she had lost the child during birth. At this time he did not know about Samuel's ordeal or his death.

Dennis returned to the house on Central Avenue in Seekonk, while the members of The Body were having a yard sale; he went inside to investigate. There was something going on and no one would talk to him. He found a ten page journal describing Samuel's ordeal and how he finally wilted. He left with the journal.

Dennis returned again September 18th and tried desperately to convince his wife to leave. While the others locked themselves behind closed doors. The members refused to come out until he left. Michelle would not leave the security of the religious sect. Dennis threatened that if she did not go with him, when he returned he would have the police with him. She still refused to leave.

At midnight that night of September 18th all the members of The Body packed their things and headed for Maine. They had been to Maine on a previous trip; to Baxter State Park, and they had declared Maine as the True Holy Ground of God. The new Jerusalem. Their destination was The Matagamon Region in T6-R8. The two infant bodies packed away in wooden boxes in the trailer.

Were they running away from the threat Dennis Mingo made about going to the police? And had they found a secluded spot to hide out while they decided what to do with the bodies? Why Matagamon? An Indian name from the Penobscot Nation meaning beautiful water. Was there a mysterious calling about this region that drew them to it without the members ever being aware of it? The same mysterious call that beckons all new comers to the Matagamon Region. Perhaps this call explains why so many unexplained events happen here. What a place this would be for a final resting spot for all eternity. As soul to sit each night on the shores of Matagamon Lake and listen to the loons.

Is this what The Body had in mind or were they simply looking for an out of way place to bury the evidence. They all will have a lifetime now to decide for themselves.

*   *   *   *

The group entered the park at the South gate through Millinocket and were in the park for two days before arriving in T6-R8; arriving there on September 23rd, 1999.

The group stayed at Matagamon for fifteen days and then on or about October 8th they left and went to Allagash, Northern Aroostook County. They stayed at the Walker Brook Campgrounds.

While they were at Allagash, they took a drive towards Canada but fearing the trailer would be searched at the border crossing and the dead bodies found, they turned around and returned to the campsite at Walker Brook. Here they had a discussion what to do with the bodies. Mark Daneau was looking at a map and suggested the Freeze-Out Trail in Baxter State Park.

Jacques made the decision to return to Matagamon and bury the babies there. They arrived back at Matagamon on October 10th, 1999 and stayed in a log cabin there instead of tenting out. On the 11th, a Monday morning Roland drove Jacques Robidoux, David Corneau, Tim and Mark Daneau to the Freeze-Out Trail at Troutbrook Farm. The four men lashed the two wooden coffins to two poles, as a travois and hiked to the Little East Campsite and then up along the Freeze-Out Trail towards Grand Pitch on Webster Stream.

A gravel knoll was found four hundred paces from the cookie rock, in The Freeze-Out Trail, and a compass course of 230 degrees. A small grave was dug under a tall pine tree and both bodies were buried. Before leaving, the gravel was brushed out and pine needles and dry leaves were scattered over the freshly dug hole to camouflage the grave and two branches were placed on top.

*   *   *   *

The group returned to Massachusetts and Dennis Mingo made good his threat. The police arrived and searched the yard and the inside of the residence, but no one would tell him where the two babies had been buried. Only that they had been buried.

Jacques and Karen Robidoux, Tim, Mark and Roger Daneau, David and Rebecca Corneau, and Michelle Mingo were asked where the two babies had been buried and they all refused to disclose the location. The judge found them in contempt and all were taken into custody. On October 20th, 2000, David Corneau had had enough of sitting in jail. He didn't like being separated from his children. He agreed to show the authorities where the two babies were buried.

On October 24th, 2000, David Corneau led a contingent of police officers, attorneys and Game Wardens to the base of a tall pine tree atop a high knoll not far off the Freeze-Out Trail near Grand Pitch on Webster Stream. Corneau showed the authorities the spot and Sergeant Roger Guay instructed his dog to work the area. Reba immediately indicated that she had hit upon the scent of a cadaver by lying on the spot on the ground. A hole was dug and a small wooden box containing two small bodies was removed.

On June 14th, 2002, Jacques Robidoux was found guilty of first degree murder and sentenced to life in prison without parole. His wife Karen Robidoux was charged with second degree murder and her case has not yet been tried in Superior Court.

Michelle Mingo was also charged as an accessory to assault and battery on a child. Her case has not yet come before the Superior Court

*   *   *   *

Is there something mystical about The Matagamon Region that attracts the bizarre, the curious and eccentrics and the unexplainable erratic behavior of some? Or is it as the individual said, who thought he was My Lord, stated that this region is so peaceful and tranquil. That people come here looking for peace and tranquility and searching for that oneness with God.

The End

Other books by
Randall Probert

A FORGOTTEN LEGACY
ISBN 978-0985287283

AN ELOQUENT CAPER
ISBN 978-0985287245

COURIER DE BOIS
ISBN 979-8521727926

KATRINA'S VALLEY
ISBN 0-9667308-3-6

MYSTERIES AT MATAGAMON LAKE
ISBN 979-8884124110

About the Author

Jim Randall is a fictional character but his stories and experiences are mine. Some of the characters are real and some are fictitious. While writing and reliving those experiences, I began to wonder if I had made the correct decision to retire.

Every October I make a journey from Uncle Royal's cabin down to the old Eagle Lake Tote Road to Webster Stream and Little East, and as I stand there by the old bridge, the vibrations of that era reverberate through me and tears come to my eyes.